ALL OTHERS MUST PAY.

ALL OTHERS MUST PAY.

A novel.

SHEILA PARIS KLEIN

Charleston, SC
www.PalmettoPublishing.com

Hardcover ISBN: 978-1-68515-824-8
Paperback ISBN: 978-1-68515-825-5
eBook ISBN: 978-1-68515-826-2

This novel, *All Others Must Pay.*, is a work of fiction. All names, characters, incidents and locations are either products of the author's imagination and creation or used in a fictitious manner. Any resemblance to actual people living or dead, or to events or conversations is purely coincidental.

Also by Sheila Paris Klein

In the Cave Of Memory
Bone Needles, a poetry anthology
The Lost Language of Dust

TABLE OF CONTENTS

To my wonderful family

AVALANCHE

You can no longer sleep, maybe ever again it seems. You can no longer listen to the others in sleep. You can no longer think of the arguments and the burnt coffee and the knife that was thrown and the crack of the rifle. Then maybe you go outside in a bathrobe and the fur moccasins you found on the porch, and you wash your face, streaked with dried blood and ash, in the snow. You wash your face in the snow, limp across the meadow, cross over the frozen creek and scramble up the slope on the other side. You prop yourself in the lee of a pine tree.

You turn around and look back at the cabin. From this distance it is a box of innocence, a snow-covered roof peak, a flirt of smoke rising from the chimney. It is still in darkness, but, far above, the top of the mountain is in full sun. You watch as the slice of sun slides down the slope knowing it won't reach the cabin for another hour.

Two of the other six had left even before you. Two are still deep into a sleep that comes from abundant alcohol, excessive vitriol and unimaginative but frantically overblown sex. One is humming loudly, and one is unconscious and could not be wakened although your attempts were cursory and purposely ineffective.

Somehow the bathrobe is much warmer than you thought it would be, although it is now stained with blood you washed from your face. You are happy to lean against the tree and wait for the others to wake. Someone opens the door and wanders to the side of the house. You imagine you are a marksman holding a rifle, ready to pick him off, and then each one of them, as they emerge from the cabin. Instead, you are the only member of the group who might eventually be sober enough to cook breakfast.

Way up in the valley, a mile above the cabin, you see a wall of snow fold in on itself and begin to roll slowly down the slope calling more snow to its flanks as it gathers momentum. It is lazy and careless at first, hitting a flat spot on the ridge and hesitating as if it has finished its run. But then it folds over the edge and slides silently down the mountain.

There is a wide swath of time in which you do nothing. You scratch your eyebrow and readjust your left leg to make a sturdier perch against the tree. You watch the wall of snow leisurely ripple down the mountain flank, taking trees and boulders with it. It sends a mist ahead of itself that settles on your skin, light and fragile.

Could it be that you are new to mountains and sloped terrain and a snow pack that has disintegrated from the melt and freeze cycle? All of that knowledge should have been part of the cursory Welcome-to-Trout-Cabin tour and lecture which took thirty seconds but only if you were the first in the door and not the one carrying the case of vodka. Or are you the one who knew all along that avalanches in early April are inevitable but maybe not in this spot on this particular day? And what the fuck do a bunch of poets know about snow anyway?

All of that has to be processed before you know for sure that you are the one, the only one in fact, sitting against a tree and watching an avalanche launch itself towards that cabin full of mildly distasteful people. It is on your head to do something or not. You choose something, and begin the scrambling and yelling modeled on an idea of what people do who are trying to help. But you and the speed of sound have collided and your voice is thrown back down your throat.

The sound follows the destruction. First the tree trunks slice through the cabin walls carrying slashes of clothing and quilt with them. Then the popping sound of their uprooting careens down the valley like those rifle shots. Last, the roar of snow and its immeasurable mass blot out all seeing, all thinking, all hearing.

You are white and frozen and buried, a hunched ball, the bathrobe a tent over your head, your bare legs encased in snow, the fur slippers torn from your feet. You are deaf, blind and numb. You are probably alive, possibly alive; but more likely you are dead. You wait, trying to figure it out. They will have to thaw you out anyway, because you're not officially dead until you are warm and dead. Unless they don't find you until spring when you are a soggy clump of rotted flesh and liquid intestines.

Then you wonder if you might be alive. But you're not sure. You want to move at least a hand or a finger because that might mean you are alive. But you are afraid to try because if you can't then you are most likely dead. You're certain you can't move if you're dead. But maybe you can be alive and not be able to move. Then you notice you are breathing. You are alive!

There is a mad scramble. Somehow you have moved a hand and an arm and the head that is definitely yours. You keep hunching your back until you feel some snow slide away, and it is colder and wetter than it was just a second ago. You thrust your head up as fast as you can; you breathe real air. There is a sliver of light and then you are chest up in the snow digging fiercely to get yourself out.

There is scrabbling in the direction of the cabin, one side of which is still visible. The rest of it might be there under the snow or might have washed down the ravine and be lying sideways in the road two miles away. You don't know. A fox emerges. She is followed by her two kits. They scramble out of a hole in the wall of snow and stand dazed and blinking. The fox sniffs the kits and nudges them with her snout. She leaps a path toward a line of trees that are, amazingly, still standing, and the kits follow.

Then you hear the scraping of metal against ice.

RUSSELL

TWO YEARS EARLIER

IN THE COMPANY OF POETS

"**H**ow did your grandmother die? If she is still alive, kill her off." That is how Russell Cooney began his post for his on-line poetry group *frombadtoverse* one hot July night in Colorado. He was sitting on his porch in shorts and a T-shirt using his grandmother's favorite remedy for excessive heat— a table fan blowing over a bowl of ice cubes. It was totally ineffective.

In a few minutes he would head up the river-walk to the boarding ramp for the Colorado Cruiser and jump in. When the river was flowing well enough he could float all the way home to his own canoe pullout with a can of beer in one hand and a waterproof flashlight on a lanyard around his neck. He doubted it was possible on this night. Whoever thought there was no summer heat in the Rocky Mountains didn't know Colorado. This night was hot, it was humid, there was a smoky haze in the air from several forest fires a hundred miles away and the black flies were swarming.

He swatted two flies off his thigh and closed the computer. He knew he would get some comments immediately, but he liked to ignore those. The assignment stood as written and pretty soon people got to work and produced something—on topic, off topic, brilliant and lucid, hackneyed and turgid. It didn't matter. What mattered was submitting. If you didn't submit for three consecutive assignments you were cut from the group. It really was the only way to get poets—chronically lazy, uninspired, under-achievers—to actually sit down and write something. Because, as Russell pointed out, an unwritten poem in your head, no matter how brilliant, was worthless.

At this point in the life of the group, there were four other members. Russell only knew their email names, just as they only knew his, the DivineR, but he had made little bios of them, just for himself. There was Edgar, who seemed to be middle-aged, city born and raised, and probably had the same management job for thirty years. He would take the longest to submit, but his poems had clarity and a unifying point of view, even though they were often so fucking depressing other members had suggested he go for counseling, forgetting a basic tenet of the group—assume nothing is personal.

There was Jacine, who was probably Asian and resigned but resilient. The group usually liked her poems. He did as well. It was clear from the poems that English was not her first language, but he knew nothing more about her. She wrote about a childhood in Korea with imperfect grammar that was either genuine and charming or invented and offensive.

Emily was a fast responder. Her poems had lift and spirit and would weave around the topic. Most of the time he wasn't sure she had even read the assignment until she zoomed in and did a pretty good job of nailing it.

Sarah was a strict abider. She, he assumed it was a woman, read the assignment, usually included the topic in her title and worked her way through the concept in a totally professional, stilted way. If he had to assign them life stories, she would be the lawyer, Emily was probably a dancer, Edgar had some kind of corporate job, and Jacine was the mystery.

Russell was a mid-level college instructor who allowed his students to call him professor since it was really depressing for their parents to be paying $60,000 a year to have their children taught "Elizabethan Literature Exclusive of Shakespeare" by *Mister* Cooney. No one in his group or any group, ever, made a living writing poetry. But Russell had a far more lucrative profession. He was a dowser, a finder of water, a diviner. It was a career that should have died at the latest in the 1950's, but still had traction, because there actually was a science to it although it had nothing to do with the rods. There was also a mystery to it, an archaic kind of charm.

Just as some people had their homes designed according to Feng shui, consulted astrologists, hired shamans to carry smoking weeds around their rooms or had their auras read by mediums, there were people who believed in using diviners to find water. Many of them were moving to Colorado and building large homes on undeveloped land. They saw the diviner as a connection to the western past, particularly because they eschewed its true staples: working the land, respecting nature, and being faithful to fulfilling only their needs. Once a house was more than a thousand square feet, angled for the best satellite and Wifi connections, with materials imported from other continents, savvy transplants needed a connection to the land. Russell Cooney was that connection.

Edgar Frankel, was not a corporate type at all. He was a skilled mason and his specialty was paths and patios. He worked all over the country in museums, old estates, large office complexes, universities. He stopped telling people he was a mason after the Dan Brown novels were published because people assumed he was *that* kind of a mason and how could he make a living at it. So he reverted to a core description. He was a bricklayer.

Emily Bishop was the youngest of the poets, on a gap year from a master's in writing program. She was the proprietor of a childhood lemonade stand she had re-purposed as a mobile poetry concession offering free poems for specific people—jugglers, podiatrists, ethicists, bee-keepers. No matter how arcane her offerings, an hour never went by without a customer. Some days there were lunchtime lines, particularly if she were near a lobster roll truck.

Sarah Ryder, had been a theatre major in college and was thinking of going to law school once her husband retired from the Air Force and her daughter graduated from college. She never considered herself a poet but it was an easy way to indulge her dramatic flair.

Jacine, Olivia Park, actually was in law school and posted poems sporadically and certainly not during exam season. Russell had guessed she was Asian, and he was right. Her parents were both immigrants from Korea.

■　■　■

The morning turned out to be a better beginning to the day than Russell Cooney had expected. There was a note in his mailbox when he stopped at the English office on his way to being late for his second class of the day. He had missed the first class completely, and he wasn't even hung over. He was certain the university kept him on as an adjunct professor because his most recent novel, one that sold only 2,710 copies, had been short-listed for a national literary award. It did not win. The novel that did win sold fewer copies than his, but no matter.

The note was a final plea from the chair of the department who had already had her secretary text him twice. "Dr. Blau needs to see you today. At your earliest convenience." It was neither early nor convenient when Russell opened Blau's door and stuck his head in. "What'cha got for me?"

"More than you've got for me. That's a certainty."

"You're as adorable as ever."

"And you're as transparent as ever." Marisa Blau motioned him into the room.

"Would you sleep with me for fifty dollars?"

"Am I paying you or are you paying me?"

"Either way. I'm easy." He dropped into a chair and threw his leg over the armrest. Russell no longer had any real interest in her sexually. The banter was the vestige of a four-year affair they had when they were each married. Now that she was divorced after twenty years of marriage and he was separated from his third wife, they were both too available.

"Something's come up. Well not really. Something's come up that was a long time in orchestrating. It will also be a long time coming to fruition so I'm giving you plenty of notice," Marisa closed her laptop. "I'll be leaving in two years. I'm leaving after seventeen years at this prestigious institution. Not that I'm going anyplace more prestigious. My boys have been in Vermont now for several years, and they are clearly settled. So, I'm moving to Vermont."

Russell actually wagged a finger at her, "You know, we always used to tell our friends the minute you move to be near the kids, they will move somewhere else. Even if they begged you to move there."

Marisa nodded. "I have a job. In fact, I have two jobs. I'll be chair of the department at the college and I'll also head up their new Sanctuary for Displaced Authors."

"Is that a thing now? It's the third college I've heard of this month repositioning itself as a socially aware mecca and no, I'm not coming with you."

"You certainly are not. That wasn't even in my mind."

"So am I on loose gravel here. Am I going to have to suck up—and I mean it literally—to a new chair. Not that I didn't enjoy every minute of our fling together, if you can call four years of insane fucking and that time under the hors d'oeuvres table at the faculty retreat a fling. But I digress."

"Oh my god, you are such a schmuck."

"But a lovable schmuck?"

"Of course. And I love you, not least because you were the one who stayed with me when I had cancer, not my asshole husband who somehow thought it was all about him."

Russell leaned over, caught her hand and kissed it. "They should do a study on the aphrodisiac properties of chemotherapy. And what kind of person fucks around on his wife when she has cancer?"

"The same kind of person who fucks around on her husband when she has cancer." Marisa flipped her hands to the side. "All right. Let's get to the point here. No you are not going with me to Vermont. And no you probably are not going to be sucking up to another chair, because I want you to be the new chair. That's why I'm telling you now. So you have time to position yourself."

"You and who else?"

"Right now just me, because I needed to talk to you first. Do you want this?" she held up her hand. "Before you answer, let me give my best argument. Job security. If someone else is chair, you will actually have to become a responsible adult rather than that persona of yours who does a half-assed job. Admittedly you do it with such brilliance and insight it's better than what most people do when they are really trying," she smiled. "Let's face it. Anyone else would have fired your ass long ago. So, what do you think?"

Russell leaned back in the chair. He looked up at the ceiling and pulled at a chunk of faded brown hair. "Yes. And as Molly Bloom would say 'Yes and yes and yes and yes.'"

"So, you know, you're going to have to do some work for this?"

"Oh, God, not the 'P' word."

"For certain the 'P' word. Don't you have anything in the works? I mean all of us are always just months away from publishing that blockbuster book we've been working on."

Russell was not someone who over-published. In the twenty-three years he had been at the university, he'd written four volumes of poetry, six articles in scholarly journals, the afore-mentioned novel that was passed over for the literary award and one true best seller—an adult Valentine's book, *A Bear Time Bed Story.* It was the darling of upscale gift shops for five weeks, mostly because of the illustrations (not done by him) rather than the story line. Still, he and the illustrator happily split the hefty seven-figure net. The following year's book, *A Bear for All Seasons,* was a little too spiritual and somewhat sappy. Full-frontal language and arch references were the totems in gift books that year, and an upstart volume, *When in Doubt,* written by a high school student, had sold a million copies in a week and a half.

Russell had leaned into his dowsing business to enhance his life-style and started the on-line poetry group. His acceptance of hardship and long-range plans were part of his DNA. His ancestral family had come west from Pennsylvania in one of those fabled, misguided treks to California that mimicked the Donner party but without the flamboyant cannibalism.

That was much too earthy for the Cooneys, who were well-educated, well-off construction experts, heading to California to build houses for the people who were heading to California to outfit the prospectors. They were, essentially, in a tertiary business meant to profit from those who profited from people looking to make a killing from their own hard labor. Unlike the Donner party, the Cooney family exhibited remarkable restraint in the face of death on the cross-country trail, burying every single one of their relatives in an almost perfect physical state. Not one bite mark on a thigh.

Sitting opposite Marisa, Russell knew he would need a long-range plan to secure the chairmanship. The immediate choice was an anthology of poetry, exactly as he had been toying with on the website. In fact, exactly as the website stated—*frombadtoverse*. He had his work cut out for him, as some hackneyed writer coined long ago. Then again who was he to claim creative genius with a book title crafted from the dung-dump of language banality?

EDGAR

PERSPECTIVE

"I like poems because they can't fix anything; they only make things worse." That was Edgar Frankel's personal statement for the online poetry group *frombadtoverse* he had stumbled upon in his search for the hobby his daughter had urged him to pursue after his wife died. Edgar was a bricklayer. He laid brick for walls, fireplaces, driveways, arches, chimneys, and, most satisfying of all, paths and walkways, where his understanding of design, shape and angle made him a master.

He was sitting at his kitchen table jammed against the window wall of his small apartment overlooking the Hudson River. The building, set on a massive platform over the Cross Bronx Expressway, rumbled and rattled and jiggled all day and most of the night from the ebb and flow of traffic.

From his chair Edgar could see the upper level of the George Washington Bridge. He was waiting for a shipment of 50,000 bricks to be transported across that bridge and up Hudson River Drive to his current project. There, a crew would supervise the unloading of the seventeen pallets brought from Tennessee. Then the foreman would call Edgar, but only if it was still daylight. Sundown was the start of the last of the autumn Jewish holidays for Edgar, *Simchat Torah*. It was a major holy day for many Jews and a special one for Edgar. This year he was to carry the Torah through the synagogue and out into the street for the joyous celebration that commemorated the reading of the end of the Torah and the reading of the beginning of the Torah. All in one blessed day.

Edgar picked up his binoculars and scanned the traffic just starting across the bridge. There. He saw the truck, red cab, bricks on pallets covered by a canvas tie-down in bright green. Exactly the same as when it left the brickyard in Chattanooga. But not exactly the same. The tie-down was no longer taut. Edgar could see a tear had started in the front corner on the driver's side. The canvas was rippling in small waves as the truck accelerated across the bridge. Edgar stood and leaned across the Formica kitchen table. His immediate instinct was to open the window and shout something, but, of course, that was useless. He picked up his phone and called Hickey, the foreman. "There's something wrong with the truck."

"Nothing wrong." Hickey said, chewing on something. "I just spoke to the driver. He's on the bridge."

"I know. I can see him. There's something wrong. His tie-down is ripped and ripping some more it looks like to me."

"So, the pallets are strapped," Hickey assured. "It's a beautiful day. What are you worried about, rain, a hurricane?"

"No. I don't know. Maybe the speed will dislodge the bricks. I don't know."

"Drink your coffee and come up here in about two hours. We should be unloaded by then."

Edgar watched the truck move slowly across the bridge. He could see what the driver could not, that a break in the oncoming traffic was allowing trucks and cars heading west into New Jersey to speed up. The driver was still stuck in his present, watching the last of the slow moving cars meander past him going no more than fifteen or twenty miles an hour. *I can see his future*, Edgar realized. *I can see the future of everyone on that bridge. If there were a big gaping hole in the bridge on the New York side, I could see it and they couldn't. I would know they were going to their doom, and they wouldn't.*

Edgar had sat at this table for fifteen years, facing the window, even when Ruth was alive. He had watched the traffic crossing the bridge thousands of times. How many futures had he witnessed? Most often, maybe ninety-nine percent of the time, it was a boring, uneventful future. They drove onto the bridge, came into view where he could see what was ahead of them and drove the length of the bridge without anything happening at all. *How many futures had he witnessed? How many accidents, missed exits, flat tires, stalled cars?*

He knew there were people, lots of them, who had seen his future. Not in the way the doctor knew about the hopelessness of Ruth's disease, but in the way the people on the tenth floor of the building could see the rigging giving way beneath him while he still thought it was sturdily in place. It was a fall that could have killed him but only left him with a broken leg.

He bet there were people who saw the crazy-pretty woman on the 59th Street subway platform puckering her lips right near his ear before he felt the kiss (not so bad, but embarrassing, and she didn't smell that good up close). For certain there were those two hunters in the small plane above the Snake River who could see the rapids he thought were still a mile away (exhilarating, totally joyfully, exhilarating and his first honest feeling in the three months after Ruth died.)

On the bridge, the oncoming traffic was light. As trucks sped past, the green canvas flapped harder and the tear got bigger, whipping against the two front pallets. He saw one of the straps snap and slice into the air above the bricks. A pallet shifted, its front corner jutting out over the edge of the truck bed. Surely the driver could see it in his mirror. The truck seemed to slow down. Edgar thought it must be stopping, but instead, it was just straining to the mid-point of the bridge as the oncoming trucks sped ever faster past it. The canvas flapped more wildly. Certainly the drivers behind him were honking their horns, but he knew that meant nothing in New York, especially for a truck driver accustomed to being chastised for going too slow, or turning too wide.

He had the phone in his hand to call the driver, but stopped, stunned, as the truck reached the mid-point where traffic opened up on the inbound side, and it picked up speed. The pallet was now clearly well over the edge, although the bricks were still bubble wrapped together.

"Watch it, watch it," Edgar mumbled and then shouted because he could see farther than the driver and, clearly, the cars 100 feet ahead had slowed down. "Don't, don't slam on those brakes!" He shouted. But there was nothing else for the driver to do and as he downshifted to avoid slamming into the cars ahead, the pallet tipped off the truck, taking the one below along with it. The plastic wrap broke and 6,000 bricks tumbled into the oncoming lane.

The truck lost its center of gravity and lurched to the side. Two more pallets fell as cars and trucks swerved out of the way, facing the unanswerable question—to speed up or stop in order to avoid the demolition. Within ten seconds the truck jack-knifed across the bridge, and five pallets went over the edge, still bubble wrapped, into the Hudson River. Edgar stood on his kitchen table looking down at the rubble for a long time.

His phone rang. "What the fuck. Did that just happen?"

"It's on the news already?"

"You bet. Holy shit. Well, that'll teach me to second guess you." Hickey was laughing.

"This isn't funny."

"I didn't say it was. It's possibly tragic. It's almost certainly tragic."

The George Washington Bridge was closed in both directions. Edgar could see ambulances picking their way through strewn cars; he was certain people would be carried out. The news helicopters circled, but Edgar did not turn on the TV. He didn't need anyone to interpret what he saw. Drivers, stunned, startled, panicked. A woman reaching back with one hand to touch an infant seat. A man in a Lexus in front of the accident talking on a cell phone. Two small dogs running back and forth along the back seat of a Honda. People, out of their cars, running away, running to help.

He saw a man reach into an empty car and grab something. He saw a car go over the railing. He saw two girls help a woman get children out of a van and carry them to the Manhattan side. He saw cars behind the accident make U turns through a break in the concrete divider and try to head off the bridge, back to New Jersey, fighting against traffic still streaming onto the bridge.

As evening came on and the sky darkened Edgar saw his own reflection in his kitchen window. He forgot it was his night to carry the Torah, that the congregation would be waiting for him. That a few would be worried enough to want to call, but had left their phones at home. That someone would eventually shoulder the Torah, carry it outside and hoist it over his head, up, up to the three-quarter moon. People would dance; they would chant blessings. The Torah scroll would be held in eager hands and unrolled slowly around the crush of congregants until it encircled them completely.

Someone, but not Edgar, would read from Deuteronomy, *"And Moses went up from the plains of Moab unto the mountain of Nebo.... And the Lord showed him all the land of Gilead....*

And the Lord said unto him, this is the land which I swore unto Abraham, Isaac and unto Jacob saying I will give it unto thy seed: I have caused thee to see it with thine eyes, but thou shalt not go over thither."

To see far beyond but be unable to go thither. To see because of a vantage point what others could not, but not be able to reach it. Only to witness—the destiny of Moses, and, on this night, of Edgar.

EMILY

ALL OTHERS MUST PAY.

Emily Minerva Bishop pulled the plywood stand out of the trunk of her car. She stood it up carefully on the triangle of grass between the entrance to the bank drive-through window and the sidewalk.

It had once been a lemonade stand crafted by a dedicated and adept father for five year-old Emily. She uncovered it one day in the back of the garage and, in a sudden stroke of brilliance, repurposed it. Two by fours held up a large board that framed the front of the stand. The bottom half had a counter space hidden by what Emily's grandmother would have called a modesty panel. It was perfect for "Lemonade 25¢". Now it held the permanent sign for Emily's new endeavor, carefully inked in with a Sharpie. The upper board, supported by the two by fours, had another hand-lettered sign with an empty space and two cup-hooks.

At the trunk once again, Emily pulled out a large plaid plastic bag she had bought at the farmers market and rifled through the boards inside, pondering her selection. Even though it was a beautiful autumn day, crisp and acid clear, the trees were still green and filled with abundance. The bank manager had just added a row of orange chrysanthemums that attractively framed her space. She selected her sign, hung it on the cup-hooks and then stepped into the street to make certain it was straight. Satisfied, she struggled her cell phone from her jeans pocket, took a picture and then began punching in the date.

The top of the sign now read **"Free Poems for: Millionaires."** Below, on the plywood skirt, the permanent red letters stated **"All Others Must Pay."**

She turned to a boy carrying a messenger bag and tapped him to a stop. "What's today's date?"

He pulled one ear-bud out, "October tenth. It's a Chinese lucky day."

"What?"

"You know, ten ten."

Emily narrowed her eyes. "Are you a geek?"

"Permanent and indelible. So, I guess I don't get a free poem."

"Nope. But you can pay."

"How much?"

"Anything you want."

The geek boy handed her one dollar and eighteen cents.

"Come back in an hour. I'm not set up yet."

"I can't. I'll be somewhere else. Here's my email. Just send me something."

"What do you want it to tell you?"

"Something I don't already know. Also, your hair is really pretty."

"This is my Monday hair for millionaires," Emily twisted a lock of red fuzz behind her ear with the matchbox car earring. "Wait. I have to take your photo."

Emily had no illusions that this project was going to make her a millionaire, but it *was* going to get her a Masters in writing. She would return to school, refreshed and awakened, in February with her work documented and a sheaf of new poems. Or perhaps this project, begun just as the summer heat had dissipated, would end when the weather got colder and she needed to go indoors.

One of her first poems was written for a carpenter.

What Dreams May Come

Like all hill houses ours is shanty to the street
low and tan
its tile roof hunched below the trees.
But here is its magic: Just enter.
Open the doors that shake against the mistral
and tumble into vastness
of house, of trees, of canyon, of hawks, of coyote.
Of glass too fragile to hold me back.
Decks too wind-raked to warm my icy feet.
On nights with no moon when sky and ravine are
mobius strip, I cannot tell the difference
between dreaming and flying.
Like hawks—wings clipping
rafters as they spiral down to rabbits
cowering amid ice flowers.
When tumbling into lunacy
is more than possibility.

■   ■   ■

"I'll take my free poem." He was much older. Grey hair, receding hairline, briefcase, jacket over his shoulder.

She looked up from her pad.

"I'm a millionaire, and I'd like my free poem. I can prove it."

"You don't have to. I trust you."

"Why?"

"Why wouldn't I? You can be a millionaire. It's okay with me."

"Can I choose which poem I want?"

"It's not written yet."

He pointed at the pad. "So you're writing it now."

"No, how could I be? It's a poem for *you*. I'm generous and gullible but not clairvoyant. I didn't know *you* until *you* showed up. So?"

"I want a poem of possibility and adventure."

"See, you figured it out. Come back at two. But I have to take your picture."

"I can come back tomorrow."

"Tomorrow it won't be free poems for millionaires day anymore."

"What will it be?"

Emily looked at him. "Your poem will be ready at two."

Emily posted her service, her encounters and her poems on-line every afternoon. She actually wrote the poems directly in her laptop but very few of her clients wanted to receive them in that form. The whole game was to be given a handwritten poem in a kind of ceremonial way. If they waited, Emily would ask them to stand off to the side while she created their poem. She would hand-write it clean once she was satisfied with the draft on her laptop, fold it in thirds, place it in a blue envelope and affix an easy-peel sticker to close the flap.

She was glib and casual with most people who stopped. But she was learning this slightness of character did not suit all-comers. There were people in real need who saw her sign. Hesitant, doubtful, they stood in front of her stand. They never asked why she was there, why she was providing such a valuable service.

Most of them were men. Not, she realized, because she was a young, slender redhead with a really fresh smile, but because they believed they had no way to express the anguish, the love, the despair, the grieving, the guilt, the fear that was making them more than slightly crazy. Maybe a poem would do it; maybe a drink or four would do it; maybe a reckless car race down the Pacific Coast Highway; or a very large bet on a heavy-weight fight, or a bar brawl, or a gun—but maybe a poem would do it after all.

■ ■ ■

Another day.

"My brother died in Iraq."

"Do you want the poem to be about your brother or about how you feel?"

"I..."

"I know, you haven't thought about it yet." Emily waited. "Can you tell me where you were when you found out?"

"I was playing in my band. I know this is weird, but I play an electric oboe. We only meet once a week after dinner at this guy's garage down the street. My wife came to get me with the car. I mean it was only half a block away. I knew something was wrong because why wouldn't she walk or just call if she needed me. We had to go right to my parent's house. Anyhow, that's how it was."

"Okay. That's okay." Emily soothed.

"Is that enough? I think you need more to write a real poem. I mean it's not going to be one of those two line Japanese things is it? I never understand those. You know: 'White sand, stretch my heart, even tigers cry.' Or how about: 'Snow clots on broken ground, I need a raise'", the alive brother is laughing.

"I mean those poems are demented. But my brother was really earnest. He had a cell phone. We spoke every morning—morning for him anyway. He would say, 'All suited up. Waiting for incoming.' But that's not how he died. His truck was hit by a blast from an IED and rolled over in a ditch. Eight guys. He was the only one who died. They brought him home, and he looked perfect—perfect."

"I will try to write a poem that helps."

"Should I wait? I don't want to wait. You know, inhibiting the creative process and all that. I don't want to see you thinking about him and me. I'll come back. When should I come back? Can I come back in an hour?"

Emily nodded.

"It says free poems for oboists. By the way, I don't think you spell it that way."

"Is that why you stopped?"

"Uh huh. I'm out of work. I can't afford to pay for a poem."

The oboe brother left. Emily began: *My brother's boots, summer-tight on my feet/ want a more forgiving heart than I can hope for.*

EDGAR

NO PERSPECTIVE

Saturday: "Ed, the bricks are here. Bad as it is, the bricks are here. We are waiting for you to show up. Uhh. Yeah. Maybe it's still a holiday. I think it's a holiday. Anyways. Call me. We gotta get this thing started by Monday."

Monday, 9:20am: "So, it's Monday. Where are you? It can't still be a holiday. Aren't they only two days? I asked Flusher. He said two days tops. So where are you?"

10:05am: "It's still Monday. You ain't here. Call me."

10:25am: "Your kid helper laid out the bricks yesterday to do a color match. What's with that idiot anyway? Do you know he only eats tuna fish—ever? He stinks. But the bricks are all color matched. Just waiting for you, buddy."

10:52am: "Hey, you got that thing PTSS—you know post-traumatic whatever. Come on buddy. It's not your fault. Just cause you saw it from your window. I mean. THE BRICKS ARE HERE. The job is waiting on you, pal. Tuna hammered in some frames this morning but he can only do so much. They're not paying the big bucks for him."

11:05am: "You not here in two hours, I'm coming over."

■ ■ ■

1:00pm: "Don't even tell me you ain't in there. Your car's in the lot. I can hear noise in there. I can smell Chinese. I saw the delivery guy leaving your building. Open the fucking door, you asshole."

"I'll just keep calling. Open the fucking door."

"Open the fucking door."

"Hey you hear that banging. That's me you fucking moron. Open the fucking door."

1:22pm: "See you take the phone off the hook, I call your cell. Open the fucking door. Ed, you're a grown man. Don't make me talk to you like a fucking teenager. It's embarrassing. You're making me look like an asshole. Open the fucking door, please. I know you're all right. I can smell the food. Please, open the door. Please."

1:55pm: "Okay. One more chance and then I'm leaving. I am outside your door. Standing in the hall. I've been here for an hour. I even took a break and sat down. Some lady came by in the next apartment and couldn't get her keys out. I held her packages. She's good looking but I think she's married. You know her? Maybe you could ask her out—if she ain't married that is. You need to ask someone out. I think you've been going downhill since Ruth died. This truck thing is just the end of the spiral. So, now you can let it all go and come back up. At least you're not drinking. But you're not the kind, right. I mean your kind don't drink do they? So you're sad. So you feel guilty. It ain't your fault. Not any of it. Not Ruth or the truck. Okay, so it just beeped."

"It's me again. Thanks for not shutting off the phone. So, like I was saying. A truck leaves with a load of bricks four days ago in Tennessee. You're there. You see it leave. Four days later, it's crossing a bridge. The tarp comes undone. Just cause you see something doesn't mean you're responsible. I seen a lot of things. I saw you fall off that scaffold. Jesus that was fucking awful. But I didn't feel responsible.

"I saw Joey being born. They had to pull him out so fast because his breathing wasn't right. I mean I never want to see anything like that again. I never would have if we hadn't gone to that birthing class. Rita asked me to be there like those other husbands. I mean who does that? What is it with guys who want to watch some doctor guy stick his –aw you know. I was there and I saw Joey come out. Right from the start I knew something wasn't okay with him. But even though I saw it and even though I'm his father, for God's sake, I still don't think it was my fault. Another fucking beep."

"Okay. Last call and then it's Tuna. I saw that chopstick come out from under the door. So is this your fortune: *Your life will give meaning to others.* Or do you mean it's my fortune. Anyway. Edgar, one last time. Open the door. If you screw me over, and I lose this job, we are both in the crapper. If I can't get work then you can't get work. Awright. I hear the lock turning. Now! Open! The! Door!"

"Thanks for waiting," Edgar opened the door.

"No problem. That woman next door really is good looking. She married?"

"She's a lesbian."

"You shitting me?"

"Yes. She's married, and she has a boyfriend. I don't think there's room for me."

"They're shipping more bricks to replace the pallets that were lost," Hickey walked into the apartment. "I didn't think you wanted to go back down there."

"So, Vitalia isn't so bad, is he?"

"Tuna? Naw, he's reliable at least. There before I am every morning."

"That's because he gets dropped off by the Village. You know, the recovery program."

"You shitting me again?"

"He's a senior in college. Wants to be an architect." Edgar nodded.

"So, which is it? Never mind. I really don't give a rat's ass. As long as you come back."

"I can't."

"You can't?"

"I prefer not to." Edgar sat down on the couch.

"I don't know what that means."

"I prefer not to."

"What are you, Bartleby the Scrivener or something?" Hickey smirked. "Oh, you think I never read anything? Junior English, Sister Brody. I got 610 on my language SAT's, 730 on my Math. Accepted at Fordham, you douchebag."

"I still have some soup left."

"I ate. Let's not confuse this with a social call. Or a *shiva* call, because that's what you look like. No shoes, no shave—are the mirrors covered? Hey, remember that *mikvah* we built in Brooklyn, the one with the yellow brick?"

"I think there are people still down there." Edgar was lacing his shoes.

"That's not what the police think. They pulled up only one car, and it was empty. So, the people must have gotten out."

"They were trapped. They washed down the river. People were reported missing."

"How would you even know that? You're making stuff up. The police got calls from forty-two families. You think forty-two people went over the side of that bridge? And they were all in that one car?"

"War wonton. Lots of chicken still left." Edgar held out the soup carton.

"So, turn yourself into the cops, you feel so guilty."

"I called them. They said they'd get back to me."

"Of course, because you have just become one of the twenty-nine other psychos who call every time there's a murder or a missing kid or a bus crash. My brother says the seventy-first in Brooklyn gets five calls a day from psychos who confess."

"How do the police know they're all crazy? Maybe they are guilty?"

"Guilty of the Preppy murder? Of killing Lisa Steinberg? Of stabbing Kitty Genovese?" Hickey took the carton. "I'll eat it if you put your shirt on. Is it still hot? And none of that green stuff, just the chicken. Don't bother to shave. Well maybe you should. And shower also. You smell worse than Tuna."

Edgar sighed, "The temple didn't even call to find out what happened."

"They got busy."

"You're the only one who called."

"No one else knew you weren't where you were supposed to be."

"The neighbor's boyfriend hid in my apartment one afternoon when her husband came home early. Nice guy. We talked about music. He's a Republican. You don't meet a lot of those in New York. I knew that tarp was loose."

"Edgar. That tarp was loose in Tennessee? Seven hundred miles away in Tennessee? Four days away in Tennessee? And, by the way, it doesn't take four days to drive from Tennessee. So, where was that truck? It went through six or seven truck weigh stops. It stayed at four motels. It spent the night somewhere while someone's husband was out of town. Let it go."

"I should have said something."

"I'm leaving in ten minutes. Take a shower. I'll drive you."
'I have my car."
"I'm driving you. Then I'll know where you are."

SARAH

THE FAULTS IN OTHERS

Now that Samson Trout, Sarah Ryder's husband, was retired, he could no longer claim to be a resident of Nevada. Not unless he actually wanted to move there, which he didn't. He had only lived there six months out of his entire career, assigned to the Air Force base. In fact, while he was on active duty he could pick any state in the country to call home. Why wouldn't he pick the one with no state income tax and low auto registration fees that also gave its citizens the right to carry a concealed weapon, not that he ever did?

It was clear, though, in which state Sam and Sarah were now going to declare residency: Colorado. After thirteen moves in twenty-four years, Sarah wanted to go "out west" and spend the ten years until their retirement skiing, hiking and kayaking in the real outdoors rather than the "ersatz wilderness" of central New Jersey.

They had a good and pleasant life in New Jersey. They bought a summer bungalow at the Jersey shore in a town that was untrendy and low key where unheated five room beach houses were affordable, especially if you had free housing on base. Over the years, the bungalow and the town rose to the level of a destination, with single-location restaurants, clothing stores and specialty chocolate shops taking over stores on the scrappy boardwalk that once displayed straw hats, inflatable beach toys and racks of sunscreen.

The sale of this bungalow (improved over the years with central air conditioning, two slate-floored bathrooms and sisal carpeting) would finance the house they were going to build in Colorado. In fact, there was a bidding war for this sizable piece of land separated from the beach and the Atlantic Ocean by a narrow two-lane road. Many buyers saw the property and put in a contract without even walking into the house.

"Why would they do that?" Sarah Ryder complained, getting into the realtor's car. She wriggled out of her down coat and pulled off the wool watch cap, freeing dark brown ringlets that settled haphazardly on her shoulders.

The realtor, David Front, who was also Sam's best friend, shrugged, "They want the land Sarah. The house is irrelevant."

So, they're going to tear it down."

"Yep, eventually."

"What a waste. And what a waste of all the time and money we put into renovating it. Could we at least take the cast iron tub with us? And the light fixtures?"

"We'll negotiate. But think about whether you're even going to use them in the house in Colorado. You know, different climate, different state, different state of mind." He pulled into the parking lot of a seaside restaurant. "Hotdog?"

"Mmm. And ice cream."

They ordered at the drive-up window and ate in the car, too comfortable to give up the warmth of the heated seats for a hard wooden booth inside.

"Too bad you're my best friend's wife."

"That's just a state of mind. Too bad you're gay. Or is that also just a state of mind." Sarah licked mustard and chocolate ice cream from her fingers.

"No that's the real deal—with or without a current man."

"I want to leave and I don't want to leave. All at the same time."

"Hey, Colorado's *your* dream. I think Sam would just as soon stay here."

"So, did you and Sam ever, you know, fuck?"

"Jesus, Sarah, don't you have a filter?"

"Not when I'm with you."

"Why is that?" David was angry.

"Because you don't have a filter. You are willing just to be who you are. With a relationship, without. You never pretend, or talk about a mysterious 'partner'. You don't care if people know you cruise and go to underwear night at bars. So, I don't care when I'm with you. I would never say anything like that to anyone else. Not even to Sam. And I would never dance on the boardwalk or eat hotdogs and ice cream at the same time with anyone else—not even Sam."

"I know. I'm blessed. Here, let me kiss you."

"What was that? Did you just put your tongue in my mouth?"

"I might have."

"You are such an idiot."

■　■　■

Sam was in Colorado. He and Sarah had already picked out the one hundred and fifty acre plot of land for sale by owner, sixteen miles outside of Boulder. It was Sam's job to make the final review and negotiate the price.

"Want to see the cabin?" The owner offered.

Sam shrugged. "Okay." Sam didn't want to see the cabin at all since they had already decided on the location for the house. It was on the front five acres of open land five hundred feet from the road. The cabin the owner used was accessible only by a mile long rutted one-lane dirt road that meandered through the forest. "Sure, I'll see the cabin."

He offered an interest he didn't really feel because he was negotiating with the actual owner of the land who probably had a lot of pride and a lifetime invested in his hunting get-away.

"There it is. Just push in the door. I never lock her. People would just break in when I wasn't here. I'm never here."

It was, in fact, just as stated, a small cramped cabin that smelled from burnt wood. No décor in this one. Just logs on the outside and a few plywood walls on the inside. The kitchen was on a short wall of the open front room, which did have a fireplace, maybe the building's only source of heat. The bathroom, with plywood walls and framing studs painted white, was next to the kitchen to consolidate the plumbing. One bedroom was across the living room, small and dank, the walls hung with imitation western motif blankets to keep out the cold. There were two other rooms at the back of the house that held a hodge-podge of tools and broken furniture.

The owner followed him inside. Sam was ruminating on how to present his lack of interest in the building without jeopardizing the deal.

"So, look, I'm going to cut some little off the price since you're going to have to spend money to tear this dump down. Let's say, ten thousand," the owner said suddenly.

"Yeah, that would be right," Sam agreed. "Can I give you some money now? Is a check okay?"

The owner nodded.

Back in Boulder, Sam settled into the corner table of a local coffee house and called Sarah. "So, we're set. The deal's been made. He came down in price a little and we're actually buying about a hundred and fifty acres including a half-acre on the other side of the highway where he has his mailbox, his trash bins and leases out space for a billboard. So, we'll have to make sure when we site the house that we can't see the billboard in the winter. He gets $4,000 a year for that lease. I gave him some earnest money, and I'll have an engineer out there tomorrow. And I saw the actual cabin this guy had been staying in. God, it's a total dump. We'll probably wind up tearing it down."

"Do you know that people are coming to see our house and not even going inside?" Sarah answered. "They know they're going to demolish it without so much as checking to see if we have a Viking oven or whatever the new trendy thing is nowadays. How disrespectful."

"Well, this is not the same thing. This place is unlivable. You wouldn't let Beany stay there even though he was a total mutt and besides he's slightly dead."

"So, are we about to mirror faults that we dislike in other people?"

"No, we dislike the faults in other people that mirror the ones we already have."

"Just don't tear it down until I see it," Sarah hung up. And laughed.

■　■　■

The prospect of designing a house from ground-up was what appealed to Sarah. Free military base housing was free for a reason. No cost, no upkeep, but also no renovations, no permanent decorating changes. An officer and family got a clean, plain white house with two and a half baths, vinyl floors, vinyl windows, flat wooden interior doors, stained a uniformly dingy dark honey color, and sometimes a garage, sometimes a carport, sometimes neither.

Sarah learned how to make do from seminars held by Air Force housing advisors. One year, she and her daughter, Bethany, enhanced the white tile in the kitchen with colored paper and decals of flowers pasted on with liquid starch. As long as they didn't wet the tile, the design stayed true, until the humid Florida summer left it oozing onto the countertop. In another house, they bought cheap carpet runners at Home Depot and tacked them down on the steep stairs with double edge carpet tape.

Their current base house was a cut above with a front porch, a garage and a kitchen with an island and brand new, solid white countertops that were a knock-off of a famous brand. In addition, someone had exchanged the very practical back door for an elegant Dutch door with mullioned windows on top and double wood panels on the bottom.

There was not a single other decorative touch from any of the houses they occupied in their twenty-four years of marriage to the military that Sarah wanted to keep, except this idea of a Dutch door. A Dutch door to let in the sound of the outdoors, the wind and the smell of rain, but still keep her safe and sequestered.

To Sarah, that was the essence of marriage, the Dutch door that let in everything enticing, but kept her safe. She could say those provocative words to David. She could lean in and kiss him, or maybe someone else, for that matter. She could plan exciting and even dangerous adventures—contact travel agents for round-the-world flights, call universities to find out about their doctorate programs, apply for jobs in any off the grid place that struck her –Addis Ababa, Ulaanbaatar, Tashkent. It didn't matter, because she was married and couldn't go, couldn't do, couldn't commit to anything.

She had put maximum effort and energy into the beach house, and now that the little town had become trendy, finally, they could reap the financial benefit. It was long overdue. For twenty-four years they had planned carefully. When Bethany applied to college her aptitude and grades were the only consideration because they had the savings put aside to pay for the best college she could get into.

That was one of the things she and Sam had done right for Bethany. It probably made up for all of the many things they had done wrong, according to Bethany. When Sarah married Samson Trout, she decided to remain Sarah Ryder. It could have been because it was the height of the women's liberation movement when that was the cry—don't take your husband's name. Although, actually, Sarah thought, what women were keeping were their mother's husband's names, especially Sarah, whose parents divorced when she was twelve. Even her mother stopped using Ryder once she re-married.

So, there was Bethany's despair to deal with. "How could you have let me be called Trout," she asked her mother the day after her twelfth birthday, while they were walking up Main Street.

"Please don't let your father hear you say that."

"What, he doesn't know my last name?"

"He doesn't know that you don't like your last name."

"Bethany Louise Trout. It's awful. Even my initials are awful—BLT. I'm a fish and a sandwich."

"Who even thinks of that?"

"What? Everyone thinks of that. Everyone thinks of every stupid thing about every other kid."

"So, you're BLT. What about kids called 'Shorty' or 'Squinty' or 'Three-finger Joey'"?

"Oh my God, Mom, this isn't *The Sopranos*. Kids are called names like Brainiac, or Techy, or, get this, Wench."

"Wench? Wench? Do I hear an allusion to Shakespeare?"

"Just never mind. Never mind. I'll meet you at Delia's Attic."

"What do you mean, you'll meet me. I'm going there too, right now."

"OMG. I am NOT letting anyone see me walking down the street with you. That is so lame."

"So, if you weren't being called BLT or fish, you'd be 'Easy Ryder.'" Sarah yelled after Bethany, following ten feet behind all the way to Delia's.

"I don't even know what that means," Bethany shouted back and quickened her steps.

OLIVIA

MY MOTHER AND ONE
LOUSY NICKEL

My parents, Chae-soon and Chul-woo Park, have owned the grocery store on Jackson Avenue for more than twenty years. Its sign still reads Sloane Fine Foods but now everyone in the neighborhood calls it the Korean market because that is who we are. We do the things all Korean markets do. We keep our flowers outside, guarded by thick plastic walls (even in twenty degree weather), stock a salad bar in the middle of the center aisle with fresh salads made in the back by my mother every morning, and have jars of kimchi shipped in from Seoul in the refrigerator case. We also still give credit to customers we know when they send their children in for one or two items, so they don't need to carry money.

We keep the credit card numbers of a few families as well. When they call in an order for delivery or call ahead to have salads or smoked brisket ready to take home, the bag is waiting for them at the register, their card already charged. "Easy in, easy out," my father says to each one as a greeting instead of "good evening."

Twenty-four years ago, when my parents first came to America, they and, in time, my grandfather Park, worked for Mr. Sloane.

My grandfather was stationed at the front of the store be-hind the long counter. He used an abacus to tally the groceries, and he was faster than Mr. Sloane and his adding machine.

"Grandpa, you can't add with that thing and then show them how much they owe on them beads. No one understands that," Mr. Sloane would say, and my grandfather would nod. "Use the adding machine and give them the slip of paper." So, my grandfather would tally their groceries on his abacus, punch the total into the adding machine and give them the white slip of rolled paper, tearing it off carefully into a neat square.

Mr. Sloane lived in the back of Fine Foods with his wife who did not work in the store. She had long red fingernails. She smoked cigarettes all day long, lighting one from another. Sometimes she had two burning at the same time. She had a crooked back she tried to hide with a piece of fur with paws she wrapped around her shoulders. When Mr. and Mrs. Sloane bought Fine Foods in 1961, they put in air-conditioning right away, even in the storeroom, so Mrs. Sloane could wear her animal in the summer.

My sister, Cecelia, and I spent our first two years in playpens made from paper towel cartons in the storeroom of Sloane Fine Foods. Mrs. Sloane would come and visit us every afternoon, and feed us slices of cut up apple from the fresh fruit bins at the front of the store. The paws from her furry dead animal would brush against our cheeks as she bent down to wrap our fingers around those slivers of sweet, crisp fruit.

By the time my parents bought the store, everyone knew what a Korean market was and even asked for the special pears wrapped in little plastic mesh cases. For many years, my mother refused to stock them. She and my father *did* add fresh coconut and guava and long Chinese eggplant to the vegetable display on the right side of the door.

For a long while we extended credit to Mr. Sloan's customers, using the same tallying method. Mr. Sloane, and then my mother, would take a small brown paper bag and have the customer write his name, address and phone number on the top. Mr. Sloane, and then my mother, would lick the tip of a pencil and add up the items the customer wanted that day, keeping a running total on the bag. People could pay off their debt a little at a time. Their money would be put inside the bag and filed alphabetically. The first of the month was the time for a true reckoning, when everything written on the bag had to be paid. Then, that very day, the customer could fill out a new bag, and begin buying on credit again.

People on credit kept their purchases small and basic—milk, eggs, bread, cigarettes, sugar, soap, packaged chopped meat and chicken thighs, tomato soup—as if their imagination and culinary skills had fallen on the same hard times as their purchasing power.

My parents worked hard at the store, but we did not live in the back. We kept our apartment three blocks away where Cecelia and I shared the one bedroom. My parents slept in the dining el off the living room in the kind of apartment that is now listed in the real estate section as "Jr. 4," meaning if you were an optimistic person, you could consider the el off the living room (which was behind the galley kitchen) as a room unto itself, because it actually had a window.

In my parent's "bedroom", a gold frosted white metal chandelier hung over their double bed. They kept their folding clothes in cardboard boxes covered in blue-flowered adhesive paper that were stored under the bed—five for my mother and three for my father. The clothes that needed to be hung, my mother's three church dresses, her winter coat and my father's one gray suit, were stored in our bedroom closet along with my mother's most valued possession, her traditional Korean dress she wore every Christmas.

My sister and I hung our school uniforms and jackets in the closet as well. We had two tall dressers painted light green for the rest of our clothing and our collection of Disney princess dolls.

We were old-school Korean, still using our Chosun names, Sook Yan and Ok Yan, at home and in Korean Saturday school. But my parent's closest friends, Maxwell and Shirley Lee, told them to Americanize our first names so we would fit in at St. Joseph and Mary Catholic School. I became Olivia and my sister was renamed Cecelia. To "keep up with the times" as Shirley emphasized, my parents became Jacine and Charles.

Maxwell was my father's childhood friend from Korea who had moved to New York ten years before my parents. Shirley was born in the United States and was fervent about her status as a "native" and, thus, more knowledgeable about New York "ways" than any of us. So, my parents also listened to her when she urged them to keep living in the apartment when they finally bought Sloane Fine Foods rather than moving into the vacant one behind the store.

"Even though you will save money, that is a backwards move. Only foreigners do that," she pronounced, neglecting the fact that the Sloanes, third generation Americans, had lived behind the store their entire working lives. Then, using my mother's ranking system Shirley proclaimed, "Living behind the store is number ten. Having your own apartment is number six." She tapped my mother's hand, "But buying your own house, that is number one!"

Our parents set up the apartment behind the store just for us sisters. The front room still had the kitchen along one wall where my mother made the foods for the salad bar every morning. Once preparation was done for the day, it was our homework room. The back room, which had been the Sloane's bedroom, was our playroom. We were the only children in the neighborhood who had their own playroom with a bathroom right next door.

Every afternoon, we went straight from school to the store, changed out of our plaid skirts and white blouses into our play clothes and sat down at our matching desks and did our Sister Agnes English homework, and our Sister Fernanda math homework. Our science teacher, Mr. Lahey, never gave us homework. We did our history homework from Sister Bing in study hall.

We were very lucky sisters not to have a brother. My father had a son with his first wife. Although he never spoke of them, we knew they had died in Korea during a cholera epidemic. As brother-less sisters, all our parents' hopes were placed on us. Even though we were Buddhist, we received communion at St. Joseph's and learned our catechism so we could go to "a number one school" as my mother called it and wouldn't wind up at a "number ten college," specifically a Community College on Staten Island. My mother said this with exaggerated enunciation to emphasize what a number ten fate that would be. "You do that, you will have no car," she warned. "You have to take the ferry boat and pay one lousy nickel. That is how bad it is."

My sister and I did not look like sisters at all, if you got past the fact we were both Asian, which took the nuns and the kids at school a while to do. Even though I was older, I was shorter and smaller in every way. Small feet, small hands, small round classic Korean face with a very typical bridge to my nose. Cecelia was tall and broad. Her face was round and flat. Her skin was darker than mine and her hair was long and thick and lustrous while mine was wispy and drab.

My entire hand was the size of her palm, but my mother assured us we were both perfect, each in our own way. She showed us how to rest our left foot in the space between the wrist and elbow of our right arm. "See," she explained in Korean, "it fits perfectly. You are each correctly proportioned."

Then she measured our outstretched arms from fingertip to fingertip. "The same as your height. You are both perfect." Perfection is very important in the Korean culture. Midwives in the home country once kept drowning buckets next to delivery beds for infants born with obvious deformities.

Cecelia and I are eleven and a half months apart. I was born on January 2 and my sister was born November 16. In the New York City School System, where the cut-off for kindergarten was December 1, that meant we were both in the same grade at school.

My mother spent our entire childhood putting the fear of mediocrity into us. The idea that we would wind up at "number ten college" was always held out as the worst possible failure. Although we didn't socialize with a lot of other Korean families, we did meet them at Saturday school, where we learned our language and heritage, and celebrated our Buddhist traditions. Whenever an older sibling of one of our Korean classmates went off to college, mother would make her pronouncement. "University of Maryland, a number six school," and she would make a face. "University of Pennsylvania, that is a number two school. University of Princeton, a number one, very number one."

My sister and I eventually both went to very number one schools. "To go to Stanford and Amherst," my mother said, proudly. "Your father and I we will pay. We have the money. And, now," she announced, "such smart girls must marry number one smart husbands and have number one very smart children. But only two each. Because children are expensive."

We were all sitting in the homework room behind the store, drinking sodas and tea after school. She thought for a moment, "You should even have girls. Girls are very good children. They are smart. In America, girls take care of the mother and father when they grow old."

While our mother may have lacked nuanced English, she was a magician at finance, calculating the cost of each semester of college and deciding where to find the money. That's when we discovered she was invested in the stock market, that she owned bonds.

She had actually gotten in on an IPO suggested to her by one of Fine Foods' regular customers. Using two separate accounts, one under her name and one in my father's name, she managed to buy 7,000 shares at the opening price. She sold them the next day for a profit of over $100,000 in less than twenty-four hours. That money, plus twenty years of careful savings, paid for our colleges and, four years later, my law school tuition. By then, Cecelia had married what my mother believed was a number one husband and was pregnant with her first child.

My father was a quiet man. His English was actually better than my mother's, but he was wary of making any mistakes, so he spoke only Korean. He very rarely spoke directly to us, using our mother as the intermediary. "Tell our daughters they cannot go into the playroom until they have done their homework," he would say to our mother, even though he was very proud of the room he had created for us. It had been the Sloane's bedroom when they owned Fine Foods, but now it had a stage at one end of the room with curtains operated on a pulley system like real theatre drapes. My father built seating along the walls that were actually boxes with hinged tops to store our games and toys.

Each section had an image painted on top: games, dolls, art supplies, dress-up clothes, sports equipment (which for us were balls, jump ropes and roller skates). "Tell our daughters I found Monopoly money in the dolls' section," Father instructed Mother. He patrolled the playroom every evening like the meter maid on Jackson Heights Boulevard, checking for errantly parked items.

When we were born, our father was already fifty-one years old, our mother thirty-three. After my father became a widower, his aunts and sisters wanted to arrange a marriage for him quickly. They introduced him to many young women, but my father was stalwart. "You can find her, but I will choose her," he told them, according to my mother.

Five years later, my father then thirty-one, was introduced to my thirteen-year-old mother. He fell in love immediately, but my mother was despondent. As a dutiful Korean daughter, she had to obey her parent's choice for her. According to her, she ventured only a very timid, "But he's an old man. He has gray hair. My mother says, 'You must marry who father choose for you.' But *your* father was very smart. He said, 'We will wait until Chae-soon older. She is not ready. I don't want kicking, screaming baby in my bed. She can't even cook noodle properly yet.'" And our mother giggled because "noodle" didn't only mean noodle.

"And so he wait and wait and wait and many times I even forget he is waiting and I am waiting."

In the meantime, my mother went to school sometimes. Most of the time, though, she was needed in her family's small pear orchard, which had thirty-two trees and produced about a hundred bushels of pears each year. Every pear on every tree was precious, protected from bruising and from birds by a waxed brown paper bag. Many of those bags were tied on by my mother. She climbed up the ladder to each branch and tied the bags on with red string. At six or seven dollars a bushel, it was just enough to support the family—my grandparents, my mother and her five brothers. All of the boys were more valuable because they would carry on the Ahn family name and also care for their parents in their old age, in the true Korean way.

When my mother could go to school, in between bag tying and harvesting, she excelled in mathematics. So, her ability to navigate the financial intricacies of budgeting, purchasing and bookkeeping at Fine Foods and in the Park household was not so strange.

In Korea, my father's family was much more affluent. They owned a small market in their village and another larger one in Itaewon in Seoul, where many of the American servicemen and their wives shopped. My father understood very well what Americans would buy and was always prompt in putting up hand lettered signs he ordered from the Gunnery Sergeant's wife on base. CORN FLAKES, HOSTESS CUPCAKES, BRECK SHAMPOO, MODESS.

By the time my parents married when mother was nineteen and father was thirty-seven, she knew many things about Korean housekeeping. She tied her own brooms from dried hay, washed and sun-bleached her bed linens every week, and stored a year's worth of rice in a double-sided metal bin that kept it free from damp and vermin. She could make three kinds of *kimchi*, including my father's favorite with Napa cabbage, chili paste and fermented seaweed.

My parents moved into a small two-room house behind the Seoul market. My mother kept the books for the shop. She and my father made *kimchi* every November during the three-day "*kimchi* holiday." Then, almost all of the small shops closed—even the ones that sold gold and jade jewelry and made leather coats for foreigners and Japanese businessmen who would fly over from Japan for gambling weekends at the new resort an hour outside of Seoul.

My father would take the earthenware *kimchi* jars out of their storage holes in the ground behind the house. He would clean off the dirt residue, wash them and set them on a raised platform in the weak late autumn sun, until they were dry. Meanwhile, my mother would chop two hundred pounds of cabbage, spinach, garlic and green onion. She would grind pepper, salt, mustard and spices into a paste and add several secret ingredients specific to the Ahn family *kimchi*.

This ritual persisted long after they came to America, and I remember the stifling odor of all of these ingredients. The odor permeated the apartment for weeks in its strongest form and lingered for months on some of the dishtowels and the earthenware bowls my mother used for the mixing. The two *kimchi* jars were kept on the fire escape in the winter and in the unused dumbwaiter in the summer.

Even though my mother was an obedient and dutiful wife and daughter-in-law, an excellent housekeeper, and an equal participant in the managing of the Park markets, she was the worst kind of wife in the Park family, the worst kind of wife in their corner of Seoul—a seemingly barren one. My father was still in love with my beautiful mother, whose pale skin, aquiline nose and thick black hair with a hint of auburn were much admired. Nevertheless he was depressed and angry. He had lost a son and a first wife and waited years before marrying my mother because he did not want to force himself on her. But despite her beauty, her intelligence and her fertile birth year (the ox) she produced no children.

The herbalist in the Park home village offered special remedies; the Buddhist priest offered prayers; the Korean doctor at the university hospital in Seoul could not explain why my mother could not conceive and suggested that a change in climate might be desirable. The American doctor at the community outreach clinic in the village found no clinical problem, writing in her chart that my mother probably had a "hostile womb environment."

This was the paper my mother carried with her when she came to America. She was planning to bring it to her first appointment with the American doctor at a hospital in Queens, when she realized she was pregnant already and had almost certainly become pregnant when she was still in Korea.

I was born seven months later. My parents left the market in Korea in the care of my father's younger brother, Sing Park, planning to go back after the change in climate cure worked and they had a few children. Uncle Sing was not a good businessman. He did not have a head for numbers, and the earnings from the store became progressively more meager.

When the market in Korea closed, Grandfather Park was put on a plane to live with his oldest son in this place called Queens. My parents were thriving. They had their two little girls, and a combined income of over $25,000.

EMILY

THE FLIGHT OF GIRL

Emily had been sending poems into *frombadtoverse* since she was in high school. TheDivineR responded assiduously to each one. She soon noticed that TheDivineR responded much more quickly to poems written by women or written by people she assumed were women based on their email signatures. Sometimes TheDivineR ignored poems clearly written by men as near as she could tell.

But Tanner thought otherwise. "Letch," he had told her. "He's clearly a letch."

"What makes you think it's a *he*? I think it's a *she*. You know, like the divine Miss M. Maybe she's a feminist. Maybe poems written by women are just better or this divine person just likes them better."

"No! Letch. I know it. We'll test. Give me one of your poems. I am going to send it in as 'HemanJack.'"

"You are so fucking lame."

"What? Okay, I'll be 'pussylover'." Tanner was cackling.

"You're such a smuck." Emily sniped.

"It's schmuck, idiot. You can't say 'sh' can you?"

"Shut up," Emily was annoyed. "SHUT UP. See I can."

"Oh sore spot, sore spot. That doesn't prove anything. Say shrimp."

"Ssrimp. And you're an asswipe."

50

"It's shhhrimp baby, shhhrimp."

Emily swung at him but he caught her arm, pulled her next to him and kissed her just like he'd seen guys do in the movies. Between movies and rock songs, Emily and Tanner knew exactly how to run a relationship. There was the playful part where the boy is indifferent and the girl is sharp-tongued. This could be moved along two ways—a segue into interested respect, then beginning attraction, and finally deep, enduring love, or intimacy and sex fueled by indifference and boredom. Emily and Tanner leaned towards the latter. They believed they handled it pretty well with a mix of sarcasm and disdain. They smoked and drank publicly to maintain their tough images but didn't do much of it when they were alone.

"You are such a fifties girl," her friend, Teresa, told her. "It's *Rebel Without a Cause* and *Grease*."

"I don't even know what you are talking about."

"Ask your mother."

"My mother?"

"Doesn't she spend her time eating bonbons and watching old movies?"

"No, my mother, for your information, spends her time winning big at poker and selling houses. She doesn't drink, smoke, eat bonbons or fuck as near as I can tell—except for once. She's an automaton who asked me whether she should get a divorce when I was still in kindergarten. When I started to cry, she just looked at me with this certain kind of oh-my-god look and said 'I can see you are too immature for this conversation.' I was five. I still sat on my lunchbox when I waited for the school bus."

"That is such bullshit. How do you even remember it?"

"I remember it because it is one of my mother's favorite stories. She tells it all the time. It's like a marker of how cool and shrewd she is."

"Do you write poems about this?"

"No, I write poems about butterflies. Of course I do."

"No wonder this divine guy is all over you. He can smell your...."

"What? Pussy?" Emily hooted.

"No, your vulnerability. Listen if this guy ever even suggests that you meet him anywhere or that you start writing to him directly rather than through the website, you tell me right away."

"Yes, St. Teresa. Do you know you were martyred?"

"All saints were martyred. You can't be a saint otherwise."

Emily was already writing directly to TheDivineR. The first poem she had sent him was the one she wrote to shock Mrs. Norris in Creative Writing, a class she took because she needed the three credits and because it met first thing in the morning leaving her with a double lunch period to hang out with Tanner.

My Poem
By Emily Bishop ☺

So, while I have his dick in my mouth
he's talking about this poem we read
in English Lit today. Something about
A fly that died.
The one that Mrs. Norris told me,
In front of the whole class,
I should be "attuned" to—

she's such a wench—
because it was written by another,
very famous Emily, to make it clear,
of course, that's not me
because I am not famous—
even though everyone in school
knows me because I am the one
with the real tits and the real
long red hair, not like
my friends Madison and Britney
(who are the best, really they are.)
And Tanner goes to me, "It makes
you think about, you know,
like when your grandma died."
And I really don't want to think about that
so I bite down on his dick
just a little to shut him up.
Not that he's my boyfriend or anything
because that would be sooo boring.
But he drives me to class everyday.
My grandma died so still.
One minute she was humming to herself
lying in bed and the next she stopped
and let out this big breath and I sat
and waited and stroked her hand
and pushed her shoulder to make her
breathe and I called her name,
her real name—Lily—
But she never breathed again.
And I wouldn't even have known about
Charlotte's Web, or how to sing harmony,
or about putting that dot of white liner

on the inside corner of my eyes
to make them look bigger.
If it wasn't for her.
And in the yearbook they wrote,
"She came, they saw, she conquered."
Under my picture, which made her laugh.
So here's my poem, a la Emily Dickinson:
There was silence when she died
The moon was on the wane
I couldn't believe I didn't cry
I'll never see her again.
And I have to push Tanner away
at the very last minute
and it's all over his pants.
Because the thing I am definitely not
going to do is
swallow.
By Emily Bishop, CWR 601, Room 412.

Mrs. Norris handed back the poetry assignment a week later, with no comments on Emily's paper. She asked some of the girls (girls again) to read their poems. Emily was sure she was going to have to have a "consultation" with the guidance counselor and maybe even the school psychologist when Mrs. Norris asked her to stay after class.

"Mrs. Norris, I really didn't mean to insult you."

"Talent, my dear."

"What?"

"Talent. You could be a good poet. A good poet one day. If you keep working at it."

"Mrs. Norris, I mean I called you a wench in the poem but I really...."

"Not interested. Am interested in the poem that has so many levels to it. The poem within the poem—a brilliant touch."

"I mean a lot of it is not really true, I was just...."

Mrs. Norris put a hand on her arm, "Irrelevant. Doesn't matter. True. Not true. Keep writing. Submit. Get comments. Keep writing. Show me more if you want to."

Emily waited, her unmarked paper in her hand.

"You can go now."

Mrs. Norris gave a few more poetry assignments which Emily made an effort to complete in line with what the other girls in the class were writing. Then they moved on to short stories. But, on her own, she had begun to write what she called real poems. She submitted to a few sites but eventually narrowed it down to *frombadtoverse*, where she always got a very appreciative reception.

■   ■   ■

Emily packed up her stand early. Clouds had moved in and rain was in the forecast. Not too many people asked for a free poem when it was raining and certainly no one paid for one. The "All Others Must Pay." sign was not for Emily to make money. She didn't care what people paid her. She was much more interested in why people would pay when it wasn't their day. Was it to overcome grief? Was it because they didn't think it would ever be their day? Was it because they believed they would wind up paying for everything anyway whether in money or love or pain?

She usually decided in the morning which poems were going to be free that day, but tonight she was going to make some new signs for categories people had suggested. Free poems for: nuns, vegans, amputees, (No she wouldn't do that one. It would seem too weird, and no one would stop at her stand.) How about free poems for: sculptors, tailors, belly dancers? Free poems for motorcyclists, booksellers, Kabbalists, morticians, golfers, philosophers, potters (she would take either kind), longshoremen and drunks (she might never hang that one. She didn't see much value in having a conversation with a drunk, although she'd probably had lots of them and didn't know it.)

Emily blogged her experiences that day, posting her poems and photos and then sent off a poem to *frombadtoverse* rather than to Russell directly because she wanted to get general feedback, particularly from the newest regular, Edgar.

Loose Men and Tight Women

Past innocence it's not hot enough
On a soft bed
With dimmed lights
And some salsa idea of music. Better
Dressed for something
Quick and tawdry
Fingers tearing silk
Standing against a wall
With the news on real loud.

> TheDivineR: *You, my dear, are too young for such jaded views.*

Emily: *Critique the poem not the poet. That is one of YOUR guiding precepts. It doesn't matter whether I learned everything I know from A Child's Garden of Verses or from Kim Addonizio.*

Sarah: *I didn't think anyone remembered that book. Robert Louis Stevenson, wasn't it.*

Edgar: *We're off topic here. Let's get to the critique. I like it. It's sharp, tough. Like the word tawdry.*

TheDivineR: *A Child's Garden of Verses? This group is more like "The Grown-up Jungle of Calamity Poetry." How do you even know who Kim Addonizio is? But, to get to the poem because Emily is right. It's tight, it's tough and the title is the best part.*

Sarah: *Agree. The title sets up the poem so we know exactly who's doing what and why. It's enticing, very sexual.*

TheDivineR: *Not exactly. We may know who's doing what but we don't know the point of view. Man? Woman? You tell me who's writing this. I don't know if I can tell.*

Jacine: *Of course you can. It's a woman. If it were a man he'd be talking about what was being done to him. "Fingers tearing silk" that's a woman's fantasy. Don't you know nothing.*

TheDivineR: *Now I do. But the "against the wall" part.*

Sarah: *There are walls and there are walls. I've got a house with a wall that is begging for someone to do something to or on or in it. Oops. Did I say that out loud?*

Edgar: *Yes, but you were only talking about the wall. Or were you?*

Emily: *Hey, I've got a poem here and so far all we've been doing is impugning my age, speculating on sexual activity and talking about a wall. What about the poem itself? I would like some critical comment here.*

Sometimes that was how it went. She could imagine these people logging into the group site every afternoon, or rather afternoon for her, evening for some of them, since she was sure at least one of them, Jacine, was a New Yorker. Maybe Edgar as well. She knew Russell lived in Colorado, just outside of Boulder. Sarah she couldn't even guess about. Mountains somewhere maybe.

The next day, Russell posted an assignment: "Look at the wall next to where you are sitting. Now imagine a door in that wall. What does the door look like? Is it big enough to walk through? Put a good handle on the door because you are about to walk through it. Take your time. Write about that wall, that door and what is beyond."

Edgar submitted within minutes, as if he had been waiting for a prompt to get to this poem he had written a while ago.

The Door in the Wall

Lately my watch is losing time.
I am minutes behind without meaning to be
And the conversation has moved on to Trollope
while I linger at the axe in Trotsky's skull.
I called my long dead sister last weekend and,
even though a Mr. Beal was patient,
neither he nor his angry wife knew
what to feed the egret that is the color of sky
and wants so desperately to lick my heart.
The house with the crown moldings and
the egg yellow nursery no longer exists.
Nor does Boolean logic, the fate of the Aztecs
or the word for the thing you use when it rains.
Gray men and highlighted women
imprison me in sidearm embraces,
swear they are the lithe and bony children
whose smell I can inhale in old pillows.
I know the sound of remorse,
the way to stir chocolate with my tongue
until I am in Bruges, the bounty of two lovers,
the first twenty-five lines of Chaucer
and that April in Baltimore filled with
the measured passion of a blue-eyed chemist,
I still have that and call her soul mate.
But I am bound for assisted living
where the nurses will smooth my skull and
stretch the corners of my mind so tight
I can translate Celsius into Fahrenheit.

TheDivineR: *Who are you in this poem?*

Sarah: *What does it matter?*

Jacine: *Is a poem fiction or life?*

Emily: *Both, I think, although it may not be our lives. Is it your life?*

Edgar: *Not yet.*

SARAH

NO ONE'S RIGHT ALL THE TIME

One of Sam's Air Force Performance Reports had stated he was General Officer material. But that optimistic evaluation, true at the time, never came to fruition, since Sam lacked the one qualification many of his fellow Colonels had—battlefield experience. Some quirk of timing had kept him in Germany during the Iraq War. By the time he was a senior officer, he was needed stateside for his specialty—weapons assessment and procurement. Without battle experience he would never be promoted to General.

Sam served out the four-year commitment he made when he accepted the promotion to full Colonel, and then it was time to retire at sixty-percent pay and take a civilian job. But it really wasn't a civilian job. A large consulting firm wanted him for his knowledge as well as his Top Secret clearance. They hired him immediately. They were happy to assign him to the Boulder office where he would soon be the civilian lead on a weapons procurement project.

By then, the land for the house had been purchased—a one hundred fifty-three acre parcel bordering public land on one side and a secondary road on the other.

"Ain't life grand," the site engineer sang out at their first meeting.

"It sure can be," Sam agreed over a celebratory beer in Henry's Best Saloon and Hardware, on the outskirts of Boulder.

"So, the land is good. The site for the house has good slope, drainage and no tree clearing needed. If you get the diviner out I bet he'll find water within a hundred feet."

"Are you serious? The diviner?"

"Sure. How else you gonna know where to dig the well?"

"There's got to be some scientific way of finding water," Sam asserted.

"The diviner is scientific. He's right one hundred percent of the time—the one I'm going to give you is anyway."

"No one's right one hundred percent."

"Well, give or take. But that's the way to go. Trust me on this."

"Is that how he makes his living?"

"He's a poet."

"No one makes a living as a poet."

The engineer ordered two more beers, "Why, he was the poet lariat of Colorado once."

"Laureate."

"That's okay, too. You'll meet him; you'll like him; you'll trust him. And he WILL find you water."

Sam shrugged and took out his cell phone, "What's his name?"

"Russ Cooney, and here's his number."

Sam found out Russ Cooney actually wasn't the poet laureate of Colorado, never had been, but he'd had several books of poetry published (by a university press) and his family owned the largest copper mine in the state. They made a date for the divining when Sarah was going to be there because he wanted her to witness this piece of arcana.

He phoned her. "This is what you have been looking for. The authentic west. Diviners, cowboy poets—why, I bet he even goes to that annual cowboy poetry event in Wyoming each year."

"It's in Nevada, you fool, your home state. Don't make fun of it. Sandra Day O'Connor was the keynote speaker one year. They get thousands of people. It's in the middle of winter and below zero there some nights and all the hotels in Elko are filled."

"First, it's not my home state, just my state of legal residence. And B, if Sandra Day O'Connor had time to go to the cowboy convention, she should have stayed on the Supreme Court."

"Be that as it may. She was there."

The divining was set for June 16th, when Russ Cooney was sure the ground would have thawed. Sam bought Sarah a book of Cooney's poems. Maybe they would ask him to autograph it.

■　■　■

The May assignment *frombadtoverse:* "Write a poem about *the* house. You know what I mean. It's the one you still think about whether you ever lived there or not. Whether it was where you spent your childhood or passed by everyday on your way to work or had illicit sex in. *You know the one.*"

TheDivineR was right. Sarah didn't hesitate.

Going to the Dogs

I have taken to reading the tales
of the concubine Lady Murasaki
in the kitchen.

There is something
in her bittersweet language
that goes well with scallions
which I mince recklessly into everything
while I catalogue her opulent obis
and calculate the upheaval in changing palaces.
We once peered through
the locked gates of Balmoral,
barred because the Queen was to reside.
A trip she postponed for weeks.
Her kitchen cooked dinner every night
in expectation, and then fed it to the dogs.
Sated, they slept deep,
warming the old Scottish stones.
Their dreams hovering in the misty castle air.
I sieve a sauce of raisins and green onions
over the lamb, while my husband sets the table.
I carry the platter carefully. My steps are small,
in consideration of a concubine's small feet.

"What do you think?" Sarah asked as Sam finished reading the poem and was about to read it again.

"I'm blown away," Sam nodded. "Blown away. This is so much more than what I thought poems were about. And we were at this place. At the same time. Looking through the same gate. Is this what happens?"

"What?"

"That we are in the same place but not having the same experience?"

"I don't know. I've never thought about it."

AVALANCHE

You are still struggling to right yourself and run toward the hillock and the sound of metal scraping. But you are moving like a mote of dust in the sunlight. You lift one arm and examine its gooseflesh and its stringy ligaments outlined across your muscle. You turn your head cautiously from side to side checking for damage, wondering at the cascade of lights in your left eye. In the profound silence after the smash of the avalanche you hear a trickle of water, the faint crunch of gravel, a gearshift and a motor. A truck has blundered into the scene and the driver has jumped from the cab into knee-deep snow. He is shouting.

"Who's there? Who's that? Did you get out? Where's everyone."

You'll answer in a few minutes, you think, running your tongue slowly across your teeth to make sure you didn't break any. You know it's really easy to break a tooth if you clamp your jaw too tight, and you think you might have done that when the avalanche hit you. You blink your eyes a few times and wrinkle your nose.

"Are you hurt? Can you move?"

In a minute, you think. *Jesus, can't you see I'm busy.*

The knee-deep man is scrabbling towards you, shading his eyes. "Is that you?"

Now, there's no need to say anything. He'll figure it out. And he's pulling at you, "Say something. Where's everyone else?"

You nod carefully at the mound of snow.

The man snarls, drops your arm and pushes his way towards where the cabin might be. It is now time for you to move, to get up and look helpful and worried and overwhelmed and angry, just like the man racing ahead of you.

"Did you get help?" you rasp. "You went to get help. Did you get help?" And then you even know the reason he left, because he took the bleeding girl with him although no one thought it was that serious a wound since it was from a hunting knife. It was definitely not from the shotgun that had left two jagged holes in the roof, but maybe that happened later. Much later. You are not sure.

The man is back in the truck shouting into the satellite phone.

EDGAR

DOUBTS

That scene on the George Washington Bridge was something Edgar's mother, Estelle, would have called "taking advantage of the gift." The family gift. What Edgar simply thought of as the advantage of perspective or at its most intense, a hyper-awareness, his mother always insisted was the family gift of clairvoyance. Not the casual clairvoyance of *I was just thinking of you and here you are calling me.* No, it was the full-blown clairvoyance of mediums and past-life regressionists; of people who hold séances and not just talk to the dead but also have the dead talk through them to their living relatives.

It was the gift of people who go into deep trances and bring messages in foreign languages, the gift of people who assume the voices and personae of dead mothers and fathers, of dead children, of dead lovers and speak assurances to the living and tell them not to worry, that all is well.

His mother would hold sessions in their Brooklyn living room and the attendees would recognize the voice, the language, and the sense behind the vague predictions. They would cry and leave happy. His mother was an honorable woman who never took money for the sessions or accepted gifts. She greeted the participants, strangers from as far away as Milwaukee, or the Bronx or Dublin, once a month on a Thursday evening and served them a special tea she learned to make in Lithuania.

They sat on cushions around the marble coffee table in the living room. Estelle sat on a low chair at one end of the circle, a scarf over her head, her hands palm up in her lap as if she were accepting a newborn. There was no music, no atmosphere beyond the dimming of the lights. On warm nights, the noises from the city would wind through the open windows—cars honking, snatches of conversation as people walked by in the street below, ice cream trucks – but that didn't matter. Estelle didn't care, the visitors didn't care, and the ghosts didn't care.

Until Edgar was twelve he believed in his mother. On séance day he would set out the cushions and heat up the water for the tea. He would take people's coats in the winter, or offer them little paper fans in the summer that he made from folded up newspaper. He would help the older people down onto the cushions and help them up after the séance. He would hand them tissues if they cried.

His mother was always tired after the sessions, so he would wash and dry the teacups and put them away. Estelle would take a bath and go to bed. The next morning, she would be as energetic as she always was. Dressed by six, she would have breakfast ready for his father who would come home from the night shift at the newspaper press. She would wake Edgar so they could eat together. At seven-thirty she would walk with him part way to his school and then go off to the subway for her job as a court stenographer.

Much later, Edgar wondered if her day job was the real root of her gift. Maybe transcribing the lives of people and their dealings with a treacherous world that left them in the midst of lawsuits, or criminal charges or custody battles or divorces, made her exquisitely sensitive to the secret plights of strangers. She could hear the hidden stories they no longer remembered, stories that made them weak for wickedness, too sensitive to wrongs committed against them, or too eager to blame or be blamed. But that was long after he stopped believing what she did was mystical in any way.

When he was thirteen, it was no longer acceptable for his mother to walk with him to school, or even to the end of the block. It was even preferable that she was not in the same elevator with him as he met his friends in the lobby of their apartment building. He would see her walking on the other side of the street as he ambled along joking with his friends, a woman in a sensible coat, with low-heeled shoes and a kerchief carefully tied around her just curled hair. The coat was too short and the skirt of her dress dangled about two inches below. She carried an oversized handbag that held her wallet, her extra glasses, an umbrella, her lunch and a novel she was reading. She walked a little stooped over as if she were looking carefully at the ground to make sure she didn't fall.

To Edgar, she looked so ordinary, so without any specialness. She was just a very average, sensible woman on her way to a mundane job she had been doing for almost fifteen years. It took all the magic out of her séances. The guests were just ordinary people whose coats smelled from mothballs, the old teacups were mismatched with fine cracks in the glaze, the tea was bought in bulk from a tiny shop in Manhattan and the cushions were flat and worn and had to be aired out each week because they smelled like people's behinds.

Nothing in these people's lives was interesting, Edgar was certain, which was why they latched so diligently onto his mother's contacts with their loved ones, almost shaking in their eagerness to believe. They nestled into his mother's vision as if they could lay their heads against her chest and be soothed and cuddled into some special place that was lost to them long before the mother they were seeking had died.

Mothers were what they longed for, but it wasn't all mothers they got. They got dead husbands who weren't so much missed as regretted, distant fathers who were never so reassuring and accessible when they were alive. The got mysterious relatives whose only identifier was an initial they didn't recognize. They got unspecified protoplasmic angels who stood on their shoulders and would guide them through darkness into the light. They got unrealized talents that were going to fall on them like rain and make them whole and appreciated and fulfilled.

Edgar's mother's special talent was that no spirit ever brought bad news. There were a few torturous moments perhaps, an illness that would in the end make them stronger, a lost love that would be found. No fire, no flood, no bankruptcy, no prison, no accident, no cancer, no heart attack, no ungrateful children.

All was good in the world of Estelle and her gift until Edgar's father died. His death was the most ordinary thing. He sat down in his brown tweed club chair after dinner one Wednesday evening and died. He didn't cry out in pain, or clutch his chest. He didn't even twinge with unease. He sat in his chair and watched "Jeopardy" until the double round began and then put his teacup carefully down on the side table, which also held the TV guide from the local newspaper, and his reading glasses, and he died.

By the time Estelle finished washing the dishes and calling her mother, the body was slumped and cool. She dialed 911. The EMT's came and said Adam was dead and then carted his body off to the hospital, anyway, with an oxygen mask strapped lopsided over his nose and mouth, where the doctor said he was definitely dead. He was buried Friday morning.

There was a service at the mortuary led by the rabbi from the temple around the corner from the house. The rabbi knew Adam well and gave a touching sermon and many of the sixty people there cried. They told stories about how they met him and he was always a gentleman and how lucky to die like that without pain and sitting in your own chair in your own home after a nice dinner but how sad for the family and what a shock and it was a good thing Estelle had a steady job because Adam was a wonderful man but not such a good provider and maybe he had a little life insurance policy and was the newspaper going to do anything for him and you never knew. It could happen to any of us.

Everyone knew not to ask Estelle about Adam until after *schlosheim*—the thirty days when one's soul is in limbo after death. Before that she couldn't contact him because he was nowhere. After that, he would be somewhere and Estelle with her special gifts would surely be able to find him.

"Have you heard from Adam?" neighbors asked.

"No," Estelle would answer.

"What, with your gifts, no news?"

"What news? You mean like what's the weather like, or has he seen anyone we know?"

"You know, like what's it like over there."

"There is no over there. There is no place with streets and traffic and diners where you can order Belgian waffles or anything like that. The dead are in a spiritual world. There is no substance."

"But can't he tell you stuff? Don't you want to know?"

"I prefer not to," said Estelle the scrivener, just like Bartleby.

"But that's your gift."

"A surgeon does not operate on herself."

Edgar believed Estelle would not use the gift to find Adam because she was afraid she would fail. The gift worked for other people because they could forgive Estelle, the intermediary, for getting things wrong, or at least not quite right but she would discover the limits of her power if she tried to reach his father and failed.

■ ■ ■

"I'm going to Morocco," Estelle told Edgar, six months after Adam's death.

"You mean Morocco like in Africa? Where in Morocco?"

"You know, Morocco. You mean like which neighborhood?"

"Morocco is the country."

"So, what's a city in Morocco?"

"I don't know. Maybe Casablanca?"

"That's a movie or a bar or something, not a city."

Edgar came out of his bedroom with the *Rand McNally World Atlas Imperial Edition, 1968*. "See, here's Morocco. Let's see. Okay, there's Fez, Tangier, Marrakesh, Rabat and Casablanca."

"That's it. I'm going to Marrakesh. I need to see a mystic."

"You are a mystic."

"Edgar. I am not a mystic. I am a clairvoyant. There's a difference. A big difference. I'm a clairvoyant. I can only see what's there. I can't change anything. A mystic can change things."

"You mean like voodoo or a witch doctor. Where they give you amulets and blow smoke in your face and take your money and your jewels because they're tainted, and they need to purify them?" he pushed his glasses higher up on his nose. "Do you know that Morocco is right opposite Gibraltar, right across the Straits of Gibraltar? And of course, you never get them back—the money and the jewels. Wow! Algeria is huge compared to Morocco. It's bigger than most of Europe. Can we go there too?"

Estelle wrinkled her eyes. "Well, I really didn't plan on taking you. Masha and Feldshuh said you could stay with them upstairs."

"You mean the sour soup sisters. I'm not staying with them. Their house smells. They smell. And WHY WOULD YOU EVEN TALK TO THEM ABOUT THIS WITHOUT TELLING ME? "

"Stop shouting! And you used to love to stay with them."

"Yeah when I was six! And I didn't know any better, and I thought that people who walked their cat on a leash and had live fish in their bathtub were fun."

"Don't exaggerate. They only had live fish for Passover when they made gefilte fish, and you like gefilte fish. And the cat's dead."

"I'm sure they have another one. And all of this is not the point. You can't go to Morocco by yourself. You don't even know where Morocco is. And because you just can't because you're just not that swift—I'm sorry Mom but you're not. I'm just going to say that in general people who go into trances and speak to dead people and who want to go three continents away to have their fortunes read, they are just not up to taking care of themselves in the modern world which isn't even the case here because Morocco probably isn't even the modern world but the ancient world but anyway. You need a chaperone. That's all."

"You're in school."

"School is very overrated. I'm in junior high school. Do you know what junior high school is? It's not school. It's an experiment gone way wrong. Nobody cares what happens in junior high school. It's like limbo after you die except it's not thirty days it's three years when you really can't be seen by anybody except other kids and ticket sellers at the movies who can't decide whether to sell you a kid's ticket or not so you have to scrunch down a little so you look short enough. Besides, I speak French."

"What's that got to do with it?"

"Okay. That settles it. If you don't know they speak French in Morocco, you cannot go alone."

"The mystic is Jewish. She probably speaks Yiddish. I can speak Yiddish."

"What's the mystic's name. Or is it just any mystic."

"Ha! Yamara Azaria. I know exactly who she is. Azaria, yes, or Azara. Just the same. In Marrakesh. There's an article about her in this magazine. And I wrote to the author and he answered me and gave me her address and her telephone number, and here it is."

"You have her phone number? Let's call her."

"Don't be ridiculous. You can't just dial a phone number in another country. They charge you lots of money to do that and what if she's not there? And you need to talk to an operator! I think that costs money, too. And then it's the middle of the night. It's the other side of the world. It must be the middle of the night."

There was no time zone map in the atlas, so Edgar could not argue this. "Why are you going to see a mystic?"

"I'm not well."

"We don't go to see mystics when we are not well. We go to doctors! You know like they tell you that you have strep throat or a gall bladder and they give you medicine or maybe even surgery. I bet people go to mystics in Morocco because there are no doctors."

"No, I am not well in a different way. There is a spirit inside me, and I can't release it. It's a weight that weighs nothing but takes up a huge amount of space. Haven't you seen that we don't have visitors anymore? Once a month for twenty years people come to me for comfort but ever since your father died, nothing. I need someone to release this weight. And I believe this woman will do it."

EMILY

THE POETRY QUILT

Emily's days were taken up with her poetry stand but her evenings were empty. With four weeks of summer left and nothing to inspire her, she decided to tackle a new project. Although she had never sewn anything before, didn't own a sewing machine, and couldn't even imagine the kind of work that was involved, she decided to make a poetry quilt. She wasn't sure what exactly it was going to be, but the uncertainty of the whole project added a frisson of excitement.

She went to the local fabric shop on Laurel Avenue that specialized in quilting. She discovered fabrics were organized by theme: princesses, castles, unicorns; barns, horse stalls, pastures; musical notes, saxophone players, piano keys; geishas, teahouses, white cranes; zebras, elephants, tiger stripes. Bolts of them in every shade of primary and secondary colors. There were fill-in fabrics in plaids, dots, squares, swirly prints, and stripes. They were sold by the yard or bundled into swatch packages for those who couldn't organize a theme themselves.

She found a woman name-tagged Ellen and described what she planned to do.

"How is this going to be a poetry quilt?"

"I don't really know."

"Well, let's think about this. Is it going to have poems written or embroidered on it?"

"If I do that, then I am stuck with the poems that are there."

"Well, whenever we make a quilt, we are stuck, as you say, with only what's there. Once it's made, it's finished. It's a quilt forever just the way it is. If we want it to be different then we make another quilt." Ellen seemed the sort of woman—earnest, dedicated—who not only sold quilting fabric, but who made quilts, probably many quilts and gave them as gifts to children and grandchildren and friends. Emily needed to be clear this most definitely was going to be the only quilt she ever made.

She brought the fabrics back to the house and dumped them onto one of the dining room chairs. The wind was picking up in the canyon below. She watched the live oak and the eucalyptus, already battered on one side from decades of wind coming over the Santa Cruz Mountains, bend yet again. Their windward sides were shorn of leaves and large branches.

"This is not working," Emily muttered, laying out the fabrics in a pattern to try possible designs before she actually cut into the yardage.

"Did you put the pads on before you started this mess? And by the way, I'll need the table cleared off by tomorrow afternoon." Gretchen Bishop stood in the doorway squinting at her daughter, who was backlit against the setting sun. "You know you are always welcome here, but, frankly, you show up and the mess follows."

"Sorry, I'll move the whole thing into the downstairs bedroom as soon as I get it worked out." Emily apologized.

"What is it anyway?"

"I'm making a quilt. I've never made a quilt, and this is my moment."

"Grandma Minerva made quilts. You don't remember her do you?"

"No, but I know I'm named for her."

Gretchen smoothed the fabrics on the table. She moved the pieces around trying to make sense of the design and finally placed the scene of a field of lavender in the center and ranged the other fabrics around it.

Emily looked on, "How did you know to do that?"

"Well, if you think about it, that's the fabric that tells the story and quilts usually tell a story. All the bits and pieces complement it—the toile, the checks, the French words. You need some more, and I don't know if I would use the striped fabric at all. But if you must, get it in black and white instead," Gretchen stepped back and looked at the rearranged pieces and nodded approval.

Emily searched back to the last twenty years of conversations she'd had with her mother trying to remember any time when Gretchen had made a suggestion, or a pronouncement or even a throwaway remark without giving Emily permission to ignore it. "That' s a first for you."

"No, it's not, I told you my grandmother was a quilter. I used to watch her and she would let me help her lay out the fabric and…"

"That's not what I meant. I mean that's a first for you. You actually suggested that I do something. You stepped in, thought I was doing something wrong and tried to correct it."

"Your life is your own. Everything you do is your own. I don't meddle. Thank goodness you have always been very independent. If I have ever told you anything it has always, always been framed as a suggestion you could take or not. As you saw fit," Gretchen looked at her earnestly waiting for corroboration.

Emily saw in that moment exactly what had been the guiding principle of her mother's parenting. *Emily is sooo independent. From the time she could talk she has never asked my opinion about anything. I have even given up making her breakfast or picking out her clothes. She knows exactly what she wants. There is no use in interfering.'*

Gretchen had done a superb job of convincing herself, her parents and Emily's father, before they got divorced, and Emily herself, that Emily was just an independent, self-starter. According to Gretchen, Emily was the guardian of her own life. She was the principal decision maker in everything from where she should go to pre-school, to what she should eat for breakfast, to whether she needed to see a doctor when she had a fever.

But, finally, here was her mother taking a toehold in an Emily event. It was only a quilt, but there was her mother, putting a tentative hand out to touch and suggest and influence and become part of something of Emily's.

They stood around the dining room table for a good long while arranging and rearranging the fabrics. "How about if we do some cutting now?" Emily asked.

"Okay, let's go for it. We won't really know whether we're headed in the right direction here until we get the pieces placed."

They cut the fabric into foot square pieces and arranged some more.

"It's looking a little sparse, maybe. What do you think?"

"It's up to you, but I think you're right. It's also maybe a little repetitive. That's not necessarily bad, but I think right now it's looking as if we were too cheap to get enough fabric, or to get enough of the right fabric. Let's go shopping." Another suggestion from Gretchen.

They arrived at the shop just before closing time. In a hurry, they rushed through the store piling bolts of fabric on the counter. They bought another five yards of fabric and left ten minutes after closing time. Ellen, the shopkeeper, followed them out and locked up. "Thanks so much for waiting."

"That's okay. I'm not meeting friends for dinner until 9:30."

Gretchen and Emily looked at each other, "Dinner. We should have dinner. We haven't had dinner together all summer."

The summer evening was chilly and Luna Cafe had lit the fire in the pit on the patio. They ordered wine.

"When my grandmother died, I still had some of the quilts she made me, but when I got married I gave them all away. I don't know why I did that. I really liked them. I kept them folded in my closet. I was afraid to use them, but I would check on them once a week to make sure they were still there. They were right next to my special doll with hair I could comb and my Nancy Drew books," Gretchen took a long swallow of her wine. "When I got married, I thought I couldn't be that girl anymore. I was marrying such a grown-up man. Your father is ten years older than I am, as you know."

Emily nodded, digging into her veal saltimbocca. Unbelievably, her mother had never told her about her childhood.

"I was already the object of so many jokes because I had to cancel our engagement party. I got the measles. His sisters made such fun of him, marrying a girl who could still get the measles. Somehow, I thought once I got married I would no longer be the girl who liked all that stuff in my closet. I would be a woman. My face wouldn't break out anymore. My hair would get straighter. I wouldn't sweat and have to change my blouse in the middle of the day. I thought I would like cuddling and being kissed and hugged. I thought I would be a wife and would know what to do." Gretchen motioned to the waiter to bring her another glass of wine.

"Nothing like that happened. I didn't know how to be a wife. What do I buy? What do I wear? What do I do about dinner? About furnishing and cleaning and keeping a house? Mail would come to the house. I had never gotten mail before.

No, I did get mail twice—my college acceptance, and then the bill for the first semester, wrongly addressed to me which I immediately handed over to my father." Gretchen stirred her risotto.

"And then I got married. No college after all. No living away from home. I went from my father's house to my husband's house," Gretchen continued. "You see how I said it. I never even thought it was my house. It was this house with grown-up furniture and someone who came to clean once a week.

"I read cookbooks all afternoon trying to decide on the most basic dinners—broiled chicken pieces with green beans and baked potatoes. Shrimp cocktail in little jars. I bought them at the supermarket and then transferred them to special glass cups with pointed bottoms that were supposed to nestle in bigger glass holders filled with ice cubes," Gretchen laughed. "It used to take me an hour just to transfer the shrimp and chip the ice cubes into smaller pieces."

"My biggest accomplishment was dessert. I made two things—brownies from a mix and dump cake—canned cherries with a package of yellow cake mix dumped on top and covered with pats of butter. Oh, and I baked it of course. Don't make a face. It sounds awful, but it was delicious. Didn't I make it when you were a little girl? Oh, I guess I had stopped cooking by then."

Six glasses of wine later they wound their way up the hill and went straight to the dining room with their new finds.

"See, I think this works much better. How are you going to make this a poetry quilt?" Gretchen was pinning the fabrics together. Somehow, the design, which had started out as only a vague concept for Emily, now looked charming and connected. It looked, indeed, like a quilt. A well thought-out professional quilt that had proportion, compatible colors and a certain artistic sense.

"I don't know," Emily realized that she had never said that to her mother before. It was her job to know. If she didn't know, then her mother would have to do something for her or about her or with her. Emily always knew. That was the story, *'Emily always knows what she wants. I don't even go clothes shopping with her anymore. She is so good at picking out exactly what is right for her.'* Even though Emily's appearance sometimes belied that fact, they both stuck to the myth of Independent Emily and Unneeded Gretchen.

"Do you want to print the poems right on the quilt?"

"I thought I did, but then I am limited to only those poems."

"What about if we had pockets for the poems? We could have pockets with fabric that depicted the kind of poem inside. Like trees, or flowers, or animals, or children, or stars."

Gretchen had never read any of Emily's poems. "I don't usually write poems about those things."

"So, then what?"

"Sex, death, failure, loss, anger, love, insanity."

"You know, I don't think the quilt store is going to have any fabrics like that. Can you just see it: I'd like a fabric that combines some despair with a little bit of anguish. No? How about misogyny with a touch of genocide? Radical politics and drugs? Maybe just some sun-bleached animal skulls and a whip?"

"Let's sleep on it. I'll get up early and clear this off for your dinner party."

"Fuck it. We'll eat in the kitchen. Oops did I say that out loud?"

Emily giggled, "Did you, in fact just say that? Did Gretchen Bishop actually say fuck it?"

"Not Gretchen. Come on Minnie, time for bed."

They pinned the quilt the next morning. "Are you going to sew these?"

"How else?" Emily shrugged.

"Anything else it seems to me. Can you find stuff that will stick them down, like iron them on?"

Gretchen was at the computer. "Okay, here we go. There's something that glues fabric. Isn't that fabulous. You can just glue everything down."

"I'm not going to glue this together. That's so permanent. What happens if I don't like it?"

"If it's permanent you'll just have to decide to like it. You can do that." Gretchen assured her.

"No, *you* can do that. You've always been good at making things work for you by deciding that's how they have to work. You always did that with me."

"What can you mean? I always accepted you for exactly who you were."

"Accepted me! You are the least accepting person I know. You made me the way I am, and you made me the way that most suited you."

Emily looked at this mother she had always thought was so capable, so put together, with hair that was indeed very straight, and flawless skin and impeccable management skills; even the cleaning people called her Madame. This mother was always going somewhere, meeting someone, giving the sitter instructions, kissing her father dutifully on the cheek when he came home, and, after they were divorced, accepting a kiss from him when he brought Emily back on Sunday evenings.

"To be really honest, you're the mother who was never quite awake for breakfast, couldn't fit Open School Night into her schedule and would send me with the cleaning person to buy school clothes."

Gretchen marched out of the room. In a moment, Emily saw her through the window in the side garden behind the pool sitting in one of the big lounge chairs with the terra cotta cushions. The morning sun just reached her feet; the rest of her was in the shade, snuggled against the long row of camellia bushes that separated the house and the gardens from the steep hill and the canyon beyond. Gretchen sat motionless in the chair, her eyes closed, her legs straight in front of her for a long while.

Emily rambled around the kitchen. Made tea. Emptied the dishwasher. Ate three cookies. Rearranged the knives in their block until they were all in their correct slots. Each time she finished a task she went to the window to check on Gretchen, who was still as a sleeping bird in her chair. She went into the dining room to examine the new fabrics and suddenly Gretchen was there.

"I did make you the way you are. And I am proud of it. I knew my own limitations. I knew that I could not be the kind of mother I saw all around me. I used to tell myself I just didn't have that kind of temperament. What I knew was that you had to be able to do for yourself because you could not rely on me." Gretchen was absently moving the fabric pieces around.

"I think at some point early on something that was supposed to develop in me never did. Some sort of chemical lack or missing neuron because Gigi and Papa Wit were really good parents to me. So, I had to make you the right kind of child for a parent like me. I said you were independent because that's what you had to be. I said you were decisive because that's what you had to be. Your father and I had arguments all the time because I thought he babied you, and I was so worried that you wouldn't grow up to be independent."

"When did you know this about us?" Emily was stunned.

"Not for a long time. Not, probably, until you went to college. I think the day you left you freed me. Because until that day, I worried you were not going to make it. That you were going to be swept into the world of marriage and children before you had a life." Gretchen shook her head. "The day I left you in your dorm I knew I had succeeded. And then I was freed because you were freed."

"And now?"

"And now my wonderful girl, I am sorry I made light of what you wanted from this quilt. You can make it anyway you want. *We* can make it anyway you want. We can sew it or iron it or tape it or just leave it pinned. I'm okay with it any way. Because you've made it. You're a whole, complete centered person. And maybe I am, too. Or maybe not yet or ever. But you my precious Emily, you are."

Emily bent to the quilt pieces and moved them around, folding them into smaller squares and triangles.

"What do you all say? TMI? Too much information." Gretchen swept a piece of hair off Emily's forehead.

"No, TMD, Too much drama. If you made me this way then you certainly took away my drama gene."

Gretchen moved a few squares of cloth. "This might be a way to do it. Did you ever sleep with Tanner?"

"I blew him. But no, we never screwed."

"Did he do you?"

"Yes, he did."

"Pretty enlightened for a sixteen year old." Gretchen nodded.

"I would say."

"Your father was my first. But I guess you could figure that out. Big mistake."

"Is this the part where I put my fingers in my ears and sing so I can't hear you?"

"I meant big mistake that I never had sex with anyone before him. I never could see how good he was until I left him."

Emily covered her ears and began to sing, "La-la-la-la-la. I can't hear you. I can't hear you."

"You're all the same. The one thing you can't acknowledge is that your parents have sex."

"Oh god. Leave me my illusions that you did it only once—to get me."

"But you used to count how often Rick and I...."

"Not my dad. That's different."

EDGAR

THE GOOD MOTHERS

The flight to Morocco took fourteen hours with a stop in Paris where they changed planes and Edgar ordered breakfast in French from a wheeling cart. One of the sour soup sisters had a heart attack and her daughter came to stay on the foldout couch that could have accommodated Edgar. So, for certain, Edgar could not stay with them. It turned out the mystic was, indeed, in Marrakesh, and Edgar was there to supervise his mother, who could not read a map or speak French. Her single most helpful skills on the journey were her careful walk and her view of her feet, which kept her from falling in the cobblestone alleys.

The map for the Jewish quarter, the Mellah, had been drawn for them on a torn piece of paper by the clerk at the hotel. "Where you see house which has balconies, then you are arrive," she explained.

And there they were, stucco houses, side by side, or, more exactly, blended one into the other, with intricately carved wooden balconies. Rows and rows of them lined the narrow streets. The houses had haphazard designations. Some had numbers, some had Roman letters, some had Arabic symbols, a few still had Hebrew signs and many had painted-over or sun-bleached *mezuzahs* on their door frames.

The Jewish population of Morocco had shrunk from a quarter of a million before World War II to only twenty thousand in the mid-eighties, as a result of the creation of the State of Israel in 1948 and the huge emigration wave after the war. But Yamara Azaria was still there according to a letter Estelle had received from her a month before their journey. The letter was written in both Arabic and English, and Edgar had a feeling that Yamara had written the Arabic and then found someone to translate it into English.

A slender, dark-haired woman, Yamara was waiting for them with tea and small, very sweet cakes drowned in honey that stuck to Edgar's fingers and left streaks on the sides of his pants when he tried to wipe it off. Yamara did have a translator, her teenage daughter Talia, a few years older than Edgar, who spoke a decent version of English with a very pronounced Liverpool accent, as if she had studied with one of the Beatles.

The letter had asked Estelle to bring specific gifts with her—American lingerie, jeans and T-shirts in a small size and anything with an American sports team logo on it as well as a "sweeter" shirt (as she wrote, but Estelle was sure she meant sweat shirt) from Harvard (which took three weeks to arrive.) Edgar thought that maybe the gifts were all for the daughter, and maybe were added to the letter without her mother knowing, but, as Estelle said, "In any case...."

The inside of the house was cool and white, sparsely furnished with low wooden benches covered in striped pillows, small carved tables, and hanging oil lanterns. The doorways were arched in the Spanish style. Edgar and Estelle left their dusty shoes at the door. The red and white tile floors were smooth and cool. They began with tea, and the honey sweets, the giving of presents, and the offering of cool cloths to wipe hands and faces. An hour later Yamara was ready. Edgar gave his mother a what-I-said look when Yamara told her to remove her jewelry and anything metal she was wearing, but then she handed it all to Edgar to hold, took Estelle by the hand and led her away.

Talia came and sat beside Edgar. "Don't you need to translate?"

"There won't be any talking. My mother will communicate in other ways."

"What does she do?"

"She does what she does. It is not the same for each. Sometime she can pull the spirit out very quickly. Sometime the spirit is not a spirit but like a piece of a body that doesn't belong. Umm—a tumor. And she, I don't know, she can take it away."

Edgar played with his mother's bracelets and her wedding ring, which he had stuck on his thumb, twirling them through his fingers and tossing them from hand to hand. He held the four of them by one edge and fanned them out and then crossed them one over the other to make an open globe. As he was juggling them, the wedding band slipped off his thumb and rolled away. He slid off the bench to see if he could find it, but it was nowhere.

He poked at Talia. "Help me find it. I can't tell my mother I lost her wedding band. She'll be so angry. I wasn't even supposed to come with her and now she'll say she was right and I should have stayed home."

Talia had crawled under the long benches and now pushed her way up. "It's not there. It must have rolled into a space behind the wall. I'm sorry."

"You can't be sorry. It's my fault, but you have to find it. Do you have a stick? Maybe we can get a stick in there to get it."

"In where?"

"In the wall. And then we'll push it along until it stops in a corner and we can dig in there and get it."

"You're a silly person. I don't know where it is, and there is no place to put a stick. When the maid comes back we will tell her to find it. That's her job."

"It's her job to find things people lose?"

"It's her job to do everything."

"Is she a slave?"

"Of course not. She is a woman we pay to work for us. She has a room here to sleep but today she has time for herself."

"Does everyone have a maid?"

"No, not everyone. You either have a maid or you are a maid."

"I need that ring."

Talia poked his arm, "Fariba will find it."

"So what exactly does your mother do in there?"

"She heals people who have broken souls."

"My mother says there is a spirit inside her, but I can't see it so I really won't know if it leaves her." Edgar swung his feet back and forth and tapped his knees. "This is exorcism. I saw it in a movie. People scream and vomit and spin their heads backwards while it's happening. They need other people to hold them down." He jumped up, "We should go in there and help."

"My mother does not need help. She is a mystical person who cures people without even touching them. Sometime she is not in the same room with them."

"Did you ever see her do it? Is she teaching you?"

"There is no teaching unless you have the talent. She says I do not have the talent."

"Do you think you do?" Edgar pressed.

"I want to go to America to become a dancer, or a teacher or a waitress. I do not have the talent. If I did, I wouldn't want to do anything else."

"In America you can't have a maid unless you have a lot of money." Edgar was sure of that.

"Yes. I can. I will find a maid to work for less money."

"You can't. You have to pay them a certain amount. It's the law."

"You cannot have a law to say how much money goes into someone's pocket. Nobody knows that."

"Yes, they do. The government knows that. You have to tell them, and then you have to pay part of it to them. It's called taxes."

"That's ridiculous. America is freedom. You can do anything there and nobody can stop you. You can live anywhere, not just with other Jews or Muslims or Christians. And you can be anybody you want just because you say you are! It is such a place!" Talia was definite.

Edgar couldn't argue this. It seemed to him if you lived anywhere else except America that would appear to be the truth. It was only when you lived there you knew you could only do the one, maybe two things that were possible for you. You were born and soon after you began to become who you were. Very quickly the possibility of being a bareback rider or an astronaut or the son of Philippe Cousteau or the mayor of Pittsburgh was not going to happen. Instead you were just Edgar, and the most you could hope for was to be the Edgar of all Edgars, whomever that was going to be.

Yamara came into the courtyard. She sat down next to Edgar. Talia translated. "Your mother is sleeping. We must wait for her to wake up."

"Did it work?"

"The healing takes place sometimes in a moment sometimes in a week. Right now we don't know which. Your mother may be able to tell us when she wakes up or she may not know yet."

"So, if it didn't work do you do it again?"

"There is no again. If it doesn't work than it will not work. There is only so much one can do." Yamara shrugged.

Yamara reached into her pocket. "Here. This was in your mother's hand when she fell asleep. It rolled onto the floor, but I found it." She handed Edgar the wedding band.

They heard singing in the next room. "'You are my sunshine, my only sunshine. You make me happy when skies are gray.'" And then laughter. Loud laughter that sounded more like shouting but then subsided into giggling. Edgar jumped up and started for the door but Yamara held his arm.

"Don't go in just yet," Talia said, translating for Yamara. "That is part of her healing. We cannot frighten or wake her because it will disturb her journey. She is letting go of whatever is holding her. She will be healed. This is the first sign."

The three were finishing dinner. Edgar was wondering where to go for the night —stay at the house, go back to the hotel—when his mother suddenly appeared at the table, picked up a glass and drained it, motioned for more and swirled her arms over her head. "I think you lose weight when you sleep. Don't you? Is that a fact or did I just make that up? Edgar you look so pale. You should get some sun. This is the perfect place to get sun, don't you think? Let's get some sun." She walked over to Edgar and took his head in her hands. "Your ears are on backwards. How peculiar."

Edgar looked at Yamara.

"This is normal for some. She will be fine in a few hours."

"I am fine now. Thank you so much for my life. You have cured me," Estelle reached for Yamara and hugged her. "I am free."

Edgar took his mother's hands and brought her over to a lantern. Her face was flushed, her hair fluttered with static electricity. In the lantern light he could see that her blouse and skirt had hundreds of small singe marks in them. She smelled of smoke and burn. Something was bulging from her pocket and in spite of the nauseating fear that fell over him, he reached in and pulled it out. It was a white rock the size of a peach. He held it up in front of the lantern and saw it was crenelated, like a brain and unevenly weighted so that it rolled in his hand. Cool to the touch, initially, it began to heat up until he yelped in pain.

Yamara jumped up from her chair and knocked it from his hand onto the floor where it shattered and emitted a billow of smoke.

"Quick, outside!" she ordered, pushing them through the shuttered doors into the courtyard. Edgar heard pieces of the stone popping like firecrackers. And then it was over. They waited a few minutes in the courtyard. Edgar looked up at the sliver of moon just visible over the roof. The night sky was an isolated square filled with stars, more than he had ever seen in New York, more even than he had ever seen in the Hayden Planetarium, where there weren't real stars anyway but just the abstract of stars created by the astronomers to tell a story.

Way later, Estelle and Edgar left the house with Talia, sent by Yamara to guide them back to their hotel. The temperature had dropped thirty degrees. They shivered as they picked their way through the unlit streets. The desert wind roamed the alleys of the Medina, swirling cones of dust into night air. The crescent moon did not give off enough light to guide them and even with expert Talia, it took them almost an hour to find the hotel.

"You cannot go back home tonight," Estelle advised. "It is too dark. Look how long it took the three of us to find the hotel. Does your house have a telephone?"

"Of course we have a phone. Even in Morocco we are modern people."

"Call your mother and stay the night. You will sleep in Edgar's bed. He can sleep on the sofa."

In the morning, while Estelle was still sleeping, an elaborate breakfast was delivered to their room. There were perfectly formed eggs, their dark yellow yolks glistening in a pond of thick cream, fat pastries coated in honey and nuts, coffee in little copper pots with wooden handles, and a chafing dish with something that looked like grainy oatmeal sprinkled with raisins.

There were, also, all the things the hotel thought Americans ate—thick pieces of toast with pots of butter and jam, dry flakey cereals, and something that looked like bacon. There was an earthenware pitcher of milk sitting in a basin of ice. Talia took a tiny cup, poured some coffee and scooped an egg onto a plate. She handed it to Edgar who was munching a handful of cereal.

Talia had slept in her clothes, but Yamara had given her a small duffle bag to take with her, and when she reached in to get a comb Edgar saw clothing and some books and papers. Edgar was accustomed to watching his mother get ready for work in the morning and knew the efficient way she combed her hair and twisted it into a shell-like knot that curved from the base of her neck to the crown. Some hairpins, a swoop of lipstick, and she was done.

Talia took her time, her hair spread across her shoulders and down her back as she combed and combed, shaking her head to lift it into shape and stopping to unsnarl a knot. She was tall and slender like her mother but her hair was golden brown in the sunlight with wiry strands of copper that sprang out of the mass. He wanted to touch her head and squeeze her hair into thick clumps but he knew the two of them were beyond the age when he could. He sat silently and watched as she gave one final shake, grasped the hair behind her head and with a few strokes and swirls tied it into an elaborate braid. She fastened the end with a thin ribbon she wound round and round and knotted.

"I must go home now."

"I'll walk with you," Edgar offered. He was glad his mother was still asleep. She would say it made no sense for Edgar to go back to Talia's house. He left a note.

"Have you always lived here?"

"Yes, for twenty generations my mother says."

"And before that?"

"You want to know before that. You want to know where my family lived four hundred years ago? Do you know where your family lived four hundred years ago?"

"Of course," Edgar lied. "We lived in Russia." Edgar certainly knew that could be a lie. His grandfather had faded pieces of paper in a foreign language that had official stamps on them, and if he looked really close he could make out the date as 1863, but they were written in Roman letters, so clearly they were not Russian.

"Well, we didn't. We came from Spain. Almost all the Jews in Africa came from Spain when Queen Isabella and King Ferdinand kicked us out. And you know what, I read that Americans thinks Columbus came to America because he was an explorer, but I think he was kicked out also. Maybe he is a Jew, too."

They turned a corner and there was the house. It was completely shuttered, and the gate in front of the courtyard was locked. Talia rattled the gate, and pulled the rope that rang the bell inside the walls. "Fariba will come."

They waited. Talia rang the bell again. "Fariba must be on an errand. Mama must be with a customer. We will try the garden gate. It's Monday and the house man is off but maybe he left it open."

They walked to the back of the house, but the gate was locked as well and there were two garden carts parked in front of it with upturned hoes as if to ward off intruders. Talia rattled the gate half-heartedly.

Edgar wished he had a watch, but after they waited a while he could see the sun had shifted significantly, that shutters, gates and doors around them were opening and closing and the street was busy with comings and goings. Talia's house was silent and locked. "Don't you have a key?"

"No, I do not need one. Someone is always here."

Edgar climbed into one of the carts. He jumped up and grabbed the top of the wall and pulled himself up. He dropped to the ground inside and Talia followed. The door to the house was on a hasp with no lock and by gently rocking it back and forth they were able to open it.

Inside, the house was silent and neat. The cushions were in place; the beds were made, except for Yamara's, which was tilted up against the wall, its bare mattress sagging inside the frame. Talia gasped.

"Wait right there," Edgar directed. He grabbed a stick used to hold open the shutters and gingerly poked at the mattress. Edgar had watched mystery shows on TV at home and he knew not to touch anything but to look for signs of a crime *like blood on the mattress* he thought. But there was nothing. "Check your mother's closet. Are her clothes there?"

Talia looked. "I can not tell. There is stuff here but I can not tell if everything is here."

Edgar was warming to the task at hand, "See if your mother's favorites are there."

"Well, her favorite shoes are here. Those are the ones she wears for special dinners. She would not wear them now anyway. Her special dress is here, oh, but her coat is gone and her purse. Her purse is gone!"

"But doesn't that mean she just went shopping?"

"No, Fariba goes shopping."

"Your mother doesn't go shopping? Everybody goes shopping."

"Not my mother. She does not leave the house. She has, she has—- she just has things that keep her at home."

"Ever? Ever?"

"Well," and Talia was crying. "She never leaves the house. She does not say she will not leave the house. Sometime, she even makes a plan to leave the house. But then she never does. Something always happens. Then she has to stay home. Sometime she has a fight with me. One time we were to go to the movie. She got angry with me and yelled. Then she said I made her upset and I can go by myself. What is the fun of going to the movie by myself? So that is it. Something terrible has happened."

"Let's call the police." Edgar urged.

Talia shook her head. "We will wait before we call. We are not on the favorite side of the police. They think we are the cause of trouble because some people are prejudice to Jews. The police think if we would go away they would not have to protect us."

"We'll call my mother. She will know what to do."

Estelle did not know what to do. She walked through the house with them looking at everything very carefully, touching nothing at first but then picking up a few things and running her palm over them. "Where is the dress your mother wore yesterday? Find it and bring it to me."

Talia brought back a dress. Estelle spread her fingers and ran her hands over it. She crumpled it up and shook it out. She smelled it gingerly and then brought it into the courtyard and held it up to the sun. "We must call the police. Where is the woman who works here?"

Talia shrugged.

Estelle's tone was harsh. "That's not an answer. You know her name. You know where she lives. We must find her and talk to her. How can you find her?"

"I can ask the woman who works next door. They are friends. I can give her money. She will sneak and find her."

After an hour, Fariba came running, carrying a bag. Talia caught her arm and Edgar could see she was questioning her about when she left, where she had been, where her mother was. Fariba started to cry and could not stop.

"She says my mother sent her home last night. She told her not to come in this morning but to go to the shop and bring the things in the bag. These are things my mother never asks for because they are too expensive and hard to find," and Talia held up European coffee and twisted bread rolls and canned sweet milk. "Fariba does not know where she is."

"We will go to the police station now." Estelle said, taking Talia's hand.

The police station was almost empty. A policeman in a uniform with several medals on his chest and stars on his epaulets came out to speak to them and then brought them back into his office to fill out a form. Then he went back to the house with them and did a complete search. There weren't many places to look. The house only had seven rooms, sparsely furnished, and three closets. Lots of small cupboards and cabinets, but these were only good for clues not for finding bodies.

The police asked Talia if anything was missing or out of place, but Fariba was the one to answer that. "No," she said. All was as always. But maybe Yamara's special bag was missing. The one for treatment. Fariba went to the staircase and carefully removed one of the wooden risers. The space was empty.

There was a long conversation that Talia explained after the police left. "He says that it is on purpose. My mother left of her own free mind because she took her purse and her bag and her clothes. There is no sign of another person or a fight or someone who forced her to leave. He knows what she does, and he says she probably went to help someone. She will return when her work is done."

Talia paused. "My mother never goes anyplace. Only one time did she leave the house. When I broke my arm. She went with me to the hospital. She never left my hospital room. She slept in the bed with me until we came home." Talia was crying and then Estelle was crying.

"Where is the rest of your family?"

"My grandmother died last year. My aunt and uncle moved to France. But they are not really my aunt and uncle. My mother is the only child just like me. So they are just people we called Tanta and Oncle out of respect."

"You must contact them."

Talia found a recent letter from them in a desk drawer. The return address was General Delivery in Marseilles, which meant, Edgar learned, it stayed at the main post office until someone came to pick it up. Talia wrote to them the next day but Estelle believed it would take weeks for any response.

They all stayed at the house for the next ten days. Fariba did as well, because she would not leave them to make do on their own. Estelle and Edgar went for a walk one evening to decide what to do.

"She is only fifteen. She cannot be here on her own, even with the maid," Estelle offered. "What about money? There doesn't seem to be any or if there is Talia knows nothing about it."

Edgar had been thinking about this. "So, we only have two choices. We can all stay here with her until we find out what happened to her mother. Or," he paused. "We can take her back with us."

"That's what I have been thinking, but I don't know how to get that done. She must have some documents or papers or a birth certificate. Then we can get her a passport."

Talia knew of nothing and Edgar wasn't surprised. Until he and Estelle had to get passports for this trip, he didn't know where his birth certificate was. But suddenly he did know, and he knew everything. It was all in the duffle bag that Yamara had handed her the night Talia walked them back to the hotel. He found it resting inside the door, left there when they first entered the house ten days before. He handed it to Talia. "Look inside, please."

There it was, a large white envelope. Inside were two letters and a passport, an American passport with a picture of Talia and her name, but not Talia Azaria, instead Natalie Frankel. Also inside the bag were all of the American items Yamara had asked for—the underwear, the jeans, the shirts and the Harvard sweatshirt. Just like any young American girl would have. There were English language books and a current copy of Seventeen magazine, two lipsticks, and acne cream and tampons. One letter was addressed to Estelle. It was written in English.

"I know when the American writer come to tell my story something magic will happen. But never will I think to do such a thing until you write to me and ask for help. My Talia is not a mystic. She is the ordinary girl, but not ordinary, just not a woman with the gift. She is smart and kind and pretty. Pretty is very helping in Morocco. For pretty she will marry young and have children and her husband will tell her what to do. He will buy her anything she want that will make her even more pretty. But maybe after a while he does not want her anymore—and here I speak my experience—and then what will she do.

In America she can do something. Morocco is not America but it is easy to buy some things here, more easy than in your country. So, I have given for her an American name and an American passport. I am so sorry it is your name, but it does not make enough sense for her to be with you unless. I know you are a good mother with a good son. And you are Jews. To come all the way to Morocco to see me, I know you have money. Here is money for Talia's ticket to fly with you and more money to take care of her for a while. I have left so Talia will leave. If I am not here, there is nothing for her.

I am a good mother; you are a good mother. I give you my daughter with much love. Yamara Azaria

The second letter was addressed to Talia, and Estelle handed it to her. Talia took it into her mother's bedroom to read. She did not come out for several hours and when she did they could see she had been crying, but also that she had purpose.

They left the next day.

OLIVIA

LULLABY

"**Y**our father is short of breath," was the beginning of my phone call with my mother, although she said it in Korean in order to be absolutely clear about his symptoms. "When he bends down to pick up a carton or even a piece of fruit or a box of cereal, he has to hold onto something when he stands up."

He insisted on going to a Korean doctor. That is not a difficult thing to do in New York. I found a cardiologist associated with a well-known hospital who had a satellite office two subway stops from our home and, even more important, the grocery store. Dr. Park, just like us, but that's like saying Dr. Smith and thinking two random Smiths are related. Dr. Robert Park. We had an appointment for a Friday afternoon in December.

I took the train down from school and then the subway to our stop. My parents were waiting at the store that was still open under the care of their best clerk, Eugene. I was certain he had been given copious instructions about how to manage in the two hours my parents anticipated being gone. He waved to us as we left and then ran to the open door. "Don't worry. Everything will be fine."

It was one–thirty on a Friday afternoon and since we were heading towards Manhattan the train was comfortably empty, with room for a few stroller moms and a bike rider. For all their language inexperience, my parents were wizards on the New York subway system. They knew which stations to switch at, which stairs to take, where to stand for the maximum likelihood of a seat and even how to enter a crowded car—with arms akimbo. They were also masters of the subway newspaper fold—a complex and dying art that cannot be described without diagrams. When I was a little girl and would travel on the subway with my father, he could be dead asleep and still jump up, catch my hand and get us off at the correct stop.

The doctor's office was in an old apartment building that once was one of THE places to live in Queens. Curving staircases surrounded a fountain that might have been turned on in warmer weather but was now filled with the last of the fallen maple and sycamore leaves. The lobby floor was marble, and there was a corner desk, now a repository for unwanted mail and Priority boxes, that must have been the domain of a doorman in the building's debutant years.

Dr. Park's office was painted in the muted colors of the late 1940's. It retained that era's charm of comfortable chairs, softly lit lamps and magazines carefully fanned out on sofa tables. The magazines were totally current as was the health literature rack. There was one patient ahead of us.

When my father is called in, we all rise, but he tells us to remain in the waiting room. We are thumbing through magazines, when the nurse motions my mother into the exam area. I am already thinking this cannot be a good sign when I am motioned in as well. But in the exam room, we find nothing alarming except for the language barrier. Dr. Park, who is indeed Korean, does not speak any Korean at all. He is third generation American. "Honestly, I know more Yiddish and Spanish, than I do Korean," says Dr. Robert Park, who went to Tulane University, has a slight southern drawl, pledged a

Jewish fraternity and got his medical degree in Mexico. But, he did his residency at what my mother considers a number one hospital in Massachusetts.

I become the interpreter of my father's symptoms and the doctor's questions. After ten minutes, we've reached the kernel of facts. My father's symptoms are not alarming in themselves, but further tests will be done to be certain. We will need to go into Manhattan to Dr. Park's main office. "So, not to worry. My staff will arrange everything, including a car service to bring you into the city so you don't have to take the subway." I am about to offer assurances that they can travel by themselves but my mother is already on it.

"That is very number one. We will sit in back, and a person will drive us. He will have a uniform?"

"Yes, of course."

My mother smiles and nods. "Shirley will be greenly."

Dr. Park has already turned away from us and has his hand on the doorknob.

Then my mother speaks to me in Korean. "I want to know what this doctor is really thinking. He has made everything so simple because he thinks since we don't speak English we don't understand that well." I am nodding my head, when her voice sharpens. "Please begin to translate now." And I do.

"Doctor Park, (*leaving out the disparaging aside about his parents not teaching him Korean*) we may not speak English very well (*leaving out the disparaging aside about my parents speaking enough English to have thrived in New York and being therefore bilingual*), or well enough to understand medical terms, but we are smart people. We have been in this country for over twenty years. Many people think it takes nothing to own a Korean grocery (*leaving out the disparaging aside about his parents perhaps not having enough business sense to be able to work for themselves*), but it takes a lot of hard work and a lot of special knowledge about how to order, how to stock what customers want, how to know what customers want before they know, how to sell them items they don't even know they want, yet.

"It takes being smart to know daughters are better than sons in this American world (*leaving out the disparaging remark about his parents only having a son who is so American he might not ever take care of them the way a daughter would*) and to save enough money to send them to number one colleges. Just like your parents did (*leaving out the reference to Tulane as a number three school. Aside from the fact that her grading system has always been a mystery to me, although on balance she is usually close to the mark, this is a man who is going to be treating my father and we don't want any antagonism.*) So, we thank you so much for your concern for my husband." (*Leaving out the part about how he would have more reverence for elderly people if he had been raised correctly—even though he had tremendous patience and reverence, in my mind, to stand quietly through this diatribe, taking his hand off the doorknob and turning so that he was facing my mother and even nodding at her assault, where appropriate. I consider him a model of restraint.*)

My mother pauses and Dr. Park smiles. "Will you translate for me?"

I nod.

"So, let me start by saying I do not in anyway think you don't understand the medical concerns here. Perhaps I have made it too simple because I don't want to alarm you unnecessarily. Mr. Park, I can see that you have low blood pressure and that in itself is enough reason to feel slightly dizzy when you stand up suddenly. There are tests I could perform right here in the office but they are not detailed enough to tell me why it's happening. I want to make sure you don't have what is often called a heart insufficiency or a problem with a valve. I did hear a slight gurgling in your chest and your EKG shows a long beat." He has stepped completely back into the exam room and closed the door.

"I apologize that my name which accurately told you that I was Korean gave you the impression that I speak Korean. All of my grandparents immigrated to this country after the Second World War. Of course they spoke Korean, as well as Japanese and even some Russian. However, as you may notice, each generation knows less and less of their ancestral language until by now, in me, there is no knowledge left except for hello, goodbye and thank you."

My mother is nodding as I am translating and at some point holds up her hand. "Enough," she says, "I understand."

He puts out his hand and shakes each of ours. "We will make a good plan for your husband. I need to go now. I am meeting a woman at the airport, and I am going to ask her to marry me. She doesn't know I am meeting her there, and she doesn't know I am going to ask her to marry me."

"Is she Korean?" That's my mother.

"Part Korean, part Japanese so my mother is not happy."

My mother nods. "Bring her flowers. Bring many, many flowers. Bring so many you almost look like a crazy. Be a number one man now."

Dr. Park is swinging his coat on as we all leave the building together. It is dusk outside. There are lights around the fountain that have turned it into something much more appealing than it was in daylight. It has started to snow, and my father shivers. My mother puts her arm around him, and they walk carefully down the stairs together. I am behind them, my arms outstretched in a useless gesture, as if I could catch them if they fell.

Dr. Park stands at the top of the stairs and begins to sing a song I recognize. It is a Korean lullaby, one my mother used to sing to us. My mother and father have reached the bottom of the stairs. My mother turns to look at the doctor and begins to sing as well. Halfway down, I feel caught between these two universes, the one that can save my father's life and the universe of old school Korea where everything less than a number one is a failure.

SARAH

CHANGES IN THE LANDSCAPE

One last lunch with David and then Sarah was flying to Denver. She had already packed up the house in New Jersey. David, the realtor, told her the buyers were filing blueprints for the new home they were planning for the site. This house, with the cast iron tub, the slate floors and all the special features Sarah had so carefully chosen would be torn down as soon as the building commission gave its approval. Earlier that week the handyman removed every amenity she could reasonably declare as personal property—wall sconces, drapes, doorknobs, cabinet handles, and installed builder's grade replacements. Not that she wanted anything. It was too late now. It was all delivered to a building site for the homeless.

"I didn't think it would matter that much," Sarah said as she caught David's arm and took a very sloppy lick of his ice cream.

"So is this our last meal?" He was gathering the cardboard and napkins from the bench.

"Yes, our very last meal, ever. It was so nice meeting you, and I really appreciate all our cheap lunches together. I'd like to shake your hand as a thank you and give you a gift card to Macy's. Maybe we'll see each other sometime in the future when I need another best friend for twenty years." She was crying. "I'm building an extra room on the house, like one of those things they called casitas, just for you. Because I don't know how I'm going to get through even thirty days without you."

"It better have a really great bathroom."

"It's going to be awful, with one of those crappy tubs too small to stretch your legs out. It will have a sink hanging off the wall so you have no place to put your toothbrush, which is always falling, on the floor or sometimes in the toilet. Oh and a pocket door because I hate those things, and you can't even have a hook on the back."

He put his arms around her. "Where did life go so wrong that we are not married?"

"Well, let's see. You're my husband's best friend. And you're gay."

"We could've worked around it."

She smiled into his shirt. "Now you tell me."

He drove her to the airport. She settled into a gift from the gods—an upgrade to a business class seat—and fanned out three decorating magazines on the tray table.

The man next to her was drinking tiny bottles of gin poured over ice. He asked for another and then another.

"I'm sorry, sir, I'm going to have to cut you off for now."

"I've only had two."

"It's been three, sir," the flight attendant looked down at his list. "Three doubles."

"Not at all. Ask this lady sitting next to me."

"I have no opinion," Sarah said. "I've been sleeping. I'm coming off a fifteen hour flight from Dubai," Sarah decided to lie.

The flight attendant shrugged and came back with his drink.

"And one for my seat mate please."

"Uh uh, no thank you. I'm not drinking today."

"Bring it anyway," he turned to Sarah. "Where you headed?"

"Denver," she finished tearing out the page of trendy bathroom sinks. "You do know that's where this plane is going."

"Are you only doing the D's? Dubai, Denver?"

"Working my way through the alphabet," she tore off another page.

"What'll you do when you get there?"

"Take a shower, get into bed," Sarah looked straight at him, "and masturbate."

"That's the best you can do? There's no one around to help you out."

"There could be. But I don't want any interaction," Sarah frowned. "I just want to do it and go to sleep. It's been a busy day."

"I could be someone around."

"Too late. We already have interaction."

"I'll shut up."

"Still too late."

"I'm not talking to you for the rest of the flight."

"The wall has been breached. The damage has been done," Sarah intoned.

He ordered two more drinks. Sarah drank one and tore out more pages.

On the way out of the airport, Sarah picked up an iced coffee and shoved it into the water bottle holder on her carryon.

He was waiting for her at the door to the family bathroom. He gestured and she followed him in, putting her finger to her lips and locking the door behind her decisively. A dress would have made things so much easier, so note to self for the future. She used opposite feet to pry off her sneakers, pulled her jeans down and unbuttoned her shirt. And he was there, leaning her against the tile wall.

EDGAR AND NATALIE

NANCY DREW IN BROOKLYN

"**W**hat is a roadster?" Natalie wanted to know. "Oh, never mind, there is a picture." She held up the book for Edgar and Estelle.

"What're you reading?"

"*The Clue in the Staircase*. It's about Nancy Drew. She is a girl who solves mysteries. I could do that."

"You want to solve mysteries? What kind of mysteries."

"It is when people get kidnapped or things get stolen. The girl does that, and she is the opposite of us. She has a father but no mother."

Edgar was skeptical. "How does that make her the opposite of us?"

"Well, we both have mothers but no fathers. I mean we *had* fathers, but we do not now. Nancy had a mother but she does not now. But! She has a maid. See, I tell you there are maids in America. She has a maid named Hannah. Maybe even a Jewish maid. I think Hannah is a Jewish name."

"Oh my god. I mean Talia. We had that conversation a year ago, before you even came here. Do you see any maids here?"

"Of course there are maids," she nodded decisively. "You think no one in America has a maid? I tell you there are maids here. I think someone in my English class has a maid. She lives on Bedford Avenue. I rang her bell one day and a maid answers. She wears a pink dress and a white apron and a little thing on her head."

"Maybe she was a nurse."

"No. Nurses do not answer the door; they take care of people in hospitals. She is a maid."

"Okay. But do you see us. We don't live in a house. We don't have room for a maid. We live in an apartment with a fake wall to your room made out of a bookcase. Where is there room for a maid?"

"Nevertheless!" Natalie said triumphantly, and she pointed to the word in the book. "Nevertheless. Did I say that the right way?"

"Yes, actually that was a perfect use of the word," Estelle assured her. "Good work. One day you can have a maid. Right now, we are the maids. We make the mess and we clean up the mess, so the less mess we make..."

"Nancy Drew has make-up. You can see it in the picture."

"But we don't see it all over the bathroom sink."

Natalie was triumphant. "That's because she has a maid."

■ ■ ■

Edgar was extremely nervous when they left Morocco. How could a mother and son arrive in a country and ten days later leave the same country as a mother, a son and a daughter and not a baby daughter who might have been born while you were in this other country but a fully big daughter who really didn't look anything like the other two people and who, if she actually had to speak to someone, would have had an accent and some strange way of using English words.

Edgar had seen movies of American soldiers in World War II dropped behind enemy lines trying to look like natives. The night before they left Morocco, he went through Talia's suitcase and cut out all of the clothing labels that were foreign in any way. He also eliminated all French language books after assuring her they could be bought in the States (although he wasn't at all sure of this.) He told her about Brooklyn and had her memorize her new address, the names of all New York sports teams. He told her she rooted for the New York Yankees, even though he was a Mets fan.

He told her to say she shopped at Loehmann's, she went to Midwood High School, she bought her sneakers at Modell's, she helped her mother shop at Waldbaum's and she called that mother Ma or Mom, not Mama. She went to the movies on Saturday night at the Avenue M theatre. Her favorite comic books were *Archie* and *Veronica*, and she knew that Yogi Bear and Yogi Berra were not the same person.

She had eight Barbie dolls, liked to do crossword puzzles (What are those? He explained.) She had eaten many hotdogs at the original Nathan's along with her favorite, the French fries. She did not think Orange Julius was a person (even though he might have been—Edgar wasn't sure about that.) She went to Brighton Beach, not, he repeated, NOT Coney Island. Edgar had twenty-four hours to turn Talia Azaria into Natalie Frankel, a middle class girl from Brooklyn. He had become the trainer of a secret agent.

It was surprising how easy it was to go through passport control in Marrakesh and have all of their passports stamped with their exit date. The forgery was so thorough there was an entry stamp into Morocco on Natalie's passport. Estelle kept watch over Natalie, waiting for her to cry or scream or try to run away but Natalie was either stoic or indifferent. She slept most of the way on the ten-hour flight, her legs curled under her on the seat, her head on the drop-down tray. Estelle pointed out the New York City skyline as they circled around to Kennedy Airport. Natalie looked, smiled and put her head back down.

When they landed, the immigration people were in the middle of change of shift and gave only a cursory look at their passports before stamping haphazardly on randomly chosen pages. Customs didn't seem that interested apart from shaking out their clothing looking for either money or drugs.

At the apartment, Estelle did some masterful shifting around using that magically designed dining alcove at the window side of the galley kitchen. A tall bookcase was dragged into the doorway between the kitchen and the alcove and suddenly there was a bedroom for Natalie with a fair amount of privacy that would be augmented by thick drapes hung cross the side open to the living room. Within a few days a bed and a dresser appeared, and the transformation was complete.

"Where will my mother sleep?"

Estelle and Edgar looked at each other. "Your mother won't be coming right now, you know. Remember the letter she left for me? Remember how we called the police, and we all looked for her? Remember that we couldn't find her and no one knew where she was, not you or Fariba or the police or the cousins we couldn't find either? Remember we decided to take you with us to New York because there was nowhere else for you to go and we couldn't leave you there alone?"

Natalie looked at Estelle carefully, shaking her head.

"Your mother planned very carefully for this. You had an American passport. You had American clothes she had asked us to bring for you, even though we thought they were just part of the payment for her to cure me." Estelle paused and drew Natalie to her. "You are ours now. You are my daughter. You are Edgar's sister. You have our last name, and you have a home. You will go to school, and you will know everything you need to know to be Natalie Frankel in Brooklyn in New York City in the United States of America."

Natalie pulled out of Estelle's arms and sank onto the floor and began to wail. "MAMA, MAMA. MAMA."

Estelle lay down on the floor with her and stroked her head and whispered, "It's all right. Cry and scream. It's okay. Cry as much as you want for as long as you want."

■ ■ ■

Although Estelle never had a daughter, she had grown up as a daughter in New York so she knew how life was organized. She got Natalie acne medication, a library card and a subscription to Seventeen magazine, and took her on several trips to Macy's. She went with Natalie to the local pharmacy. Mildred, the middle-aged makeup expert, advised the two of them on what products were most suitable for a fifteen year old. Mildred also advised Estelle on products for herself to keep her current among the mothers of teenage girls.

She explained to her friends Natalie was a cousin sent over from Europe to live in New York so she could experience American life. In their Brooklyn neighborhood many families had memories of aunts and cousins coming over from "the old country" and sleeping on couches and chairs for months while they found a footing in an America where everything was possible.

The biggest adjustment Estelle had to make was in revising her geographic web. Edgar roamed along a wide swath of Brooklyn and even crossed into Manhattan on occasion, but it was boy's roaming. He covered long distances on his bicycle with a group of friends whom he had known for several years. Estelle knew their parents and their telephone numbers.

The boys did what Estelle described as surface roaming. They stayed on the streets and played stickball or stoopball or threw their bikes down on the grass at the park and hung upside down on the monkey bars. They drank from hoses left out on the lawns of nearby houses and shot pieces of floor tile from homemade slingshots at soda cans on the pony walls that delineated city rose gardens. They understood the universal signals of city life—only play ball on one way streets, wear a house key on a string around your neck, go to your grand-mother's in desperate times and come home as soon as the street lights came on.

Natalie, however, was a different breed of child. Acclimating her to Brooklyn life was a yearlong project. What were girls her age doing and what did she need to do to fit in? The rules of Brooklyn were clear. If you lived in the same apartment building with girls your age, you walked to school together, but walking to school was not friendship, merely company. Girls carried their books diligently to and from home everyday, boys ran by with a ragged notebook tucked under an arm and taunted the girls as they passed.

Natalie made friends at school because she had two exotic talents. She knew how to braid her hair in many different ways Brooklyn girls had never seen before, and she developed a brief but flashy reputation as a fortune-teller. In afternoon homeroom, girls would crowd around her and hold out their palms for her to read. She would choose no more than two each day and sweep her fingers along their hands nodding and mumbling low incantations before pronouncing that they were about to meet a new boy or kiss the boy they secretly liked. Natalie knew her clients had no interest in anything that didn't involve love, or romance or, in surprising numbers, revenge.

On the rare occasions when a class had a substitute teacher, Natalie would pick a classmate and braid her hair while the rest of the girls crowded around to see what she was doing and made requests and suggestions. She even got to braid a teacher's hair one Friday afternoon.

As Natalie gained friends, she also gained Brooklyn tastes and needs. She wanted braces for her perfect teeth, she needed short socks with pompous on the back, she had to have a special brand of sweater and not just one but many of them, all far too big for her but just the way the other girls wore them. She needed little black slippers she wore as shoes on the coldest winter days and then she needed platform shoes hidden by pants that dragged on the floor and frayed

What confused Estelle the most, though, was Natalie's geography. While Edgar and the boys were surface roaming, Natalie and her friends were burrowing. They could be only a house away but huddled deep inside a closet as they gossiped about movie stars and TV programs and tried on make-up. Boys made the briefest of phone calls under dire circumstances to find out where to meet. Girls talked for hours on the phone and many of them had their own phones and even their own phone lines.

There were times when Estelle came home from work to find Edgar plopped in front of the television but no Natalie. No Natalie at six o'clock. No Natalie at seven and a somewhat apologetic Natalie at 8:10 who said, "Sorry, I was at Isabelle's, and she was talking on the phone to her boyfriend." Estelle could not understand how that was an excuse for coming home more than two hours late. One afternoon Estelle could not locate Natalie anywhere for three hours until she and Isabelle emerged from inside Estelle's closet with blue toenails and false eyelashes, way before either was a thing.

OLIVIA

STEALING POEMS

In my second year of law school my father died suddenly at the age of seventy-five. My mother, Jacine, was working on the books in our old homework room when she heard him gasp. She finished her columns of figures and walked out to the front. He was on his knees over a box of oranges that had just been delivered, his hands aimlessly fingering the dark purple tissue paper around each one. My mother called 911. Father died of a massive heart attack in the ambulance on the way to the hospital.

My sister, Cecelia was in her seventh month of pregnancy and was driving in from northern New Jersey for the funeral but was stalled for three hours on the George Washington Bridge because of a jack-knifed tractor-trailer and missed the funeral—a Buddhist ceremony held in a small teahouse in Chinatown.

My father's body was cremated. My mother was given his ashes in a carved wooden box. She held it carefully on her lap in the town car on the way back to the house in Forest Hills my parents bought two years before. She set up a small shrine in a corner of the living room and added a piece of her mother's jewelry and a lapel pin of her father's given to him by a US Infantryman in 1953. We never had a shrine in our home before, not even for grandfather Park.

When grandfather came to America, he lived with us for a short while in our small apartment. He was the first to sleep in the dining el. Cecilia and I were both in cribs provided by a Catholic charity. We shared the one bedroom with our parents, who slept on the floor on a Korean futon. My mother found some colorful fabric and wove it through the bars of our cribs so that we could not see our parents or each other once we lay down.

After grandfather moved out to live in the Korean section of Chinatown, my parents moved into the dining el. They slept there for many years even after my sister and I were in college. We had been urging them to move for a long time but at first they were against the idea.

"So close to the market now. We move, we just have a long walk or maybe even a subway ride," my mother reasoned. "Not good for the shop to be too far away. Sometimes we get early delivery. Sometimes we do the books late at night. Best to stay here in the place we know."

However, when mother's friend, Shirley, saw the listing for the town house in Forest Hills, in a *cul-de-sac* with fruit trees and lilac bushes, she literally took my mother by the hand and brought her to see it, extolling the value of what she called "a private house" in a good neighborhood that would grow in value.

Shirley talked to my mother about an "exit strategy" which, somehow, in Korean, my parents interpreted as a plan for when they would die rather than what she really meant, a plan for a comfortable life after they sold Fine Foods. It took them months to decide Shirley was right. Fortunately, the real estate market in Queens was soft that winter and the house was still for sale and even had a small reduction in price.

When my mother made the shrine for my father and her parents, I found grandfather's abacus, but she would not put it with the other mementos. "Grandfather Park was not a very fine man to me. He mocked me when I did not have a baby. He told your father take another wife, "she snorted. "So, when you born I did not use Park ancestor names, only Ahn ancestor names. Grandfather was angry, but I said I prayed to Ahn ancestors who helped me have a baby. I told him I must name the baby Ahn name or bad things would happen, very bad things, and they would not help me to have more babies."

As soon as my father died, my mother promoted Eugene, the stock boy, to the front of the store. The year before, after much urging by Cecelia and her husband, my parents had finally installed a cash register with a scanner. It took my parents several weeks to master it. The first few days, they double scanned many items and had to punch in credits to the exasperation of several customers. Eugene took over for them, but it was an awkward situation because they insisted on standing at the register with him the entire day and reading the paper receipt. In the evenings, after they closed the shop at nine, they would practice scanning bar coded items, weighing fruits and vegetables on the scale built into the new counter and punching in their codes.

Our old laptop computer was still in the homework room at Fine Foods. My mother asked Eugene to get her an email address: Omah77. At first my sister and I wrote to her, and she would read it and dictate her response. But, she realized someone outside the family was learning too much about our business, so she learned to key in her response herself. For a long time her emails were short and comical.

DEAR OLIVIA, STORE VERY BUSY TODAY. I MISSS YOU. DO NOT FAIL ANY TESTS. YOUR MOTHER

Her emails got better but we were never able to wean her off capital letters. I would wake up every morning to a new email my mother had sent –sometimes at 4:00am.

DEAR OLIVIA, SO LONG. TEN MONTH SINCE FATHER DIE. SUMMER SOFT HERE NOW. SISTER RITA TOLD—QUICK DEATH BEST FOR PERSON, BAD FOR FAMILY. MY MOTHER SAY—QUICK BIRTH, QUICK DEATH. MANY HOURS FOR MY BIRTH SO I WILL DIE A LONG DEATH LIKE WINTER NIGHT. IT ALREADY BEGIN—WHEN FATHER DIE. OMAH77.

I would read her emails early in the morning before Torts lecture. So many times they read like poems to me. Just the essence of her day, but often with something very profound in the understory. I began to play with them on the computer.

So Long

Ten brief months since father died
And summer is soft here now
Mother say quick birth
Quick death but it was many hours
For my birth. My death
Will be a winter night.
It was already begun—in the hour
When father died.

Turned this way, the poem was about me, so I would have to work some more to keep my mother's voice. When we took a break in my Torts Study Group, I went back to the poem, but was stymied on how to fix it. Although I belonged to a poetry group, I had only submitted once or twice and never gotten much feedback.

I submitted "So Long" for critique. Comments were quick to come.

> Sarah: *Seems like a haiku to me, (don't they always have to include a season?) but too long I think.*

> Edgar: *If there is emotion here, I can't find it.*

> Emily: *Good work. Welcome to the site.*

Nothing too helpful. But, ten minutes later, fresh coffee in one hand, on my way back to our library meeting room, my phone dinged an email response from the site manager.

> TheDivineR: *This feels to me like a beginning poem. Let me tell you why. The line breaks are arbitrary. Did you write this as a prose piece and then decide to turn it into a poem? Nothing wrong with that; but a poem is both more and less than prose. It has to make a leap. You made a move in that direction, by linking your father's death and yours through your mother's saying (which I like a lot, by the way). But there is no space for the idea to take hold in the gut, soul, heart (pick one) of the reader. We need another image in here; maybe when your mother said this (was she cooking, gardening, ironing —I'm sorry those are very sexist. Just find some-thing). Do you want to work on it some more? I think it is worth saving. Why don't you send another?*

I closed the message without responding and went back to study group. I never corrected the original poem, but most weeks I would send in at least one, culled from my mother's emails. According to TheDivineR, they were getting better but I never really understood why. When my mother's emails became more cryptic for a few weeks at the beginning of her busy season, right before Thanksgiving, I asked her to send me little story about when she and my father had first taken over the store. She wrote back.

HAVE NO TIME DEAR OLIVIA FOR THIS> WHY DO YOU NEED FOR SCHOOL? JUST SAY LIFE MUCH BETTOR WHEN WE HAVE FINE FOOD> YOU GIRLS NOT WORK LIKE ME> NO NITE SOIL, NO BAG FOR KOREA PEARS< NO UP AND DOWN LADDER NO WORRY YOU HAVE NUMBER ONE LIFE NO SON BUT HARD IN BEGINNING YOUR OMAH77

There wasn't much there to make a poem but when I thought about the whole process, I began to think poems weren't or didn't need to be true anyway. After all, The Times Book Review had two sections, one for Non-fiction and one for Fiction and Poetry. I submitted this poem the next day:

Korean Pear

Not bad enough we have a market
on the wrong side of Jamaica Avenue,
but our neighbor, Mr. Watson, is a number ten idiot.
Made bad news on us with his Laundromat.
Flood our food and ruin special Korean pears
And no apology—not like Korea where all
people make a good apology—so sorry.

Please accept.
Told Mr. Park a long time ago
we must move to the other side
near the subway entrance, but not quick enough
Not quick enough and now we have competition.
Korean family, like us, but young,
Many brothers all work together
Not like Mr. Park and me—old, two daughters,
But, every Sunday, we close the market.
Go to daughter and American husband,
and granddaughter Ilene, who is okay to be a girl.
Not ashamed like her grandmother.
Never gets yelled at for being stupid.
Never gets beat or has to bring night soil
To bin man.
Never, ever goes up and down a ladder
two hundred times to
tie bags on pear flower.
Make perfect Korean pears
to send to Jamaica Avenue
For one lousy nickel.
Ilene sits on my lap, touches my face
"Omah, you are so beautiful."
We don't sell Korean pears anymore.

> TheDivineR: *This is one good poem. There is a voice
> in here that is saying so much more than the poem says.
> The first stanza is terrific. Further on, the details are
> compelling but not visceral enough (do you know what I
> mean here—we want to feel the ache in the legs from 'go
> up and down ladder two hundred time') and we want*

to know something more about the bag tied on the pear blossoms—paper, cloth? And why.

Get rid of the 'Omah you so beautiful.' Expected, hackneyed, just weak. Lines I liked: 'For one lousy nickel' and 'We don't sell Korean pear any more' Soldier on my dear Jacine and write back, outside of your poem. It helps to hear the poet's voice, not just the persona's voice.

Which was the poet's voice? Mine? But I had hidden myself behind Jacine, my mother, using her voice as my own. Did I want to reveal that? I thought for a while about what it meant that I had been pretending to be my mother. That I, as a future officer of the court, schooled in the ethics of my profession, had pretended to be another person. My email address was on Yahoo, which did not have any requirement that a user use her real name. In fact, most people never used their real names; witness TheDivineR . But I had chosen to use a real person's name, or at least someone I knew to be real. And it was not me. TheDivineR had asked for a response in my own voice, but he wasn't going to get one.

EDGAR AND NATALIE

LOOKING AND TOUCHING

One Thursday, Natalie knocked on Edgar's door and walked in. She looked around the room and then sat down on the edge of his bed. "Are you my brother now? Mandy ask me."

"Well, sort of. I mean since you live here then I guess if someone asked us we could say I'm your brother."

"Mandy has a brother. She sees his penis sometime."

"WHAT?"

"She told me she walks in his room sometimes and see his penis. By mistake."

"Okay. So that' s not so good."

"But it is by mistake. That is different."

"Well, not if she keeps doing it. Then it's sort of like a mistake on purpose." Edgar pulled at his shirt.

"I have never seen a penis. Except in health class."

"You saw someone's penis in health class!"

"No, in a book. I don't have a brother except you."

"I don't think brothers are supposed to show sisters their penis."

"No, but by mistake, by mistake. Like when I walk in your room to ask you something. Then maybe if you are not dressed I could see it." Natalie put out both arms and shrugged.

Edgar shuddered. "I'm not talking about this anymore." He walked out of his room as Natalie said in a low voice. "Well, maybe later we can talk again."

The next day, Natalie knocked on his door and immediately opened it. Edgar was sitting on his bed, under the quilt.

"What do you want? I'm not dressed. You shouldn't be in here."

"Oh sorry. I was wondering when Estelle comes home."

"The same time as always. Six-fifteen."

"Oh okay," Natalie said and sat down on the edge of Edgar's bed.

"WHAT DO YOU WANT?"

"Can you unzip my dress? I can't reach."

Natalie carefully pulled the dress off her shoulders. "That feels so much better."

■　■　■

Why Estelle came home early one day a few weeks later, Edgar would never know. It was difficult to accuse a mother of coming home early for no discernable reason once she's found you naked in bed with another naked person. Estelle grabbed the first limb she could reach and dragged Natalie out of the bed and onto the floor.

"THIS IS WHAT HAPPENS WHILE I'M GONE!" Estelle was screaming at Edgar. "I can't believe this! How could you even think of doing something like this?" She rubbed her hands in her hair. "I trusted you. NO! It's not that I trusted you, it's that I didn't even think of anything like this." She mashed her palms into her face. "This is just awful."

Natalie, still on the floor, sat up and pulled her discarded dress over her.

"And you," Estelle turned to Natalie. "There are letters from you mother on the kitchen table right now. It's a good thing I came home when I did, because the mailman couldn't read the handwriting and didn't know which mailbox to put them in." She looked at them and made a choking sound.

"What am I going to do? What am I going to tell your mother? How am I ever going to leave you two alone again? Oh my god." She looked from Edgar to Natalie. "See! You can't even answer me! You have nothing to say, do you? Because you both know how wrong this is. You are wretched, wretched, ungrateful children." She pushed the quilt back onto the bed and sat down for a minute and then jumped up. She turned to Natalie, "Put your clothes back on. And you, too!" She pointed at Edgar. "This is all your fault. YOU are the one I raised. YOU know what is right and what is wrong!"

Edgar pushed the quilt away and started to stand up.

"Not in front of us!" She pulled Natalie to her feet and out of the bedroom.

Edgar stayed in the bedroom a long time. He knew his mother was right. When he came home from school every day, he would take a shower and get under the covers wearing only his T-shirt and wait for Natalie. They had always timed it right, and were dressed and doing homework by the time Estelle came home.

He waited in his room for his mother to decide what to do. The front door opened and closed and, a few minutes later, opened and closed again. He heard noise in the kitchen and the scrape of chairs. When he finally, reluctantly, came out, Natalie was sitting at the kitchen table reading her mother's letters and handing each page, absentmindedly, to Estelle as she finished, forgetting Estelle could not read Arabic. Edgar stood in the doorway, amazed. There were two cups of tea and a plate of cookies on the table as if his mother and Natalie had bonded in some secret way over the very thing she had been screaming about less than an hour ago.

"What does she say?" Estelle questioned.

"She says she is very sad about what she did. She feels it is dishonest and trickery to have forced you to take me. She says she cries a lot because she misses me. But she is grateful that I am in America. She has not gone back to the house. She has moved to Fez. She has a job in the office of a friend of hers." Natalie waved the page. "I have her address. She wants me to write to her and tell her everything." Natalie looked at Estelle.

"You certainly will NOT tell her everything! You will not upset her and make her think she has made a terrible decision. You will tell her about school and your friends. You will tell her how much you are learning about life in America and New York. That's it." Estelle looked up at Edgar, "And as for the two of you. Something needs to be done. I can't even begin to say how wrong it is for a fifteen and a sixteen year old to have gotten into this mess. It can never happen again! And, it *will* never happen again."

Estelle took a sip of her tea. "Edgar, I went upstairs to the sisters. They said they would be happy to have you in their home. I did not tell them why, just that it was difficult in such a small apartment to have two teenagers, but I think they figured it out. You will be staying with them until I find a better solution." She held up her hand. "And, there will be no back talk. There will be no complaining. You will be helpful and polite."

Edgar sighed and nodded.

"I'm not throwing you out of the house," Estelle said. "This is still your home. Every day, once I get home, you will eat dinner with us here. You can even do your homework if you wish, but the two of you cannot be alone in this house again."

She paused for emphasis, "You will be especially helpful to the sisters, since they would not let me pay them. You will sleep on their pullout couch in the living room and you will close it up each morning. You will carry groceries for them and bring the laundry down to the basement. And you will not ignore them when they want to talk to you, even if they are going to tell you every detail of their shopping trip to the grocers or how they once lived in Japan when their father was stationed abroad! Because, if this doesn't work out, the next stop is Uncle Harry and Aunt Etta's all the way in the Bronx!"

SARAH AND RUSSELL

THE DIVINER

Sarah sat in her car waiting for Russell Cooney, the diviner, to arrive and find water.

"It's not that exciting," Sam advised. "A guy shows up with two rods or sticks and follows where they point."

"Isn't there an engineer who can do this?"

"Yep, and I am sure our architect will want to use one, but my understanding is all methods are about the same."

Sarah snorted, "Well, how sad for the engineer and his five years of schooling."

"Look, if the dowser is good, it's not the stick thing that's telling him anything, it's his own sense of the land." Sam stopped in his justification. "Let's just view it as our foray into local lore. It'll be interesting."

Sam had retired, and the house on base was packed up. A new family had already moved in. The beach house sold for more than the asking price. The buyers liked the landscaping and the location, although they wished for the impossible— that the house was on the beach side. They planned to tear it down in any case and used it as a reason to make a low offer at the beginning of negotiations. They stuck to their bid until David told them there was another interested buyer willing to pay more. The couple raised their offer by ten percent and the house was sold.

The furniture for both houses was on a moving van traveling across the country. If she chose, Sarah could track the van's progress on the web. She did it once, found the truck, a little blue dot on Route 80 outside of Toledo, and then decided it didn't matter. Everything on the truck was going to spend months in a warehouse while they settled, temporarily, into their new lives in Boulder. They were perched in a townhouse with basic furniture supplied, as a courtesy, by the Air Force, since Sam had been hired immediately as a contractor because of his top security clearance.

Sarah looked up from her phone as a new, dark gray truck pulled up alongside her car. Russell Cooney jumped out and strode towards Sam, his dog loping ahead of him. Handsome dog, handsome man she hoped.

She liked the way western men looked—their skin dusky apricot, the color of life. Their hair thick and touched with yellow or else steel gray. Russell Cooney was older, probably older than she and Sam, but his back was straight and his jeans were tight. She checked her face in the rear view mirror, stepped out of the car and sauntered over to the men, so intent in talk they did not look up. Sam, however, reached for her and drew her closer to him. *This is mine* his arm around her waist said.

Russell Cooney stopped talking. Held out his hand. "I'm the diviner."

"Sarah Ryder," she shook a hand that was no larger than hers and very soft.

"I'm explaining to Sam how this works."

"Just continue. I'll catch up."

"So, I use a rod, but actually, one could use anything. Ty uses a pendulum. You could use a forked willow you find lying on the ground or a knitting needle like Par."

Sarah didn't know Ty or Par but she did know about knitting needles and really didn't think they could be used to find water. And, more to the point, Russell Cooney had ordinary brown eyes and Chiclet teeth that were either crowns or false or veneered or something. "So, you said 'you.'"

"Hmm?"

"You said 'you' could use anything. Did you mean every 'you' as in me?"

"Nicely parsed. Well, I think I was using the generic 'you' when I really meant 'I'. But, some people who know very little about the process can do it. I've heard a really good description about dowsing. Someone called it 'a mother's instinct with a read out device.' For people who really know the land, a divining rod just shows you with a rod what you intuitively know but are unwilling to believe," Russell explained carefully.

Sarah really didn't like his teeth. He looked old and a bit unkempt. She was thoroughly disappointed with this first representation of western man. "I read on the internet that scientific studies show dowsing is no better than chance."

Russell turned away and looked at the mountains behind him for a minute. "I haven't even started to work and you are critical. Why don't we try an experiment? You'll try to find water out here, in let's say, these two acres right in front of where you want to build the house. You can use any method you want except dowsing. You can look at the slope of the land, where the trees are growing, how the stars align, how fast your laundry dries. Any method you want. That okay with you?"

Sarah shrugged.

"Then, I'll do some dowsing and mark off where I know there's a stream or an aquifer. That okay with you?"

Sarah shrugged again.

"Then, you decide where the engineer will drill. At your spot or mine. What do you think?"

Sam interrupted. "We're not doing anything like that. This is ridiculous."

"No it's not," Russell countered. "We're doing an experiment to see if I am better than chance."

"I am not interested in doing an experiment. I called you because you're the expert. *You* are going to find the water and that is where we are going to drill. End of story." Sam emphasized.

"Well..." Sarah started.

"End of story."

Russell looked at both of them, Sam's arm hanging loose, no longer around Sarah's waist. Sarah's arms crossed on her chest. "And I was so looking forward to proving myself. Shall we begin?"

Sarah watched him walk towards his truck to get the rods. She was amazed at her behavior. She had, in fact, been looking forward to the diviner, to watching him, to walking the land with him, to watching the rods move and point to the spot where there was water. And then to think about this new house—which way it would face, where she might have a meadow and a garden, what she might see from each window, where she would put her Dutch door, what it would let in and what it would keep out.

Instead, she had let a little poison drip into the day, just because she wanted this man—this western man—to be a little younger, a little handsomer. She wanted his truck to be battered and coated with red dust and his dog to be golden and called Maggie and his hands to be sturdy and rough.

Sarah pulled Sam aside to make her point. "There's this thing called ideomotor response. It's where your body reacts to a mental image you have and causes a muscular reaction."

"Of course. Golf. Tennis. Baseball. Follow through with your eyes and the ball will go where you want it to go. But what's your point?" Sam was annoyed. "Let's say you're right and all he is doing with the sticks is unconsciously moving them to find water because but he can't figure it out consciously. What's the difference?"

"The difference is, we are supporting bad science. It's like giving credence to people who say there are physical character-istics that prove certain races are better at running. Anyhow, what happens if it's just a little water? Enough to prove him right but not enough to rely on for the next thirty years?"

"We'll see."

They followed Russell to the open two acres nearest the road. He was carrying a small leather sack and a forked wil-low stick. They walked up to the highest point. "Is this ideally where you want the house?"

"Ideally."

"Should we walk with you? Or stay back?"

"Either way, but if you're coming, no talking."

Russell stuffed his leather sack into his back pocket. He took hold of the willow stick by the forked ends, and holding it loosely, palms up, began to walk slowly along the hilltop. Sam and Sarah hesitated and then fell in step behind him. Russell traversed the ridge and then dropped down fifteen feet and traversed the ridge again, stopping a third of the way and giv-ing the stick even more play. He looked at the trees, scattered sparsely along the hill except for one spot where five or six of them were clumped together and then headed in their direc-tion. He stood among them for a while and then walked on.

"Doesn't that mean there might be water? If there's a bunch of trees in one spot, I mean," that was Sarah.

"That's what I thought at first, but I don't think they are clumped there naturally, since they are different species. It looks more to me like someone started a specimen grove and then gave up."

Russell walked back to the hilltop and began crisscrossing up and down. Sarah caught Sam's arm and held him back. "What happens if he doesn't find water here? I'm not relocating the house based on his say so."

"No, of course not. Then we'll find someone else to give us the definitive answer."

"So, I don't understand. Why are we doing this to begin with?"

"I thought it would be interesting. I thought you would find it interesting. Maybe fodder for a poem, or something."

"Are you thinking Wordsworth—'I wandered lonely as a cloud'. Like that kind of fodder?"

"I don't know. Maybe. It's an experience. A completely different point of view. I mean that's why we're here isn't it. Because we've done one thing all our lives—followed the Air Force wherever they sent us—and now we can strike out on our own."

Russell had stopped and was crouched down in a hollow halfway down the hill. He took his leather bag out of his pocket. Sam and Sarah ran down to him.

"I would say this is it." Russell reached into the bag and took out, not what Sarah would have expected—a knife, or a marker flag, or even a compass – but a GPS. He highlighted the location.

"What comes next?"

"We start digging!"

Sarah squinted at Russell. "Surely you jest."

"Of course I'm joking. We get the drill guys out here, and they carefully drill down and see whether I'm right."

"And if you are?"

"Then you've got your water and you can start building. And if I'm wrong, you can sharpen the guillotine." Russell sat back on his haunches and looked at her as he drew his finger across his neck as if to say, "I know everything you are thinking."

And he was right.

Even Russell Cooney didn't think there was any real science in dowsing. He knew about all of the experiments that had shown dowsers were wrong about as often as they were right and that there were much better, more scientific ways of finding water. And he had never actually evaluated his successes to see if he was any better than chance.

It just seemed to him there were certain locations, where the land sloped a particular way, where the wind blew in a particular direction, where particular kinds of trees were clustered in a particular pattern, where iron had leached out of the soil or any one of fifty other peculiarities. That's where, more than likely, there was water. It wasn't a sixth sense. It was more a knowing without knowing. It was looking at a nondescript parcel of land and seeing a topographical map. Like a skier knowing at exactly what point on a slope he would become airborne. Like looking at the snowpack on a mountain and knowing, if there were an avalanche, which way it would break.

RUSSELL

LISTENING

Russell was the next to the youngest of the Cooney children in a family of five: two older brothers, one older sister and one younger brother. Although they were, in general, a kind and close-knit family, there was a certain amount of knocking about, name-calling and pranking. Russell was the victim of choice of his oldest brother, Mitchell, and he in turn victimized Nelson, the youngest. His father called it good-natured roughhousing, boys will be boys. His mother called it bullying.

When Russell was three and a half, his mother, Martha, took him to a well-credentialed neurologist in Denver. This was after many months of appointments with local doctors and psychologist.

"He doesn't talk," she explained. "He looks like he understands everything we say, but he doesn't talk."

"Does he make sounds?"

"*No.* He doesn't talk. He really doesn't make sounds either. Sometimes we think he hums very quietly but we can't tell because when we try to listen, he stops. I mean we think he stops, that is, if he was humming at all."

"Did he ever make sounds?"

"Yes. He made the most wonderful baby sounds, but then he stopped."

The doctor took a detailed history. What was his position in the family? Did he ever have a high fever? Of course, doesn't every child. Does he rub his ears or clear his throat? Not really. Does he have enlarged tonsils? Did something traumatic happen to him? To someone else in the family? How do you punish him? Do you hit him? Yell at him? Deprive him of things? Did he ever break a bone? Has he ever been to the hospital?

Martha was appalled by the questions but she knew she was a good mother—smart, indulgent, loving—who had never, ever done anything to neglect or hurt Russell, although his siblings were another matter. Mitchell, who was eight, called him Pluto, after the Disney dog that didn't talk. Mitchell's friends wanted to call him Pluto as well but Mitchell explained only he was allowed to make fun of his brother. "What's the difference? He can't hear us."

"Of course he can hear us. Don't you know the difference between not talking and not hearing?" Mitchell was definite, "If you can't talk your mouth doesn't work. If you can't hear your ears don't work." He whistled loudly at Russell, who turned his head. "See, he can hear. That's why you can't say bad things about him."

"So why doesn't he talk?"

"I told you why. His mouth doesn't work. It's a special problem. Like people who only have one arm or have to wear glasses."

"So how do you know what he wants?"

"My mother knows. Besides, he just gets it himself."

It was true. Martha did know what he wanted. She knew when he was hungry because he would yawn really wide and rub his eyes. She knew when he was cold because he would come up to her and take her arm and put it around his back. He would curve himself into her side and shrug his shoulders up and down to spread the warmth from her body into his, and she would find him a sweater, or wrap him in a blanket.

She kept a basket in the kitchen for him to reach into when he needed a squeeze ball, or a tissue, or a hat or a picture book. He never had to tell her when he was sleepy because, like all the children, he would never admit he was sleepy. It was up to Martha to declare it was bedtime and to enforce it. The only one who ever fell asleep on his own was Nelson, the youngest.

The specialist moved on to repeating all the tests that had already been done including a hearing test. Russell sat in a high chair with his mother slightly behind him in a soundproof room. He had special headphones on. The technician had no hope Russell understood what he was instructed—to raise his hand every time he heard a sound. He was surprised Russell *did* understand and raised his hand for all but the faintest sounds. There was nothing wrong with his hearing.

There also was nothing wrong with his speech. Russell actually talked all the time. He had conversations with himself all day. He told himself stories. He sang himself to sleep. He even made himself laugh by saying really stupid things in a strange voice. He just never did any of this out loud. He was happy talking to himself in his head. He could learn most of what he needed to know just by listening to his siblings and his parents. They were full of talk. The dinner table was a field of noise with people joking, arguing, explaining, discussing. He was the listener.

He didn't even know there was anything wrong with not talking aloud until his mother began taking him to the special doctors. He could do everything the doctors told him to do. He could do a few more things the doctors didn't ask him to do, like count backwards in his head, twist his tongue all the way around, and wiggle each ear separately, but no one asked him to do those things.

He saw how upset his mother was but he still didn't think that was enough of a reason to talk. In fact, maybe it was a reason not to talk. After all, she spent a lot of time with him, reading and singing to him and watching his face for his reactions. She asked him questions all day and explained everything she was doing carefully to him. Every once in a while he would nod an answer to her and smile to encourage her.

He knew he would say something out loud, eventually. He thought about how to make it special. Come into his parent's room in the middle of the night and tell them a story he had made up? He liked the one about the skunk who could fly and ate olives. Should he say their names? Mama? Daddy? Martha? Dad? Should he sing his favorite song—*James James Morrison Morrison Weatherby George Dupree*? Who was three just like he was. And took great care of his mother. Maybe something funny, like what he secretly called the dog. It was perplexing.

But the very next day, it wasn't. He came running into the house from the backyard and held out his arm. "A bee bite me!"

Martha could have run screaming around the house yelling, "He can talk. Russell can talk." But, instead, she took a more practiced approach, "Well, I am so glad you told me. It was a good idea to use your words. So much better than pointing and crying. You are a very smart boy."

Then Russell sang the song. And that night at the dinner table he told the story about the skunk, and everyone listened to him. For a few days, everyone wanted to hear Russell talk. Mitchell would announce, "Pluto wants to speak." Everyone would stop talking and turn to him. He told stories; he asked questions; he sang the James song and three more; he asked for ice cream after breakfast and got it; he wanted to play kicking ball with Mitchell and his mother made Mitchell do it; he went to the supermarket and rode in the cart behind Nelson, telling him the name of everything Martha bought.

After a while though, he wasn't Russell who couldn't talk. He sat at the dinner table vying for a chance along with everyone else who out ranked him and could say much more interesting stuff. He decided to stop talking, but it wasn't very effective now that everyone knew he could talk. Instead of being a source of concern, he was now just called stubborn. At three and a half, his glory days were over.

WORD SALAD CONTEST

On a Saturday in March, Edgar posted a poem:

Shall I Compare

Where Moscow women huddle
in the dwindling winter sun
their fat fingers curled on flowered
babushkas, once stretched high school girls—
lithe bodies basted in Coppertone.
The drone of single-engine planes trailing
Lucky Strike banners.
At the sound, seventeen
falls on them like fishers' nets.
The odor of boy, summoned from
a reptilian brain, washes purpose
from their morning and without the sense
God gave geese they plump their lips,
ready to receive nectar.

> Sarah: *So, I get that this is about maybe a beach. And*
> *I can feel that whole summer thing but somehow it's*
> *muddled and hard for me to figure out whether this is*
> *all happening at the same time and in the same space.*

TheDivineR: *I like the sound "falling on them like fisher's nets." I also think the line breaks are muddled. Can you re-post this without the artsy attempt? Maybe "high school girls" should be "summer girls" so we know there's a switch in seasons. Although, I take that back since your title implies summer.*

Sarah: *So, can you use a line from someone else's poem in your poem and can you use an implication as a clarification?*

TheDivineR: *Yep.*

Sarah: *Well, that was a little cryptic. But now I have another question. Do you think you can learn anything by handwriting the poetry of other famous poets—sort of the way amateur painters copy the work of famous painters? Or is that completely different?*

Edgar: *Completely and utterly different. Are you kidding me? What does simply writing out someone else's words have to do with copying a painting where you actually learn something about color and texture let alone the skill it takes to reproduce the work of another.*

The DivineR: *Actually, I know this sounds crazy, but sometimes you can use the structure of a well-known poem to create your own. Sometimes copying out a sonnet, for example, can give you a better understanding of a sonnet's structure.*

Emily: *Have you ever done that?*

TheDivineR: *No, I just thought of it. But why don't we all try this: copy a sonnet but change every noun. When you get done it won't make any sense, so then you will have to go back in and change every verb, then every pronoun, then every adjective and every adverb. At the end you will have your own sonnet.*

Jacine: *I could do that. I will try. What sonnet should I use?*

TheDivineR: *There you go. How about 'Shall I Compare Thee to a Summer's Day'? The rest of you— next time you're stuck, try it.*

Sarah: *So what happens? You write something like Shall I Compare Thee to a Winter's Night?*

TheDivineR: *No, more like: When You Comfort Me It is Winter's Breath. Maybe we need an assignment like that. Take a sonnet and rewrite it. Go as far as you can, so we can barely recognize the original. Prizes for the most distance.*

Emily: *What kind of prizes?*

TheDivineR: *I don't know. A day writing with me.*

Sarah: *Why you?*

TheDivineR: *It's good to be the king. But you're right. There is no reason it should be me. But I can't promise someone else's time. I'm the only poet I've got unless we all get together.*

Sarah: *Yes. What if we all got together?*

Edgar: *I'd come.*

Emily: *Sorry, does someone want us to all get together? In the same actual place at the same actual time?*

Sarah: *Yes. I could see that.*

Emily: *I think I am going to say count me out. Unless you all want to come here.*

TheDivineR: *Where's here?*

Emily: *San Francisco.*

Sarah: *And stay where? At your place?*

Emily: *There is no my place. I'm living in my mother's house.*

TheDivineR: *I'm really warming to this idea although I have reservations. If we're going to do this—if I'm going to do this—then you, we, have to make a commitment to write. I don't want to be wasting my time. So, we will have assignments and deadlines. If we can't agree on that, then count me out.*

Sarah: *Look, I have a place. I have a cabin on my property. It might even have a working bathroom. I don't really know.*

Jacine: *You find out. We'll come.*

SARAH

THE CABIN IN THE WOODS

Sarah had never seen the cabin she offered to the poetry group. Sam had told her it existed and described its shortcomings and its dilapidated condition. She told him it could not be torn down, mostly out of anger. The house they sold in New Jersey—their lovely beach house with its newly renovated kitchen—was to be torn down by the new owners.

She took the jeep the Monday after the group email mashup on the poetry retreat. After briefly inspecting the newly poured foundation at the "big house" as Sam called it, and noting that one segment appeared to be settling unevenly, she found the rock-strewn road to the cabin, cleanly dug by early tire treads, and maneuvered the jeep through the pine forest. At the mile mark, she could go no further, stopped by a rusted out pick-up truck parked across the road. No tires, no wheels, a dangling side view mirror, a mottled oil slick patina along its flank.

Sarah backed the jeep up about ten yards to a wide spot in the road and turned it around. The pick up truck was wedged tightly between two boulders. She scaled the smaller of the two and looked down into the bed of the truck. Two foxes were curled into each other, asleep on top of a shredded car floor mat, their fur deep red and dazzlingly variegated in the sunlight. The foxes twitched as she paused and the larger one looked up. Sarah scurried over the boulder, hoping not to roust them, but when she looked back they were picking their way along the roof. They slid down the hood and disappeared into the pine trees.

Just beyond the pick-up truck, the road took a hairpin turn to the left. The right side of the road had been partly torn away. A swath of trees about fifty feet wide and a hundred yards long was matchstick flat with the detritus of road silt, boulders and gravel threaded among the trunks. It was clear even to a city woman that either an avalanche or a rockslide had come through.

On the left side, a wedge of road was still intact, wide enough for a vehicle but only if the driver was careful. Bad sign number one, she thought. Another hundred yards and the cabin came in sight. It was half log, half plank siding. Its porch sloped towards a small clearing where a seven-point buck, three does and a foal were grazing on ragweed. Chicken wire was nailed to the porch railings and a makeshift gate was angled across the top step as if to keep a child from wandering off. The gate was dangling from its top hinge, but the steps were intact and looked newly repaired. The door was ajar.

Sarah called out and waited a full minute before stepping inside. She quickly catalogued the building—scarred wood floors, sloping and worn down in several places but still intact, an ungainly stone fireplace, wide but shallow, five windows with their glass in that frozen liquid state—wavy and thicker at the bottom as gravity forced the glass down. Faded plaid curtains and interior shutters framed each window.

The kitchen was along the windowless wall on the left side of the door. An old double sink with a movable ridged porcelain top had been pulled part way out into the room as if someone were attempting repairs. A wood-burning stove that must have been top-of-the- line in the 1930's stood next to the sink. A cupboard with six open shelves leaned against the far corner. One of the shelves held a cast iron pot—the kind that might have been suspended on a swinging hook over the fireplace. Another shelf held a disparate collection of flowered china— three cups, eight saucers, two dinner plates, a soup dish with a wide rim and a matching sugar and creamer set.

There were two doors in the far wall. Stopping in the first doorway, Sarah saw four bunk beds, two with rolled up mattresses. One, though, was fully made up with sheets, a flat, worn pillow with no case and a faded dime store quilt with large, blowsy roses, its edges torn away, like the border of some continent. The walls were down to the studs. Sarah realized this must be the part of the cabin that was plank- sided, perhaps a later addition. The two windows were half open, supported by small sticks. The curtains here were newer and held to the side with tiebacks looped over cup hooks.

Beyond the second door a hallway led to two more rooms, both empty. One, an original, she assumed, was log and daub with a small window covered in a waxy paper, the other room was a plywood add-on. There was also a bathroom with a toilet and a sink. She turned one of the faucets and a narrow stream of rusty water trickled into the sink, down the drain and out onto the floor. The plumbing under the sink had been carefully cut away. Sarah decided not to flush the toilet.

The cabin was in just that middling state of disrepair where it was impossible to say whether it was being systematically vandalized or haphazardly repaired. In either case, it was totally uninhabitable. Sarah stepped back out onto the porch and sat down on the top step, now rippled with sunlight as the wind made a skittle of the pine trees. The yellow field of ragweed spread before her was alternately shaded and sunlit. The deer, grazing farther down the hill, were indifferent to her.

There was a subtle hum in the background Sarah realized must be the stream Sam had mentioned. She headed across the meadow to find it, swollen from the spring thaw. It was rife with smooth rocks and sturdy, angular boulders, in places close enough to one another to offer fording. Sarah considered crossing over but remembered Sam had told her this was the border of their property. Beyond was parkland.

She turned back towards the cabin. It was surrounded on the north and west sides by old growth pines and open to sunlight on the south and east. The windows had shutters on the outside as well, the roof of carefully layered cedar shingles looked quite sturdy and she could see the blunt, stone foundation, that held the cabin above the forest floor.

Sarah thought it might just do after all, depending on whether the kitchen and bathroom were on their way towards repair or dissolution. She was heartened by the idea that she could decide. The cabin was whatever she said it was. On its way to repair and all would soon function, wholly and beautifully as she wished. On its way to ruination and she could have it dismembered in a day.

Why she wanted to make this acceptable to the poets was a lesser question than why she wouldn't want to make this acceptable for Sarah. With the right plan and effort and muscle it could be done in a week-or maybe a month. If the road needed to be rebuilt, so be it.

■　■　■

A cabin was the place young-ago Sarah wanted to live as she played out her imaginary role as Amy in *Little Women*, for Mrs.

Moss, her fourth grade teacher. She remembered her fierce attachment to the idea she was living her life in the wrong place, a brownstone in New York's Greenwich Village where her family occupied the third and fourth floors and rented out the second to a copywriter for an advertising agency. The first floor housed her father's print shop.

Sarah walked all the way to Pearl Paints on Canal Street and bought a set of watercolors and a full-size easel. It was more cumbersome than heavy. Halfway home she had to pay Winston, a boy she knew from school, a dollar to help her carry it to her house and up three flights of stairs to her room. There she set it up in front of her one window overlooking the small backyard garden and the wooden water tower on the neighboring four-story apartment house.

She painted all that summer wearing a long flowered dress and a smock she fashioned out of her father's old shirt. When she went out of the house, she wore a straw hat with long streamer ribbons tied under her chin. She met Winston fairly regularly. He was sweet natured and rather frail looking. His glasses were too big and heavy for his face and made his eyes look really large. They slid down his nose every time he bent his head. He was always pushing them up, and the sun glinted off them, making him squint and crease his forehead. He knew a lot about American history and talked about the Civil War much of the time. They went to the movies once, and he bought her a frozen Milky Way at the refreshment stand. They held hands and ate little colored dot candies sugar-glued onto long strips of paper.

One morning, they walked down Bleeker Street, eating candy even though it was before lunchtime. Sarah wore one of her flowered dresses but held her hat in her hand, the ribbons fluttering along the sidewalk. A rat peeked its head out from around some metal pails, stuffed with restaurant garbage, set out against the curb. Sarah and Winston stood very still, watching the rat. It pulled its head back behind the pail, but a few seconds later, peeked out again.

Wordlessly, Winston took Sarah's hat. He moved carefully to the side of the pail, holding the hat low to the ground, making a round shadow. The rat peeked out again and in the instant he started to run across the sidewalk, Winston dropped the hat on him, planted a foot on two sides of the brim and grabbed Sarah's hand and pulled her onto the hat brim as well. The rat, squirming under the crown, was now trapped.

"Oh my god," Sarah squeaked.

Winston popped the last dot of candy off his strip of paper. He looked down at the hat and pressed his feet even more firmly onto the brim. "You are never more than thirty feet from a rat."

"You mean in the street?"

"No, I mean anywhere. In the street. In school. In your house. In the movies."

"That can't be. There are no rats in my house."

"Well, I didn't actually say there were. But a rat could be in the house next door."

"So, the other house has a rat?"

"It could. Or maybe the house next to that one. Or the house across the street. And even if it isn't there is still a rat within thirty feet of wherever you are," Winston nodded. "Even if it's just a rat passing by. Like this one."

They looked down at the hat crown. The rat had stopped wriggling, but they could see his shape and some of his hide through the spaces in the straw weave. "What are we going to do?"

Winston wavered, "I don't know. Maybe we should wrap him in the hat."

"I am not wrapping him in the hat! I am never touching it again, except with my feet. I don't even like doing that, and the next time this rat moves, I am jumping off."

"We can't do that. If we jump off, the rat could come right out and bite us."

"Bite us! BITE US! Then we'll get rabies, and we'll die!"

"Soldiers died in the Civil War because they were bitten by rats. They got rabies."

"You can't know about that. I bet there is no book that ever says that. That soldiers died from rats. You are making that up."

"Well, they could have."

"So, what do we do now?"

Winston leaned over and caught a garbage pail with one hand. He dragged it over to the hat and they both tilted it back and, scraping their feet along the side of the brim, made space for the bottom rim of the pail.

"Get off the brim and drag the other pail over," Winston instructed her.

The two pails sat in the middle of the sidewalk holding the brim of the hat down. Sarah and Winston watched as the rat began to squirm again.

They walked three blocks without saying anything.

"I think what you told me about the rats is really disgusting. I don't even want to go home now. Because there could be a rat next door." Sarah looked to Winston for some reassurance.

Winston pushed his glasses up to the bridge of his nose. "I bet if you listen you'll hear some scratching in the walls tonight. And you know what? That will be a rat trying to get into your room."

"You are so mean, Winston. Maybe you know about rats because you have rats in your house. Maybe you know about rats because you look like a rat. You do, you do. You wiggle your nose just like a rat, and you squint your eyes just like a rat."

"I don't care. I don't care what you say. I know I'm right about the rats." Winston took her arm and walked his fingers up to the crook of her elbow. "Creep, creep, creep. See there's a rat creeping right up your arm."

Sarah pulled her arm away and looked at him as fiercely as she could. She wanted to cry or shout at him, but then he pushed his glasses up his nose and squinted his eyes and he did look like a rat and suddenly it was all very funny, and she laughed, and Winston laughed and she grabbed his arm, "Creep. Creep. Creep."

"There were rats everywhere in the camps during the Civil War." And Winston was just a boy talking about the Civil War and teasing her about rats that were nowhere near her house and her room.

Sarah decided she couldn't be Amy anymore even though Winston was still her friend. She pushed her easel away from the window and left her ovals of paint on the sill until they dried up and cracked. She went to the stationery store on the corner and bought a red book with the word *Journal* written in script on the cover and three black pens. She was ready to start her writing career.

RATS

By Sarah Elizabeth Ryder

You tease me about rats,
Caught under hats,
And tell me they're close as can be,

Honestly you theory
Makes me quite leery
But you'll never be a rat to me.

She wrote it out very carefully on a piece of blue paper, rolled it and tied it with a ribbon. She walked the two blocks to Winston's house the next day and gave it to him along with a box of Junior Mints.

NATALIE

HIDDEN RESOURCES

In the waning daylight of a Strasbourg winter, Natalie Fouchette shoved the baguette wrapped in paper into her briefcase and picked her way around the snow splattered cobblestones as much to protect her red-soled shoes as to keep herself from slipping. The girls would be home already, doing lessons at the dining room table and chattering in their patois of Frenglish while Alex chopped vegetables for dinner.

She was pleased with her late-afternoon discovery of three secret bank accounts held by her client's estranged husband. Two were in regional banks right in "Francine D.'s" small hometown. One, the largest, was in an offshore account. The client had known her husband was concealing his true financial worth but had always assumed it was purely business craft to protect his assets from creditors and keep her at arms length from litigation.

Now the clients were in the maelstrom of divorce and Natalie was the forensic accountant in charge of their financial destiny. She had already emailed the lawyers there was possibly more than five million euros at stake. She suspected money laundering was involved, but would broach that in a private document she intended to write after dinner when the children were asleep.

Alex was the one who made the "real" money as they called it, as a partner in one of the largest banking firms in France. And "No!" Natalie had to explain to her clients, she was not permitted to use him as a resource in finding hidden money even if the goal was not always to resolve an acrimonious divorce. There were inheritance questions, dimly remembered safe deposit boxes, ancestry issues and, still, the monumental quandary of treasure and property stolen by the Nazi regime. All of those were more gratifying than deciding who got the house in St. Martin.

"Think! If I had a ten-percent finder's fee instead of an hourly," she teased Alex, popping a sliver of pepper into her mouth, "we could buy one of those chopping machines."

Alex peeled a small eggplant, "And we could also start eating meat again."

"Oh, if only that had been a money decision!" Natalie laughed and leaned over Celeste's shoulder.

"Stop, you're jiggling my arm," Celeste whined.

Celeste and Regine were inspired by their culinary arts teacher who schooled them in the devastations of eating "anything with a face." They had become "pescatarians" just a month before, refusing pork, beef and lamb, but gleefully throwing shrimp and langoustines into pots of boiling water. "How is this any better," Natalie had challenged. Twelve-year-old Regine just rolled her eyes. As a result, Natalie and Alex would sneak meat into the house and have a "supper" after the girls were in their rooms.

She first met Alex at a friend's party. Her colleague, Carl, cooked an annual dinner every New Year's Eve for the seven years she had been living in Strasbourg. The guest list varied but the menu never did: saffron mussel soup, rack of lamb, sautéed mushrooms and shallots, warm pureed pear poured over chunks of dark chocolate and many bottles of Chateauneuf-de-Pape.

That year, Alex was a new guest. He was seated next to her because he had just returned from a five-year assignment in Washington, and she was the only other person fluent in English. He liked the way she sopped up the last of the mushrooms with a chunk of bread, overstuffing her mouth. She liked the way he smelled – a combination of ginger and lime. That they had sex that very night on top of the pile of coats in the Carl's guest bedroom just solidified their initial impressions.

They spread themselves out on the king-sized bed once the girls were asleep. "Here, open your mouth," Alex urged. He placed a piece of thinly sliced prosciutto on her tongue.

"Oh my god, "Natalie moaned. "When do you think the girls will get over this? I can't take the policing of the refrigerator much longer. Yesterday, Celeste threw out the little bit of pate left over from the weekend." She took a bite of cheese. "I think need we need a wine cooler in the bedroom."

"I think we need to send them to boarding school," Alex laughed.

"Ugh."

"Well, you survived just fine!"

That was the solution Estelle had fashioned after she discovered Natalie and Edgar naked in bed. She found a boarding school that offered Natalie a scholarship not only because of financial need but because, "she would enhance the exposure of her fellow students to different cultures." Instead, they enhanced hers, teaching her about high-end shoplifting, the etiquette of meeting rich boys' parents and the hierarchy of colleges. In exchange she did all their French homework and taught them how to suck dick.

To be abandoned twice by two mothers. To have two people who loved her toss her away for reasons that had everything to do with their own convenience was a pain that never left her. She would never abandon her own girls, nor would she ever be abandoned again. She would do the leaving.

"That is not what I have in mind for them. We...I... waited a long time to have them. Because I was so worried I could be a good mother, the right mother for them. We will keep them here, as close as we can and suffer through the no-meat phase," she kissed Alex on the neck and reached for the prosciutto. "Then we will go through the recycling phase. I'm sure there will be many others after that. Eventually, they will go off to university. We will be grateful we have wonderful children and a stable home. We have done everything to make it so."

"Well, then," Alex stood up. He cleared his throat. "You need to get free of this fear."

"It's not fear. It's anger." Natalie piled the empty plates carefully one atop the other and lined up the knives. "Do you know, today is the anniversary of the day my mother disappeared."

"I'm sorry. I know that was a terrible time for you," Alex reached over and touched her hair.

"You can't even think how bad it was. I am with complete strangers who have come to my house just two days before. This is my mother's plan! To pick a woman because she is Jewish and lives in New York. She could have been a drunk, or a murderer or, or anything. But to my mother, who knows nothing of the world, she is good because she is Jewish and lives in America and has the money to come to Morocco to get help from a mystic!" Natalie was crying. "Can you imagine giving our girls to complete strangers like that?"

"No, I can't. I truly can't. She must have been desperate."

"Desperate for what? Were we in a war torn country? Were we destitute? WERE WE BEING HUNTED BY NAZI'S?" Natalie was shouting. "NO." She paused. "By the time we found each other—or rather I found her in Fez—I was beyond anger. After all, Estelle had thrown me out, too."

"But she, at least, made careful—provisions."

"Exactly! Provisions! She found a school that would take me for no money. That's not a provision. That's a calculation." Natalie shook her head. "But a better calculation than my mother. That school, those girls, taught me how to make my way in the world. Whom to meet, where to be seen. Even what to eat."

"But Estelle and what's his name…."

"Edgar."

"Edgar. They came to visit you. They didn't just abandon you."

"They came exactly three times. A month after they dropped me off. A year later for Parent's Day. I was giving the welcoming speech—which the school asked me to do in both English and French to show what a sophisticated program they had—ironic isn't it? And for graduation!

"I think Edgar felt bad. He was allowed to call me once a month, but we really had nothing to say to each other. After a while, it was so awkward, I told him I had a busy semester ahead and maybe we should just write letters. We each wrote once."

"Would you ever want to see him again?'

"NO!" Natalie paused. "Well maybe. If I ever find him I'm going to tell him what a shit he was for letting me take the blame."

SARAH

PERSPECTIVE

"You do know this is wrong on so many levels," Sam accused Sarah.

"It's just one more thing. Why not get the cabin rebuilt now while the house is being built? We have the materials, the contractors and there are no plans because it already is everything it needs to be. We'll just piggyback it onto the work we are doing here."

"No."

"How could there be a 'no' in this?"

"You have confused me with a person who says yes to crazy ideas."

"Not really. I know you are not a person who says yes. I am hoping to help you become one."

"So how is this going to work?"

"This is how I envision it," Sarah said ticking the steps off on her fingers. "You are going to say 'no.' Then I am going to say okay fine I will do it myself. Then I storm out of here and get into my pick-up truck and drive into town and buy a bunch of stuff that people buy when they are fixing up cabins. You know like a jackhammer and some of that white stuff with Vitek written on it that's all over new houses. Then I'll get a door knocker and new faucets and an espresso machine and Bob's your uncle."

She took a breath, "Oh, and I'll hire some people standing outside of the store and bring them back here. And when I come back you will manhandle me out of the truck, throw me over your shoulder and yell at me like in that movie that's sort of like *Taming of the Shrew* but it's a musical. And you will have to sing 'Why Can't a Woman be More Like a Man.'"

"Okay, so. You don't have a pickup truck, you don't need a jackhammer, that white stuff is called *Tyvek,* the musical is *Kiss Me Kate,* and the song is 'Why Can't You Behave?'"

"See, you are so much better at this than I would be." Sarah tilted her head and smiled.

"Don't play me."

"You've already been played. Twenty years ago. This is the encore."

"Oy vey!"

"*Fiddler on the Roof.* See, I do know some things," Sarah grinned.

"I can't decide if you are totally adorable or an idiot."

"Of course I'm adorable, and I may be an idiot, but I am your idiot."

When it came right down to it, Sam knew he was going to have to give in. There was the overriding effect of The Sacrifice that Sarah and all military spouses and families made that was genuine and moving. It usually meant when the career ended and the military was no longer telling you where to live and for how long, the sacrificing spouse got to choose how and when and where to spend the rest of their lives.

Actually, the construction plan worked better than either of them thought, particularly Sarah, who, despite her assertions, had no belief she could handle two building projects at once. The house, all 4,000 square feet of it, had architects plans and blueprints. It had to meet detailed codes for construction, and it also had a general contractor, Tim Purcell, who came every morning to set up the work for the day with the plumbers and the electrician and the sheet rock and insulation guys (and one woman).

Sarah's job was to choose the finishes and the embellishments. She over-ordered everything to have enough for the cabin.

"Are we making a mini-house back there?" Sam complained. "Because I am not up for that. It's a cabin. In the woods. Built on a questionable foundation and already maybe sixty years old. Why are we—you—ordering thousands of dollars in materials."

"Economy of scale."

"There is no economy of scale. Every doorknob costs x and so ten more doorknobs cost ten x. What happened to those six-packs of handles and things? Things that can be returned without a thirty percent restocking fee."

"I'll look into it. But we should use what we already have since there *is* a restocking fee."

"Let's just take the 'we' out of this. It's all you. If that's what you need to do, then I would at least like to know why. In fact, *you* should want to know why. I think you have lost perspective. You are too close. You need some distance."

What's distance? Sarah thought. She trusted the zoom-out feature on a computer. When they were looking for land, Sarah would click on listings, see the property close-in and then slowly tap the zoom-out feature to get more and more of the surrounding land in view. Just out of frame there could be a gravel mine, or a gas station; two miles away there could be a development –something called Mountain's Edge or The Colony Club. There could be ski lift towers already in position to traverse the edge of the property, or the pillars of a soon to be constructed highway overpass.

Where was the town, the schools, the storage cone for the road salt and the snowplows, the pullout where the chain guys would line up in winter for unprepared drivers? Zoom-out would tell her. Where the mine shafts, the open grazing land, the cattle? How far away do you have to be to see what's coming, what's about to be built, what's about to happen or even what is happening that no one can see yet? The flooding river, the rockslide, the avalanche, the tsunami? There are signs of impending danger everywhere if you know how to look.

How far out do you have to look to know the home you are making, the family you have borne, the life you have chosen and nurtured is *the one* and the only one? What about the parallel lives you almost lived, the ones with six children or none, the ones where you didn't marry or married the man who came along next or first, or loved a woman? What about the life where a shopping cart was your closet and your pantry and you slept in the park during the day and walked purposely down the pedestrian mall at night hoping the window display in the home décor store had changed so you could imagine your imaginary living room in imaginary mid-century modern?

Sam asked, *where is your perspective?* Sarah would say, *all I have is perspective. The only way I know anything is by standing in the one spot I make for myself every morning, which is different in every single way from the day before. From that spot I look at the second in front of me and maybe even the minute and decide what I know and what I want. I make myself believe that I am in charge of that second and minute.*

I go on through the day like that making decision after decision while someone standing on the roof or on the mountain or in a plane looking down on me can see the tree limb about to crash through the ceiling or can see nothing untoward and wants to let me know it's okay today, it's all okay, build that cabin. And that's how I have to behave. As if I have chosen to do exactly what I am doing. Just go ahead and do it and you'll be fine. But of course they are too far away to say that to me. So everyday I have to do that for myself. That's my perspective, and that's how I know I have to behave.

AVALANCHE

She was curled in sleep under the quilt the man had adjusted carefully before he left. He had brushed her silky red hair off her face and fanned it out on the pillow. He may have tried to wake her but to what purpose. There was no great plan for the day. He had gotten out of bed to escape anyway. The smells of alcohol, pot and the heady aftermath of sex were roiling his stomach. He left his clothes behind, carefully closed the bedroom door and stopped on the porch to gather random footwear before he wandered down the steps and headed across the meadow.

Far up on the mountainside a tree, torn from its perch, hurtled down the slope, its branches streamlined against the trunk by the force of the avalanche. It was the vanguard for the tons of snow rolling behind it. Other trees were uprooted but this tree was destined for the cabin window and its old glass that would blow apart easily on impact. It smashed through the window. It captured a homey plaid curtain and carried it through the cabin and out the front wall as a victory flag.

Along the way, it swept the bed with its crosswise occupant out of its path. Her arm was cradled under her in the sleep of the drugged. The combination of alcohol, pot and the last of the pills made her heart rate slow. She had just taken a startled breath. She murmured a soft "Hmm" before the tree and the force of the snow plowed her into the wall.

Bones mangled and broke, soft tissue collapsed. The breath was pushed out of her. She did not wake. In another, more romantic universe, she would have had time to murmur the name of a lover or have a scene from her childhood flood the reptilian part of her brain with the musky smell of maple leaves crushed underfoot. But there was no such reprieve. Death came in an instant.

SARAH

BUILDING REMORSE

Everything Sarah had chosen for the house and the cabin was suddenly in question in a flood of buyer's remorse. The wood floors were too light. The granite for the fireplaces was too pink. The stove was no longer on trend—a newer, more elaborate one was now being featured in three different decorating magazines. Narrow glass tile and waterfall countertops were about to be over. She had a feeling carpet and wallpaper were about to be in, just when she had rejected them. Was a Dutch door a staple or should she switch to a cantilevered one?

She was about to spend hundreds of thousands of dollars to build and furnish a house that could be out of fashion by the time she threw the last contractor out. If she'd had the energy she would have blogged about it all. But maybe that was no longer a trend.

Sarah decided she could perseverate at the gym as easily as on-site and was now spending several hours a day honing her glutes and triceps—she had given up on her abs since she spent most of her eating time standing at a counter somewhere inhaling a very satisfying high-carb diet.

She also decided she and Sam were at a crossroads. They had begun by looking at his retirement as an adventure. There was a new state, a new job for Sam, a chance to build exactly the home they—or to be more precise, she—always wanted. And, Sarah planned, a new relationship.

She compared her relationship with Sam to college. The first few years were devoted to requirements in order to establish oneself as a legitimate partner in a marriage. There was the required sex, required finance management, required pregnancy, required child-rearing, required house buying. Then came the choosing of a major and honing one's skills—was she going to major in child rearing and have a few more? Was Sam going to go career-military or leave after his four-year obligation? Were they going to plan everything together and execute it equally as best they could or create separate domains?

Now they were in the elective phase which Sarah thought would be the easiest – become a poet, or a landscape architect, take up sky-diving or bee-keeping, coast along waiting for graduation, or work to get the most out of the last year, build a relationship out of what had become twenty year habit or drift into parallel play.

After the dowsing experience, Sam seemed very happy with parallel play. Rather than being a shared adventure, Sarah had viewed the dowser with suspicion and distaste. To her, his services were useless and arcane. The curiosity she usually felt for the off-kilter, Sam discovered, only applied to experiences she orchestrated. It turned out, after all the years of leaving it to her to shape their adventures, Sarah viewed it as her purview. She viewed any Sam-initiated oddities as taking over a role she had carefully cultivated for herself.

This thing with the cabin mystified him, as did her insistence they have an in-law suite in the walk out basement. As their lives grew less complicated, it seemed everything else had to be more complicated—a house and a cabin, guest bedrooms and an in-law suite, an architect and a decorator, a new career as a munitions consultant and a new career as a what? A poet?

"Why don't you send your poems into magazines?"

"First I want to have a body of work. I can't just send in three poems if I only have three. And they need to be critiqued."

"By your group?" Sam huffed. "You don't even know these people. How do you know they're even poets? How do you know they're not plumbers or obstetricians."

"They could be plumbers or carpenters or even dowsers for all I know. I mean they are not all earning a living as poets. But I know they are poets because they write poems."

"But are they any good?"

"They're as good as I am, usually better."

She called David Front. "You know how you always called us the perfect couple—the best of both possible worlds."

"I never said that! That is beyond douche."

"You did. You did."

"Well, maybe. Maybe I said it in 1991, on the day my dog died and I thought I had food poisoning."

"In any case. We are not." Sarah whined.

"But *you* never thought you were; you're only claiming that I thought you were."

Well, we're still not."

"In what ways, and there have to be at least three."

"Okay, so we switched jobs, we switched states, we switched houses, and I thought it was going to be a real awakening but it's turning out that we needed those things. That was our matrix. So, now we are just free-floating. Or maybe I'm the one who's free-floating. I don't think Sam feels the same urgency to knit us back together. Or maybe I don't feel the same urgency. Or any urgency at all. This sounds so stupid."

"That's because it is. You haven't said a single insightful thing yet. In fact, it's one big word salad."

Sarah hung up.

Sarah called him back.

"Shit, I was going to hang up first. How do you always get ahead of me?" David complained.

"I'm smarter than you," Sarah said continuing her litany of marriage incompatibility. "We need to figure out a new way of being together, and I'm not sure Sam is up for it. I think he's done working on this relationship."

"Do you mean divorce?"

"No. I don't think that's even shown up in his brain. I mean he's done with moving forward. In his mind, we are a completed work. We are a bundle of flagging energy, mediocre sex, and lazy conversations. And I am totally with the program. I cook the same foods, wear the same clothes, and give the same half-assed blowjobs I've been doing for twenty-one years. I have the same fucking roll of fat under my belly button. I still don't shave my legs in the winter. And he has grown back hair."

"There are blow jobs in this?"

"Don't be an ass."

"I already am."

"I'm adding a casita, and I think it's for you. I told Sam it was an in-law suite."

"Your parents are dead."

"I know. Ballsy of me wasn't it."

"Well look at you!" David laughed.

"Okay. So what do I do?"

"Start by shaving your legs. And maybe a little bit more."

"A Brazilian?"

"Funny you should say that because I'm seeing a guy right now who's from Rio."

"Oh, shut up. I'm not going to talk about your romances. Frankly in the beginning they make me horny and when they end they bore me," Sarah complained.

"That's my constant state—horny and bored at the same time."

"Oh my god. I really miss you. Have you ever been blown by a woman?"

"I don't know."

"How you could not know?" Sarah insisted.

"Some people are complicated."

"What color should I paint the walls in the guest suite?"

"Have we solved anything here?" David hung up.

"Come for a visit! Now." Sarah texted.

"After my Brazilian tryst fizzles."

"I'll shave for you."

"I am not looking at your naked who ha! EVER."

"You are such a fucker."

"You're my best friend."

"I love you."

That was conversation number one. Conversation number two was with Sam who met her at the construction site one afternoon with a bottle of wine and two glasses.

"What are we celebrating?" Sarah criticized.

"It's a Tuesday afternoon on a cloudy day in January, we are both healthy, our daughter hasn't asked for extra money in a week, and we are standing in our very own soon-to-be-finished house. Let's see—you're not pregnant and our parents are all dead. In other words, we have no worries—at least not at the moment. So would you like to celebrate or do we need to have one more conversation about what's tearing at you? It seems to me you're pulling yourself apart looking for a way to be in turmoil." He poured the wine.

"Here's to reality. Here's to sanity. Here's to normalcy." He drank. "Here's to ordered, ordinary living or is that exactly what riles you about our life? Not enough excitement."

They were sitting on a stack of wallboard. Sarah stood up. "Yes. Isn't that disgusting?"

"You're depressed because you have exactly what you want. Where do you go now? That's a real question by the way."

Sarah walked around the pile of sheetrock and walked around again. "All the ways we are with each other get more and more solid each day, each year. I know everything you are going to say. You know everything I'm going to say."

Sam nodded. "You're right. So how's this—I'm actually a spy. I bet I've never said that. Or, I cheated on you and Bethany's not really your daughter. Oh, I'm sorry, that's something you would say to me. So what's the craziest thing you could say to me?"

"How about I planted dynamite in the foundation, and when the house is all finished I'm going to blow it up."

"That's better. Why don't we switch places? I'll go to the gym every morning for two hours and then hang out at the house wondering which carpenter is the most fuck-able. By the way, which one?"

"That's easy, Liam. The Irish one who climbs onto the roof without a ladder. It's kind of daring. He wears these waffle shirts. His jeans are torn. And his accent."

"See. Let's get a dog."

NATALIE

PERSPECTIVE

Natalie had known all along she would leave Alex one day. It was hard to explain why this was the eventual end to what many of their friends saw as a wonderful marriage so she just called it her "path." Alex had insisted they try to resurrect the marriage through counseling even though she promised it was useless.

"It's not going to help resolve anything, because there is nothing to resolve," she explained in their first therapy session. "I am faithful. I think Alex is faithful. We don't fight about money, or religion, or how to raise the children. We like the same movies. We like the same foods, except for snails. Oh and quail eggs. We don't like the same music, but I forgive him for that. We could be married for the rest of our lives, and it would be fine, but ...."

Alex interrupted, "How could there be a 'but'? You can't leave me and just say 'but'. There has to be a reason. A real reason. You are just stringing words together to make it seem like we're having a discussion. And to make it seem like you have a reason."

"I don't feel...," she shrugged. "I don't find any excitement. There is nothing interesting happening."

"What's your definition of interesting?" The therapist tried to intervene, but Alex waved his hand.

"So what's interesting? Being left by your mother in the care of total strangers who are forced to take you to America. Now that I admit was probably really *interesting*, as you would call it. I would say terrifying, but then that's me, a normal person who looks for a normal life." Alex was combing through his hair with shaking hands. "Who turns to a husband after seventeen years of marriage and announces she's leaving because life is not interesting? Who does that?"

"Obviously me," Natalie snapped.

Here the therapist intervened. "Natalie, if your life is not interesting, who's in charge of your life?"

Alex was pacing. "This is not about interesting! This is leaving before you get left. Your mother left you and because she left you, you lost your country, your house, your family, your language. Let's see what else? Your friends, and even the way you lived your life with servants and a mother who was always home—not because she wanted to be but because she was sick," he shook his head and walked to the window. "And you are forced to live with strangers. Literally strangers, who take you with them based on some crazy plan by your sick mother."

"Don't attack my mother," Natalie ordered. "She was a mystic, a true mystic which is rare and magical, and she could see what was best for me. She could see my future and knew there was none for me in Marrakesh without the gift. Or anywhere in Morocco as Jew.

"What would you know anyway?" she accused Alex. "You didn't even know you were Jewish until we met. And maybe I do have the gift after all, because I know when it's time to leave."

Alex turned to her. "Please let me finish. And then these people they too abandon you! The mother sends you off to boarding school in another state. Not with any regard for what's best for you. She sends you off because she has some antiquated notion about what teenagers actually do when they're left alone at home every day." Alex squatted down and grabbed Natalie's hands. "You were the victim. You are the victim. But, I refuse to let you make our daughters victims."

"I…I," Natalie stammered.

"Yes, that's right. Say 'I'. Because that is how you are thinking right now. You think you are leaving me to protect yourself. But I will survive. You have forgotten you are leaving them! Our daughters. YOUR daughters. HOW CAN YOU THINK THAT IS RIGHT? TO PROTECT YOURSELF AND HARM THEM?" He took off his glasses and wiped his eyes with his palms. "That's right. Of course I am crying. If you weren't so absorbed in yourself, you would be crying too."

"So what am I supposed to do? Abandon what I know I need to do just to make you and the girls happier," Natalie had gotten up from the chair and was pacing the room.

The therapist forced herself into the argument. "It's not them you are angry with but your mother and this other mother. Betrayed and abandoned by two mothers is a terrible, terrible hardship for a teenage girl. And I am sorry they are both dead. But that doesn't mean you can't resolve your anger. I believe this has very little to do with Alex. Sit down and let's really talk about this."

"I think better when I stand and walk," Natalie circled the room, and stopped in front of the window, her back to Alex and the therapist. "I remember waiting at the window of my room at the school for them to show up. Other girls' parents are arriving with picnic baskets and gift-wrapped boxes. A few parents even brought their dogs. And my friend Annette's parents brought her parakeet in its cage. Its name was Douglas." Natalie turned to them. "Isn't that a crazy name for a parakeet? But Edgar and Estelle never came. They wrote to say they were coming but they never did. So, Annette came to get me and I had picnic with them and the school let Annette keep Douglas in her room for the rest of the semester. He was so cute. He could sing this song called Yankee Doodle."

Alex put his arms around Natalie, "You sound so much like a sixteen year old right now. I know how hard this must have been for you."

"They called to say the car broke down. So it really wasn't their fault. But it was so hard. There were two other girls whose parents didn't come, but they were from Portugal, so no one expected them anyway."

"Please my sweet Natalie, until you really understand why you are leaving," he gulped. "Please, work on us first. I will work on us. We will see the therapist. We will try. Right now you don't know how to try, you only know how to leave. You have no perspective."

SARAH

TROUT CABIN RULES

The first email discussion about the cabin chugged around the chat room for a few days and then dropped itself into the abyss of old news. New poems were posted, critiqued and rewritten. Jacine disappeared from the group for a month. Russell posted the same assignment twice. Edgar explained in detail why he disliked every poem he submitted. Emily wrote a poem and then a short story about her poetry quilt. Sarah posted photos of the cabin and her design board of fabrics and furniture. Then it was February, almost a whole year later.

"So, the cabin," Sam started one evening. They were well into their first winter in the new house. "We built this for what? For you? For the poets who may or may not ever come here?"

"Yeah. I mean yes. Yes for me and yes for the poets. And then maybe there'll be other projects."

"Did you ever think we could be renting it out?"

"Absolutely NO."

"Well think about it. It's a vacation rental by owner thing. 'Creek side cabin high in the Rockies, sleeps'—how many?—I think we could say six. Don't you?" Sam was ticking off the beds on his fingers.

"Bands of strangers rampaging through. I—we—haven't even stayed in it yet."

"There's money to be made. And it's really year round, when you think about it. Snow stuff in the winter. Hiking in the summer. Your poets could be our first group. We work out any kinks with them and then off we go."

"Bethany could use it," Sarah offered.

"I'm sorry. Are you talking about Bethany Trout? Or some other Bethany who likes being in the woods by herself with no Internet or TV and spotty cell phone reception. You know that was the first thing she checked when we picked this location for the real house."

Sarah was stirring something on the stove, "I love this house. You're happy here aren't you?"

"Yes, very. Think about it."

> She opened up a chat with the poets' group the next evening: *Are we ready to plan a work weekend at the cabin?*
>
> Edgar: *I'm game. Where exactly are we going?*
>
> Jacine: *More to the point what exactly are we doing?*
>
> TheDivineR: *Writing! In case you've forgotten.*
>
> Jacine: *Together? I mean are we writing a poem or whatever together or are we just writing while we are together and if that's the case why are we?*
>
> Emily: *Because Sarah wants to use the cabin she spent so much money fixing. Am I right?*

Edgar: *Sarah can just get together with TheDivineR since they're so close.*

Sarah: *Who me? We're not close.*

Edgar: *No, I mean location close. You can't live more than thirty miles apart.*

Sarah: *I don't know that. How do you know that?*

Edgar: *You live outside of Boulder. He lives in Boulder. You're a poet. He's a poet. What's to know? Okay— Sarah meet TheDivineR—otherwise known as Russell Cooney.*

Sarah dropped out of the chat and accosted Sam. "Did you know that the guy who found our water was a poet?"

"Of course. I gave you one of his books." He looked up from his newspaper.

"Well, why didn't you tell me?"

"I told you. I gave you one of his books. Did you look at it? I thought you would contact him and get into his class or group or just share work."

"Did we ever have a conversation about this?"

"What's the difference? You didn't much like him anyway."

"Well, maybe I would have liked him better if I had known."

"So, now you know. Do you like him better?"

Sarah shrugged. "I have to think about it. It's a whole other thing now. Besides, I think he's the moderator of the group."

Of course he was the moderator, Sarah realized. The book Sam gave her more than a year ago was buried in one of the hundred boxes in the garage. Sarah looked him up on-line. "Holy," she yelled to Sam. "He's in wiki!"

He was now even more of what she didn't like. If she thought his look didn't fit her idea of a cowboy, it certainly didn't fit her idea of a poet. *That's the problem. He's a hybrid. Sort of like a mule.* Rather than feeling more genuine, to her he seemed more ersatz—like white chocolate.

More to the issue, she was disappointed in her carelessness. How long had she been in the poetry group? Three maybe four years. She knew nothing about any of them. *But that's the way it's supposed to be. It's not who we are but what we produce. Once we find out too much about each other we can't be objective.* Yet, someone else in the group knew more than she did about both her and TheDivineR. Edgar. So, who were Emily and Jacine and Edgar? She didn't even know enough to Google them.

Back in the chat.

> Sarah: *Before we make any further plans, I think we should know a little more about each other. I'm actually Sarah Ryder. If you Google me you will find not much except maybe for an interview I once gave for a military magazine.*

> Emily: *Emily Minerva (Minnie) Bishop. My Master's theses on Free Poetry is on the U of I website.*

> Edgar: *Edgar Frankel, and the one you find in Google is not me.*

There was no answer from Jacine. Russell Cooney responded with a link to his website and an apology to Sarah for knowing who she was all along.

■ ■ ■

Sarah spent days figuring out the logistics of the poets' retreat. When should they arrive, when to go to the cabin, how to allocate the rooms. A weekend was too short; a week was too long. It seemed to her five days was the best solution. They could all arrive on a Friday and spend that night in town. On Saturday morning they would drive out to the cabin and spend Saturday, Sunday, Monday and Tuesday writing. On Wednesday morning, they would drive back to town and drop everyone off. People could decide whether to stay on or head out to wherever. Just enough time.

She got out the decorator's schematic for the cabin to look at room sizes and furniture. She and Sam would stay in the back bedroom, nearest the bathroom. Jacine and Emily could have the dormitory room with the four beds. Russell and Edgar could share the smallest bedroom, since men usually don't care much about where they sleep, and if Russell was put out, well he had his own house to go to. If anyone didn't like the arrangements, they could sleep on the pullout couch in the main room.

Over the next week there was a flurry of back and forth over the date of the retreat that Russell had named The Calamity Gathering. Five days later it was decided and Sarah posted the agenda.

Five days, second week in April, get to Boulder and leave however you wish, Dutch treat at all stays in town, guests of the host once at the cabin, bring your own toiletries and meds. Dinner is family style, meat, veggies and carbs at every meal. The cabin has hot and cold running water, electricity, heat and a full kitchen but no dishwasher. There is NO INTERNET. Dress for cold weather and snow; snowshoes and poles provided at the cabin. Be prepared to carry your own luggage, share a room and abide by the Trout Cabin Rules:

Sarah had the rules printed on craft paper and hung inside the front door.

TROUT CABIN RULES

I.   **Shoes and boots off at the door**
II.   **No pets**
III.   **No drugs**
IV.   **No smoking**
V.   **No uninvited guests**
VI.   **Alcohol in moderation**
VII.   **Discreet sex (and please no semen on the quilts)**
VIII.   **Singing and zither playing in moderation**
IX.   **NO GUNS**
X.   **Marshmallow roasting in the fireplace is permitted**

"That should do it," she told Sam.

"You are such an optimist."

"Don't you think they'll abide by a few simple rules?"

"To you it's a few simple rules; to someone else it's the negation of an entire lifestyle!" Sam said and pressed her, "So who do you think is most likely to break the rules?"

"Russell! Russell!"

"Yeah, me too."

"And the least likely?"

"Oh, I don't know—maybe Jacine."

Sarah had thought about them all staying at the big house the first night but Sam was adamant. "Don't even think about hosting these people twice. It's enough that we've already spent about fifty thousand dollars on this cabin. Let them use it to the fullest extent of their creative juices. We'll meet them for dinner on Friday, and we'll go into town, pick them all up and take them to the cabin on Saturday morning."

"That's it. You don't want to consult a friend."

"That's my final answer. This will give them time to size each other up and decide who they're fucking."

"Whom. And me, do I get to decide."

"No, you have to take the rejects."

"And you?"

"View me as the caretaker. Or the bartender. I'll bring the pencils and the condoms. I'll watch over the fake ranch knick-knacks and make sure they don't burn the place down."

"That's *my* job."

"No. As soon as they get here, you'll just be one of them, chewing on pieces of your hair and looking studious and distracted. You'll be my college crush all over again, and before anyone else crawls into your bed, I want the first shot."

THE CALAMITY GATHERING

The town was full of the oddities upscale tourists love—hundred-year-old houses with wind chimes and balanced rock cairns, tables of farm produce with prices on wooden sticks and tin boxes for payment, quilts on racks outside fabric stores. There were local honeys and jellies in Mason jars with caps wrapped in twine and calico, and handwritten price tags on scraps of brown craft paper. It was everything that an easterner would want in a western city.

Dinner was at a restaurant that had been the mayor's official residence from 1907 until 1958. Sarah had reserved a private dining room. When she and Sam walked in, Russell was standing at the entrance talking to two Asian women.

Olivia put out her hand. "I'm Olivia, and this is my mother Jacine."

"Jacine, I've loved your poems from the very first time you submitted."

Jacine and Olivia spoke at the same time. "They are not my poem. I write emails to Olivia, and she make them poem…"

"I am so sorry I kept up this lie for so long. My mother writes me every morning and sometimes her emails are so poetic they need to be…"

They paused and looked at each other, "But I couldn't come just by myself, because she is the real author of the ideas. So when I told her…."

But actually it was when Jacine told Shirley the deception became a showdown, with Shirley pronouncing Olivia had committed plagiarism. "You are just as important as Olivia for her poems. I hate to say this as a person with no children myself, but your daughter has used you. And you know how much I love Olivia. I am shocked this law school has taught her nothing. I might expect this of Cecelia but not of Olivia, not that I don't love them equally, of course I do, but Olivia has the training in ethics. That should have told her this was wrong. Since Mr. Park is no longer alive, I feel it is my duty and Maxwell Mister Lee's to look after your best interest. After all, YOU are Jacine!"

Jacine saw the whole thing in a different way. "My Olivia did exactly right. She changed my poems so they are correct English, and she signed them with my name. Anyone who needs to find the writer of them knows to find Jacine, not Olivia. She has done nothing wrong. And Cecelia, she has done nothing wrong either. Don't be jealous, Shirley."

"What do I have to be jealous? I have a beautiful home and a wonderful husband. And no daughters to steal my good name."

But when Jacine told Olivia what Shirley had said, Olivia agreed. "I have deceived the poetry group and have stolen from you. It is your ideas and a lot of your words. I just turned them into phrases that are more pleasing to other poets. I should have told them all along what I was doing. That would have been more honest. I am so sorry mother."

Standing in the restaurant a month later and shaking hands with Jacine and Olivia, Sam whispered, "And so it begins!! It shows you how wrong you can be. No uninvited guests. First, rule broken."

"Well, technically, she was invited, just not by us."

"Are you kidding, I don't accept that. Let's see how quickly they fall."

Edgar was the biggest surprise for Sarah. Tall, with fading blond hair and a rugged tan, he was much closer to her idea of a cowboy than Russell. His voice was husky and deep, and he interspersed references to writers and poems she had never heard of with very detailed discussions of every mundane thing including the taste of buttermilk and the sound of snow chains on city streets.

Emily was precisely as she imagined. Thin with long straight, red hair, blue eyes and small, slightly crooked teeth, she had the young Joni Mitchell look. Her hair moved in a sheaf, the ends scissored straight across. Her mouth was faintly lopsided, open to the possibility of a smile at any moment. She had that perfect California unaccented accent.

Jacine and Olivia looked nothing alike. Jacine was actually dressed quite stylishly, in a fur-trimmed parka. She was short and a little overweight, but her black hair was interspersed with brown and red highlights and cut in a super chic kind of flip. Olivia had the student look. Her hair was long and straggly; she wore no make-up and had chosen a coat for warmth rather than style. It was bulky and ill fitting with large pockets that bulged with scarf, mittens and hat.

It was still a mystery to all of them exactly who had written Jacine's poems. What did it mean that the words were Jacine's but the poems were Olivia's? Russell was the least concerned. In his view an idea was an ephemeral, amorphous blob, until someone turned it into something concrete. Jacine sent Olivia emails. Olivia turned them into poems. A woman sat on a chair with a scarf wound around her head and her face turned obliquely so only one pearl earring was visible. Women did that everyday, in every century, in every country. An artist turned it into a painting. An audience turned it into a masterpiece.

Edgar thought of it as bricklaying. Thousands of bricks made in a factory hundreds of miles away were delivered to a construction site. Edgar created a pattern, built a frame, laid a base, and, one by one, placed those bricks into that pattern. It was his art that decided whether they were running bond, or spiral, or Greek key or herringbone. The bricks were a tool. The words were a tool. In fact, the further away one got from the bricks or the words, the more opaque they were. The whole thing reminded him of the perspective of a star show at the planetarium. Expand and collapse. The camera first focused on an atom and gradually moved out to molecule, to leaf, to tree, to forest, to continent, to Earth, to solar system, to galaxy, to universe and then zoomed back down to that atom.

Sarah had the most visceral reaction to the deception. Decades of military life made her sensitive to being subsumed into her husband's goals. It was always Sam's career that mattered. If she wanted a career of her own it had to be teaching or nursing or any work where she could relocate easily and find willing employers on the military base or the surrounding town, and, of course there was almost no work overseas except on the base, where she was one of hundreds of applicants—supplicants she called it. In Sarah's view, Olivia had stolen her mother's words and her story.

■ ■ ■

When they were still in the military and she and Sam used to fight, that was the issue. "Do you never think about what I might have become if I weren't a following spouse?"

"I think of it all the time. I've always thought you would have excelled at tightrope walking and mud-wrestling." Sam sniggered. "But seriously, yes I have and that's why we've always agreed that when I retire it will be your decision where we live, and I will be the trailing spouse."

"I want to be a lawyer."

"That's okay. In fact it's more than okay. When I retire we will both be forty-five." Sam paused. "If you think that's too old to go to law school, start now. I am sure we can figure something out, especially here in New Jersey. There must be a half dozen law schools within driving distance. I will help you research and apply. I'll do anything you need me to do."

But for Sarah, that support in the middle of an argument had quelled her energy. She was certain Sam would have collated everything she needed, but the process of taking the LSATs and filling out applications was tedious.

Sarah had always styled herself a change-junkie. She disliked tedium and it's cellmate, boredom. She briefly looked into what law schools were within commuting distance. There were three in New Jersey, six in New York City and another three in Philadelphia. Several were out of her academic reach, but there were at least four reasonable possibilities, and one safety. They had never lived in a place that offered so many options and Sam was right, now was the time to apply. The idea drifted around in her head for a few months, but she was too lazy to act on it. Then she was forty, and then she was forty-three and Sam was two years away from retirement and the move to Colorado. So, that was the end of that.

■　■　■

Standing in the entrance to the restaurant and meeting these people for the first time, Sarah knew the next five days were up to her. While Russell had been the leader of the group on-line, she was in charge of these actual people who had arrived at her invitation and were expecting her to make it happen. "Let's see if we can get through dinner," she groused to Sam as they were led to their table.

Russell started the conversation. "I am the actual Russell Cooney as opposed to TheDivineR who orders you around on-line demanding poems on the most annoying topics and then critiquing them as if they were your ideas for what poems should be. I offer no apologies. I think I'm less dictatorial in person, but I also think Sarah would disagree since she and Sam hired me to find water on their property. Sarah believes I was *lucky* to actually do that, whereas I maintain I have a deep well of only partially tapped talent in that area."

Russell smiled. "I am a poet of slightly above average ability in the world of really great poets; but I am stellar in the universe of ordinary poets. In my defense, I am the one who's actually gotten you to write poems on a pretty regular schedule. So, who are you and why are you here?"

"I'm Edgar Frankel, and can we order first before we go deep into psychological angst. Did anyone ever have a bison burger?"

"I don't eat meat." That was Emily.

"Is it going to be this cold at the cabin?"

"You know we should check on when everyone's flights are so we can make a plan about getting back to the airport."

"What's the average temperature this time of year?"

"Sorry but at the cabin –shower or bath?"

"What does the average matter? It's the temperature right now that matters."

Sam signaled the waiter, and they all opened their menus and ordered with surprisingly few questions and special requests. He ordered two bottles of wine for the table. Russell produced a bottle of bourbon from a backpack and handed around shot glasses. "How about a toast to a creative four days." Sam and Jacine downed their shots in one gulp. Sarah shuddered over half a mouthful. Olivia and Edgar sipped theirs, and Emily got up and headed for the bathroom.

Russell filled the glasses again and Olivia made the next toast. "To our host—Sarah."

"And to Sam," Russell added.

Edgar, still sipping, "To creativity."

Emily sat back down and reached for her glass, "And to a white out."

"Did you say wipe out or white out?"

"Or write out?"

"I'm not sure," Emily giggled. "Either I guess. What's a wipe out?"

"What's a white out?"

"I don't know what any of them are. It just sounds good."

"Wine?" The waiter poured.

Olivia sniffed Emily's coat, "Pot?"

"Maybe. Interested?"

Olivia shrugged and nodded. They both scraped their chairs back and headed for the tiny bathroom. "So, your mother?"

"I told her the whole thing and basically forced her to come. She didn't care and wasn't going to, but I guess there's a lot of guilt in our family or maybe it's a Korean thing. She spends a lot of time with my sister and her baby and not so much with me. Also, she hasn't seen mountains since she left Korea. That was a long time ago. And her friend Shirley took her shopping especially for the trip."

"Very stylish. And she's a good drinker."

"I know. New to me!" Olivia handed the pipe back to Emily.

"Let's keep it to just this one," Emily advised. "I didn't bring that much with me."

"Maybe you can buy more here."

"I'll ask Russell."

"You think he knows?" Olivia exhaled.

"Oh for sure he does," Emily nodded. "Also, did you see the way he's looking at Sarah? He is so hot for her."

"It certainly doesn't sound like it."

"What's that got to do with anything?"

"You think it's going to be one of those weekends," Olivia was whispering.

"Don 't you? Besides, we can make it one of those weekends. Who are you thinking of?" Emily waved her hand in an attempt to clear the air. She looked at Olivia, blushed, turned on the hand dryer to dispel more of the smoke and left.

Olivia glanced at herself in the mirror, adjusted her glasses and walked back to the table.

The bottle of bourbon and a bottle of wine were upended into the ice bucket.

"Two dead soldiers," Edgar nodded, hoping he sounded like he had participated even though he'd only finished his single shot of bourbon as the waiter was serving the food.

"So," Sarah continued. "We've basically lived all over the U.S. and in Germany and Japan." She picked up a knife and sliced her potato in half. "Anyway. I don't even think I'm a poet. I'm just someone who writes poems. It's sort of like someone who cooks dinner every night even if it's for twenty years is not a chef. They're just someone who cooks dinner."

Olivia looked at her plate in amazement. She had no idea what she had ordered and couldn't recognize it now that it was in front of her. She poured too much wine into her glass and muddled around for something relevant to say, "To poetry and poets whoever they are."

Sam ordered another bottle of wine.

It was at least twenty degrees colder outside. Their goodnights were quick. No lingering. Sarah had already organized them for the morning. Luggage and people parceled out between two jeeps. Russell would arrive on his own.

Sam was comfortably drunk so Sarah drove. "What do you think?" He asked.

"I'm having serious doubts."

"About?"

"About the whole fucking idea. Who are these people and why are we going to spend five days together? I'm already wrong about each and every one of them except Russell of course. He's still a total dick. I mean why even bring up that whole divining thing. Somehow he thinks he proved to me he knew what he was doing. Not."

"And the others?"

Sarah shrugged and focused on navigating a patch of asphalt coated in black ice. When she looked over at Sam, his head was pressed against the side window, and he was snoring softly. She tried to recalibrate her opinions of each of the people in the group and realized she had started out the evening by imbuing them with much more grace than any of them possessed. She thought Emily and Edgar were the ones with the most potential to surprise her, probably because Edgar said so little and Emily spent so much time smoking in the bathroom. She was going to have to clarify the Trout Cabin Rule about no smoking before yet another prohibition was sabotaged.

Sam woke up as they were pulling into the garage. Bethany's car was parked neatly next to his SUV; a total surprise, since she was not expected home until the following weekend. "Oh shit," Sarah mumbled. Her first worry was not whether anything was wrong but whether Beth would wind up at the cabin as well. "What a revolting development this is," she mimicked, but Sam just laughed. "Anything that can go wrong will go wrong."

CABIN LIFE: DAY ONE

Everyone was ready at exactly ten the next morning with a reasonable amount of luggage. They stopped and trooped inside at what Sarah referred to as the Big House to pick up a pot with that night's dinner, a stew of beef and potatoes, and a roasting pan with grilled vegetables. There were baguettes, a black forest chocolate cake and a large ham wrapped in foil. Two coolers held a week's worth of food for the rest of the stay.

Both vehicles made it up the last part of the dirt road to the cabin and were unloaded.

As they wandered inside, Sarah gestured to the **Trout Cabin Rules** sign. "Read 'em and weep folks. Just a reminder that, loose as this is, we *do* have some standards."

"Oh, this is so Ralph Lauren," Jacine said as soon as she took off her boots. She walked around the front room smoothing her hand over the dark wood table and fingering the curtain fabric.

Emily took off her jacket and left it outside over the porch railing in an attempt to air it out. She, of all of them, knew how to evaluate a property, based on decades of her mother's training. The engineered wood floors didn't impress her, but she thought the rustic décor was just the right touch, as was the stone fireplace. It took a day for her to realize the entire cabin was heated by a large propane tank at the side of the house, which was blocked from view by a shed.

Emily would be sleeping in the largest bedroom with Olivia and Jacine. Edgar and Russell would have the bedroom off the main room and Sarah and Sam would have what they called the master bedroom. There was one bathroom for seven people.

Olivia took Emily aside. "I know this is supposed to be our artistic retreat. Right? Away from civilization, so to say. We can hone our creativity and all of that. But one bathroom. I'm not a brat, but what the hell. Their main house must have four bathrooms."

"Five," Emily corrected. "But who wants to have a bunch of people you've never met in your very own house? The one you live in all the time? We all knew we were staying here."

"Yes. And it was fine with me until I saw the other house. Is there a word for this? I know it's not *schadenfreude*. But something like that."

"Envy!"

"Ugh! That's what I'm feeling?"

"Mmm."

"Oh fuck. Monstrous isn't it? I grew up in an apartment with one bathroom. I'm in a dorm now. I need to get over myself."

"Indeed." But Emily felt the same way. All these people, so little privacy.

Russell kicked open the door of the cabin. He was carrying two cartons full of bottles. He placed them carefully on the long dining table and stepped outside and shoved another carton onto the porch. They could hear his truck start and chug slowly down the road.

Sam just groaned and looked at Sarah who began to unpack the cartons, lining up the twenty-four bottles on the kitchen counter. Four bourbon, four mixers, six white wines, seven reds and three vodkas. *What exactly was the definition of alcohol in moderation? Maybe this was it, spread out among seven people over four days.* Calculated that way, it seemed less onerous. She could open one red right now and add at least a half bottle to the stew. Besides, what was a hearty dinner without a nice glass of wine? So, that would take care of three of the reds. No one would be more than pleasantly high.

They could hear Russell on the porch once again, stomping the mud off his boots and then more clinking and banging. Edgar opened the door, and there was another carton of bottles in Russell's arms with a rifle resting across the top. He set the carton on the table and leaned the rifle against the door molding. Sarah stood up and was about to speak when he held up his hand, pointed at the Trout Cabin Rules sign and said, "Bears."

Jacine and Edgar shivered, although with fear or excitement they didn't know. Sam, almost out of his chair, nodded, sat back down and grinned at Sarah who took a marker out of one of the freshly stocked and organized kitchen draws and drew a bright red line through "*No uninvited guests*", "*Alcohol in moderation*" and "*NO GUNS*." She tossed the marker on the counter and looked around the room. "Let the festivities begin!"

Dinner was exactly as Sarah had planned. It was relaxed and comforting with a fire in the stone fireplace, plaid placemats and napkins on the table and almost enough chairs for them all. Sam opted for the ottoman stacked with two pillows to bring him up to table height. They went around the table doing a very good imitation of a graduate seminar introduction meeting.

"So this is me in one sentence—a New York Jewish widowed bricklayer slightly overweight, more than slightly depressed, with pretty good biceps from lifting bricks. I'm not sure why I even write poetry, except it's easier and cheaper than going to a psychiatrist."

Jacine and Olivia, sitting across from each other, nodded, and Jacine began, "I am a widow. I own a Korean market in the Jackson Height. I have a computer. I write to Ok Yan every morning and tell her my day."

Olivia continued, "I'm in my second year of law school…"

"Yale." Jacine interrupted.

"Every morning I read my mother's email. They're usually about what she did the day before or what she's about to do. Some of them are so revealing they are poetry. I make them into poems. Then I send them to you all. They are from Jacine which is me and my mother combined," she finished her glass of wine. "When I knew we were going to meet, I told her and made her come with me."

"I *am* going to be a poet," that was Emily. "No, no—don't suck up. I'm not one yet. I'm on a break from Iowa, and I am trying to convince a bunch of really talented people at school that even if I'm not that talented, I'm creative. So here's a picture of me in Palo Alto at my free poetry stand. And there's my website. I live in the house I grew up in with my mother. If you think my poetry booth looks like a lemonade stand, you are exactly right."

"So what's this 'All Others Must Pay' thing?"

"Everyday I offer a different group of people free poems. Like plumbers, or lumberjacks, or bankers, or nursing mothers or I don't know. Whatever fits on the sign. And then people stop, and I write a poem for them on the spot."

"Does anyone ever pay?"

"Lots of people, even the ones who could get a poem for free."

"Really?"

"Yep. They can only have a poem if they let me take their picture and post it on my website. So, in the end, everyone pays in one way or another."

Sam stood up and moved to the ottoman in front of the fireplace. "I'm here to keep you people in line," he smiled, "although I'm pretty sure Sarah will do a better job than me. So, let's just say I'm here to make scrambled eggs for breakfast and maintain a decent level of testosterone in these backwoods."

They finished the entire pot of stew, three bottles of red wine, half the black forest cake and a pot of coffee.

Sarah and Emily cleared the table. "Let me wash up," Emily instructed. "It's one of my talents." She was gathering up the wine glasses, pouring the leftovers into her glass as she went and topping it off with the dregs from each of the three bottles.

Russell and Olivia were already sitting on the floor in front of the fireplace. Edgar and Jacine sat at opposite ends of the couch and Sarah plopped herself down in between them.

"… in charge of the creative program this weekend," Russell was saying. "We'll do some assignment work, some collaborative work and some free-style work. I'm hoping we can get in at least three hours of writing a day."

"Is that enough?"

"I don't know what enough is, but it's not so easy to get good work. There's got to be thinking time and wandering around time and critiquing time."

"What about this idea of being in flow and just keeping on keeping on," Sarah challenged.

"Feel free. But frankly I think it's bullshit. Most of the time when I'm working on something, I'm looking at that clock on the computer and wondering when I can stop." Russell rubbed his chin. "That sounds really discouraging I know, but it's the truth. In my defense, when I look back at the work, I really can't tell the difference between words that flowed and words I eked out in agony one at a time. I certainly can't tell the difference between stuff I wrote when I was sober and stuff I wrote when I was drunk. Unless of course I'm reading it when I'm drunk."

"And then?"

"Oh, then it's all great!"

Emily had finished the cleanup and stood for a moment deciding where to sit. Edgar tried to make space for her on the couch, but she ignored him and climbed over Sam and the ottoman to sit on the floor in the V of Russell's out-stretched legs. He pulled himself up until his back was straight against the stone wall of the fireplace only to find that this gave Emily room to snuggle tightly into his thighs. She was holding her empty wine glass. "Three hours is enough for me," she laughed. Russell moved his arms away from his sides so they were clearly visible, but Emily ignored him and reached over and put a hand on Olivia's calf. "I'm getting tired. Which bed do you want?"

Sam coughed.

"What the fuck," Sam smirked and actually rolled his eyes, when they were in their own room. "Is there anyone that girl hasn't propositioned."

"Me. At least not yet. And hopefully not you." Sarah flipped back the quilt and climbed into bed.

"Not yet. Either. But I have hope."

"It's the writer's retreat thing."

"What does that mean?"

"Half the people at those places are totally into fucking and sucking and drinking and smoking."

"Well, thank god there's the other half."

"Oh no, the other half are the ones getting fucked and sucked."

"Oh shit, and I majored in engineering."

"I cannot see you at those retreats. You can't even stand being around Russell for more than a couple of hours."

Sam pointed. "No. *You're* the one who can't stand him. Or have you forgotten."

"Did we also drink too much? Maybe I think so."

"Maybe I hope so, too. Why don't we just do what everybody else is only thinking of doing? Or at least right now."

"No, first I have to hear your predictions."

"Okay. A threesome with Emily, Russell and Olivia." Sam suggested.

"Totally obvious."

"And *your* predictions." Sam inquired as the toilet flushed in the bathroom next door. "And why the hell do we only have one bathroom in this place? You'd think for the fifty thousand dollars it cost to rebuild this place—oh yes it did—you could have at least added another toilet."

"No one has a cabin in the woods with two bathrooms! And my prediction is that I am going to suck you off within the next ten minutes."

"While I'm doing you?" Sam stretched.

"Of course not! Where did anyone ever get the idea that worked? You can't give and receive pleasure at the same time. One of you is always slacking off. Me do you first and then you'll do me. And, you had better not fall asleep. Otherwise, I'm going to wind up on my own predictions list."

CABIN LIFE: DAY TWO

The next morning, as promised, Sam had a skillet of scrambled eggs and twenty slices of bacon ready by eight-thirty as people drifted in from the bedrooms. Edgar had a room to himself, since Russell had gone home for the night. He was awake earlier than anyone else, and had already showered and shaved.

The bathroom was clearly the sticking point in the cabin. Sam had pulled on his jeans and a sweatshirt, gone outside to pee against a tree, and then washed up and shaved at the kitchen sink, using the shiny surface of a spatula as his mirror, before he cooked breakfast.

Emily, Jacine and Olivia had an elaborate arrangement about bathroom sharing. They decided showering while someone else washed at the sink might be tolerable. Sarah had no such partnership arrangements with Sam. She could not imagine anything less romantic than sharing a bathroom with him. It was much too sibling-like.

It was ten-thirty by the time everyone had eaten breakfast and dressed in some fashion. The women were sharing the bathroom with rigid discipline. The men had decided to pee outdoors even when the bathroom was free.

"Oh my God, Sam," Sarah demanded. "Can you tell them not to pee off the porch into the dirt? That is disgusting."

"It's a boy thing."

"These are grown men! What is their issue here? Let them go into the woods or just use the bathroom."

"It's not one of the rules."

"Neither is no nuclear weapons! Who could think of shit like this and make a rule about it?"

"Well you see what happened to the other rules." Sam pointed to the list, scarred with red cross-outs. "At least no one's fired a gun yet."

Sarah chucked her chin at Russell's rifle leaning against the doorframe. "Chekhov's rule—if a gun shows up in the first act it will be fired in the third."

Russell was standing by the fireplace with a rolled up sheet of paper. "Do you have any nails? Where can I hang this?" He unfurled the paper and carried it over to the nearest wall. "What about here?"

"You want to put nails into the log walls?"

"Well, what would you suggest? I need to hang this up so we can get started."

Sarah handed him a roll of electric tape. "Here. Do what you can with this."

"Find a seat everyone, and let's get started. The first thing we need to decide is do we want an assignment each day or do we want to write on our own?"

"Are we actually supposed to be writing?"

"What did you think?"

"I thought it would be more like a discussion group. Like a transfer of ideas. Kind of like life-expanding."

"Would anyone mind if I took photos?" Emily asked.

"For what?"

"I might mind."

"I'm documenting for my masters."

"What are you documenting? Us or you?"

"Me, of course, and …"

"This tape is not holding up."

"So why do you need pictures of us? Here give me the camera, and I'll take pictures of you." Olivia tugged on the strap of Emily's camera.

"Just small nails. The wood will expand and fill the holes once we're done."

"I don't need photos of me. I need photos of all of you and the process."

"Not me."

Sarah swooped the paper out of Russell's hand. And scrawled:

Expanded Trout Cabin Rules:
1. **No nails in the walls**
2. **No photos without permission**
3. **No peeing off the porch**
4. **No nuclear weapons**

She looked round the room, "Anything else?"

"Yeah, no plagiarizing."

"I don't deal with creative matters, only cabin matters."

"I have more paper, you know."

"And I'll probably have more rules."

"Let's just do a quick assignment to get us started. It's called Twenty Lines. Here they are, and GO. Line one: your most prominent feature. Line two: a line from a nursery rhyme. Line three: the last TV program you watched. Line four: The punch line of any joke. Line five: How you want to die. Line six: any foreign phrase you can spell. Line seven: a line from a movie. Line eight: the last thing you threw out and why. Line nine: a question you don't know the answer to. Line ten: the answer.

Next ten lines are the same, but order reversed and different answers, of course." Russell paused and looked at the room. "Okay. Now write a poem. You have ten minutes."

"Are we reading these aloud?"

"Yes. But no critique. We read them as is and take them as is." Russell looked at Olivia and Jacine. "Okay, so what's your deal? Are you both writing? In my book you're both here so you're both writing. Jacine you can write in Korean. Olivia you'll have to do this on your own. Get busy."

Russell looked at the dutifully bent heads and listened to the very satisfying scratch of pens. "A cabin of industry. That's what I like to see."

Sam, standing in the kitchen, walked over to the window. "Holy shit! There's a bear out there."

Pens and papers pushed aside, they were all at the window.

Sarah jumped up. "Oh, it's Cubby."

"Cubby. You know a bear named Cubby."

"Yeah, of course. He was here all the time when the guys were working. There was Cubby and a bigger one they called Mamo. She broke into one of the trucks. Looking for food I guess. I think they used to give her leftovers from their lunches," Sarah smiled. "They're harmless."

"I'm sorry. Is that the pronouncement of someone who spent most of her life in cities?"

"There is no such thing as a harmless bear." Russell asserted. "See, that's why I brought the gun."

"No one knows how to use it except you."

"I know how. Air Force you know."

"Well, I don't know how and neither does my mother."

"I know how, I think," Edgar mused.

"I want to learn how," Emily announced.

Jacine raised her hand. "Not me."

"Time for lessons," Sarah announced.

Cubby prowled slowly up to the cabin and sniffed around the foundation. He looked for a long time at the stairs leading to the porch and put a tentative paw on the second step, but then turned his head, backed off and loped into the woods. Russell picked up his rifle and made a come-on gesture and they all meandered outside.

When they were in the clearing in front of the cabin, Russell brought another rifle from the truck and handed it to Sam. I think the best place is that hill," he said pointing off to the right. "You take Emily and Olivia. I'll take Edgar and Sarah. No one wants to see a husband trying to teach a wife anything, much less how to shoot a rifle." They stopped about ten yards in front of the hill. Russell and Sam walked ahead to examine the terrain. The hill, covered in low brush, sloped sharply up from the clearing. The ground was compacted, with no boulders.

"Do you have blanks?"

"Not a chance. Why would I? This will be live ammunition. I think we'll be all right."

"You only think?"

"Okay, modification. We teach them one at a time. No one else on the field except our learner and us. Everyone else waits on the porch."

The quickest learners were Edgar and Emily. Edgar, who never would have imagined his talent at Coney Island board-walk games would have any lasting value, discovered he knew how to hold a rifle and aim even though he had only used this skill to knock down moving rows of wooden ducks. For two summers he was the "ringer" for the game every weekend.

Passersby would stop to watch him win time after time and wind up spending twenty dollars trying to duplicate his success. At first, the owner paid Edgar four dollars an hour, but after a month Edgar negotiated a better deal—ten percent of the take. One Labor Day weekend he earned four hundred and forty dollars. As customers failed and left, he would step in to convince a new audience how easy it was.

Emily, although quite slight, had a sturdy stance and a sure grip. She could patiently squeeze off a shot that almost always hit the exact spot on the berm Sam pointed to, although the recoil knocked her back a step or two each time.

The lessons lasted well into the afternoon. Some were more able than others, but eventually everyone had fired off at least a couple of shots without flinching. This was the accessible goal for most of them. As they headed back into the cabin, Jacine came out on the porch. "I want to learn."

Sam looked at Russell and shrugged. "You're up. It's your rifle, and I'm done for the day."

Russell took the rifle and guided Jacine down the steps.

"It's getting cold out there." Sam left his boots at the door. "Time for drinks?"

"Just to warm up."

"Are we supposed to be doing our poems," that was Olivia, looking at the papers strewn on the couch.

"Can you remember those ten line assignments?"

"Yeah, something about a line from a movie and our most distinctive feature."

"That's not going to do it for me."

"Wine is a good decision."

Drinking and looking out the windows at the backs of Russell and Jacine, sucked another hour out of the afternoon. They were coupled together as he taught her how to hold the rifle and steadied her arm for the shot.

"I hope this isn't rude, but do they even understand each other?"

"Oh, my mother understands a lot more English than she speaks. A lot more English then she is willing to admit. Besides, it's all about muscle lessons, not language. He can just position her the way he wants, and she'll figure out to stay there." Olivia poured a little more wine into her glass. "May I ask what's for dinner and is there anything I can do to help?"

Two hours later, a laconic dance in the kitchen had produced a salad, rice with shredded leftover beef, half of the chocolate cake and three empty bottles of a mediocre cabernet.

"I hate to say this but we're running out of wine," Sarah took Sam aside. "Are we supposed to get anymore?"

"Hell no! I'm not in the business of supplying alcohol. If they notice and care, let someone else go into town."

"Well, the only other person with a car is Russell."

"Up to him, then."

"So, why do we all write poetry anyway?" Edgar asked, after the detritus from the meal had been cleared away and they were seated in new configurations around the fireplace.

"Why do you write?"

"I'm not sure. It started out as just something to do after Ruth—that's my wife—died. I'd come home and cook dinner, which I forced myself to do every night—and then I'd be searching for something to do. So I began looking up stuff on the Internet. Just weird stuff. Black holes and string theory—which, by the way, is impossible to understand, even with the morphing diagrams, or at least for me."

"You should look at the stuff the guy from the planetarium does videos on, he's pretty good."

"So, if I couldn't get enough out of something within an hour or so, I'd switch to something else. I found out all about binturongs, and what different designs in saris mean and then I found you guys."

Emily challenged, "That's a weird reason to start writing poetry."

"Not for me. I was on a search for something, after all, and it turned out this was something. It's the opposite of what I do all day. So, it's like since I spend a lot of my time bent over a pile of bricks, I learned to do stretching exercises to counteract the muscle contraction. Poetry is a counteraction."

Jacine, still flushed from the afternoon outdoors, explained, "I do not write poetry. Only Olivia thinks it is poetry. In Korea, poetry is a serious, serious work. It has special rules and forms. Very few women can write such. Really very few men also. I have little time for school, but even then we have to learn famous poems." She turned to Olivia and recited a poem in Korean and nodded her head.

Olivia tried to translate, "My mother sang this to *her* sister and taught it to *my* sister, Cecelia. 'Sister, sister dear, dark as deepest night and smart as sesame cake. Let me hug you once again.' And yes, I am the dark one, but only my hair, not my soul." She smiled and stretched her neck from side to side.

"I'll go next." Sarah said. "I should have started to write a long time ago, only because it's so mobile. A pen, a notebook or a chewing gum wrapper, or a restaurant napkin. So portable. If I have ten minutes or a half hour, I can do something—write a poem—and finish it. It may be mediocre, but I've done something. And maybe the next day it won't be mediocre. I mean not that it's actually any different but I'm different, or it's less raw, or more raw. Or something."

Emily stood up and walked to the fireplace. "You know I write poems for other people. It started out as kind of a manipulation. I needed something to distinguish me from all the other people applying to grad school. I read about someone doing this and decided it would be my gimmick. I know it sounds calculating, but that's what grad school is all about," and here she looked to Russell.

"So, I have my little poetry stand which is charming and adorable, and on the right day, I am also charming and adorable. I figured I would get a few cute guys a day who would stop by and I could cajole them into giving me a topic and all. But then it's not that in any way." She walked over to the table to add more wine to her glass.

"I know exactly why I write," Olivia said.

"Wait. I'm not finished. People stop at my table and they are not cute guys looking for a hook up. They are real people. They're old or they're women and they don't care who I am and what I look like. I've got the way to say what they want to say. They'd never ever walked down a street looking for a person who could write a poem for them. So, if it's Free Poems for Zookeepers Day, it's just a ploy to get them to stop. The ones who really need something, they stop. They tell me what they need, and then I've got to take this little spittle of need and turn it into a poem. And sometimes I get it right."

Emily laughed and twirled in her spot. "There was a mother who came by with a little boy, and she told him he could ask me for a poem. Maybe he knew what a poem was, I don't know. He said he wanted a poem about a dinosaur and an umbrella and the sky where his teacher was. He told me his teacher used to be on the earth, but now she was in the sky. And his mother nodded, and I put a sticker on it when it was done, and I think that helped."

"Did you get into grad school?" Edgar asked.

"Yep. There's no more wine by the way."

"I'll get some. I've got to go home anyway," Russell stood up.

Jacine walked over to Olivia. She said something in Korean in a low voice, as if someone could understand.

"Are you coming back tonight?" Olivia asked.

"I wasn't planning on it. I can buy whatever she needs and bring it in the morning."

Jacine shook her head and Olivia said, "That won't do."

Russell stood up. "Which won't do. The buying or the overnight."

"Both." Jacine said.

"Oh my god, then come on then. Let's get going so we can get back here."

CABIN LIFE: DAY THREE

I think I'm awake earlier than anyone else, because there is hardly any light in the sky, but when I look over at my mother's bed, it is empty. Emily is still asleep. Every night she crashes on her bed the moment we get into the room. She is still in the same position, clothes on, her feet in their shoes dangling over the side of the bed. I lie still for a while, thinking I might go back to sleep, but it is clear that I am awake for good. There are sounds coming from the kitchen. I wash up and pull on my jeans. The door into the main room is ajar, and I sidle in to see what's going on.

My mother and Russell are standing by the stove. She is still wearing yesterday's clothes, but they are not nearly as organized as they were last night. She is rolling out biscuit dough. He is arranging eggs in small bowls and stirring a saucepot simmering on one of the burners.

When she has lined up her biscuits, my mother scoots over to Russell and nudges him with her hip, her classic signal that someone needs to get out of her way. I'm thinking she does this automatically as if it were me or my sister, but then, as she bends to open the oven, Russell reaches over and flips a sheaf of hair off her face. This is my mother and Russell! My mother and Russell!! To me it is a natural gesture between two people who have already fucked each other.

I run quickly through the timeline. We arrive and meet Russell at the restaurant for the first time. We have dinner, say goodnight and go to our hotel room. Russell goes somewhere else and doesn't show up again until we are at the cabin, and he is bringing in the cases of liquor. I am now in Nancy Drew mode. The next day he teaches her to shoot a rifle. Ah! That's where it begins.

Last night mother and Russell go back to town to buy more wine and whatever else my mother thinks she needs. But it is a quick trip, and they will be coming right back. Except maybe not. Last night, while I was sleeping, one of two things happened. Either Russell and my mother came back after spending more than enough time in town or they stayed overnight at Russell's place. Judging from my mother's clothes, the latter is exactly what happened. It's fascinating.

Neither of them has realized I am in the room yet. I am watching carefully, looking for more clues when my mother turns her head slightly and speaks to me in Korean. "Don't be so shocked. Arrange your face." My mouth is open, and I am staring; I rub my face and create a half smile. I know I am still staring but I cannot make my eyes move away.

Russell turns and gives me a wave. "Eggs benedict?"

I raise my eyebrows. He shrugs and smiles.

My mother nods her head at me, "Number one idiot." She says this in English.

"She'll be okay," this is Russell.

I am speaking in Korean. "When did this happen? How did this happen?"

"Don't judge so much. We left and went to his house. You didn't think we were here?"

"Oh my God," I say in English.

"Knowing isn't everything," that's my mother and she glances at Russell, who rearranges her words. "You don't need to know everything."

My mother walks across the room and opens the front door. "It so hot in here."

The cold air is a comfort. I am working, alternately, through embarrassment and curiosity and beginning to sweat with the effort. I can't decide whether to pursue this in English or Korean, but both choices are forestalled when Sarah walks briskly into the room and heads straight for the door, closing it swiftly. "Let's try a window instead. We don't want Cubby in here."

Sam meanders in after her.

The only thing I can think to do is set the table. My mother and Russell are conferring by the stove over different ideas about eggs benedict, which, as near as I can judge, my mother never heard of before this morning. She is advocating for *kimchi* in between the biscuit and the egg. He counters with a prime location on the side of the plate. As my trendy sister would say, "I can't even."

I want to get my mother alone so I can ask her. But I don't know how since I have never asked my mother anything like this. We are not the family that talks about things that have anything to do with our intimate bodies except for how to clean them properly, which my mother was always very explicit about. I don't know how she would have managed having a son, but for two daughters, the lessons were easy for her, including a certain amount of discreet demonstration about how and where to shave and which kinds of cloths to use for which areas of the body.

The strange breakfast with eggs benedict and *kimchi* is fine with the rest of the poets. After the clean up and the jockeying for shower time, Russell starts to corral us for an assignment or a lesson or whatever is on his mind, but it certainly isn't on anyone else's mind. Emily sits down next to me on the ottoman.

"I don't understand why you are here."

"So my mother and Russell can fuck," I laugh.

"What? Oh my God that is so good! Really?"

I nod.

"No, but really. Why are you here?"

"I don't know. There we were on line, chatting back and forth and kind of urging each other on. It didn't seem to matter that these poems weren't quite mine because I certainly couldn't know for sure anyone else's were theirs either. Also, I'm on break from school and I've never been to Colorado."

My sister and her husband had just flown to London for the weekend. The weekend! It was so sophisticated. I had never done anything sophisticated. But I am thinking all of this and not saying it to Emily because *she* does seem so sophisticated to me.

"I can't write like this, with group assignments and pencils scratching and people sighing and picking their noses and throwing crumpled paper on the floor and starting all over," Emily is complaining. She gets up. "Let's go off and do something by ourselves." She holds out a hand and I clasp it and stand up.

"Our room?"

"No, the woods. Bundle up!" She rummages through the coats. "Find yours and let's go for a walk. Do you have a tablet or anything like that?"

"Of course I do."

"Bring it."

One of the reasons I had the chunky coat was to be able to put my tablet in the pocket when I was scurrying across campus. So, in it went along with scarf and mittens in my other pocket and, at the last minute, some muffins wrapped in a napkin and a bottle of sparkling something which may have had alcohol or maybe not.

I am surprised we're heading down the road toward the main house and the highway but Emily is leading and clearly has a plan. The road is alternately icy and muddy and maybe fifteen minutes into the walk we meet Russell's truck.

"Do you think they' re missing us?" I say, knowing the one person who would notice would be my mother.

"I'm sure they're so into the assignment by now they've forgotten all about us," Emily smirks.

I am about to sidle past the truck but Emily is opening the driver side door. She leans over and looks inside. "Oh, good. Here are some energy bars. And, an open bottle of—what is Wild Turkey anyway?"

"Bourbon," I answer because, once, when the liquor store next door had a fire we sold their stock illegally, literally under the counter, for a few months until they could rebuild. It was a favor to the owner, an old Polish man who claimed he was distantly related to the Pope.

Emily hoists herself into the truck. "Oh, look, he's got some kind of a radio or a phone in here. I thought they said there'd be no way to reach the outside world once we got to the cabin."

"That's what Sarah said. Russell didn't say anything."

She pops open the glove compartment, looks inside and then snaps it shut. "Let's move on. Maybe we can get a ride into town when we get to the highway."

Although it feels like we are moving at steady pace, it takes us an hour to reach the big house. By then we've eaten the muffins and drunk the cider. We sit down on the front steps.

"Fantastic," Emily holds up her phone. "Everything was just uploaded."

"What's everything?"

"All the photos I've taken and the journal notes and maybe a few poems."

"At the cabin?"

"Sure. Haven't you been doing stuff on your phone?"

"No, we had no service."

"What does that matter? You can still do work. As soon as you get service, you can upload or send everything." Emily looks at me. "How could you not know that?"

"So what did you just send and where?"

Emily scrolls down her screen, "All these photos. See."

"That's us and the cabin."

"And the shooting lessons and here, look, the bear!" Emily is grinning.

"But we agreed not to do that. And no one else did it!"

"I didn't agree to anything. And anyway, why would I listen to those assholes—sorry I didn't mean you. They clearly know nothing."

Emily opens her tablet. "So, let's pretend today is free poems for lawyers. She looks at me expectantly. "I mean wouldn't you stop at my table."

"I don't know. It would depend on how rushed I was and where your table was."

"Let's say I'm in the Yale Quad. That's what it's called isn't it?"

"I might."

She waits.

"Okay. I would."

She waits again.

"Would you write a poem for me?"

"What would you want it to say?"

I don't hesitate, "I want it to say that I'm waiting for my life to start. That I've been so focused on my parents and my family and what I need to do to please my mother. I have not even started on my life, even though I'm twenty-three years old and in law school." I take a breath. "And my sister is married already and has a baby girl and lives in New Jersey."

Emily nods. She stands up with her tablet still open, moves to the side of the broad steps and sits down. She quickly types something and then sits for a long while looking out at the highway, where we can see the cars slip silently along. Only their roofs are visible over the long berm that insulates the house from the noise. After maybe a half hour she comes back and positions the screen in front of me.

Miles to Go

When I am young I will trespass down a snowy
Hill crashing on my belly into the trees
shake my head in wonder I am still
Thinking and watch my breath form crystals in
The bite of cold air I own, even though
The land, the hill, my life is not mine yet but
Held in some impenetrable trust I do not have the
Power to untwine.

I read it and read it again. "Is that it?"

"No one has ever asked for more," Emily says. "Do you need more? After all you said it should be a poem about waiting to start your life."

I nod because I don't want to say the poem is not nearly enough. It feels empty and distant, meant for someone who hasn't done any of the things I think I have done. I am certain there is a way to get credit for all the schooling and the death of my father and the almost boyfriend I have and being able to run Fine Foods whenever I am needed. But I don't say that because I think maybe she is right to hone it down to the snow and the cold air.

I think about the scattered pieces of other people I have never been willing to gather to me. Instead I trusted my parent's judgment that my grandfather was selfish and Shirley is a shallow gossip and the girls at school were nice but we didn't need them because we had a sister and that was so much better. It was a wonder I had a kind of boyfriend at all even though we were really friends *without* benefits.

"Do you want to key it into your tablet?"

"Sure." I certainly can't refuse. "Oh wait. There's Wi-Fi here."

We doodle around with the Trout1 website trying to figure out the password, but it's a hopeless game.

"Do you have to pee? I have to pee." Emily jumps up and knocks on the front door.

"What are you doing? You know they're not here."

"They're the kind of people who have a housekeeper," Emily supposes. She knocks again. Waits a few moments and knocks a third time, loudly. The door opens.

"Hi. Sorry it took so long. I couldn't believe anyone would be coming to the house much less knocking at the front door. Who are you?"

"Who are you?"

"I'm the person who is already in the house," the girl says. She is pulling her blond hair into a ponytail. "So, who are you?"

"We are the poets. You know, the people staying at the cabin."

"Sweet. What do you want?"

"To pee."

"What are your names? I'll check the list."

"I'm Olivia and this is Emily. There's a list?"

"No, of course there's no list." We are all looking at each other. "Well, fuck, just come in and go to the bathroom. It's not as if we don't have workmen here everyday doing something or other and peeing and shitting. Take your boots off," she instructs and leads us across the foyer to the powder room.

"So, if you wouldn't mind. Who exactly are you?" Emily is asking.

"Bethany, the daughter, the only living child of the glorious Trout union. And I'm going for it even though I don't really want to know: is there actually any poetry going on at the cabin?"

"Only in the broadest sense," I say. "Like things are going on that will become topics for poetry, although no one has written a word yet as near as I can tell." I glance at Emily. "Mostly drinking and eating."

"Oh come on, get real. Olivia's mother and this guy Russell have fucked already. Several people are flirting with other people, gender irrelevant. There is not just drinking go on, there is massive drinking going on, which hopefully will lead to more fucking, gender irrelevant." Emily holds up her tablet. "What's your password?"

"Oh, we have one for guests. It's 'wrangler'. That's with a 'w' for you city people."

Emily keys it in and nods to me, "Go on-line, and I'll send you the poem. In fact, I'll send it to Russell." And she types in "Hey Wanker, look what we've been at while you shiftless suckers blow another day."

Bethany grins at both of us. "One favor for another. So who's on your fucking list, and please say it's my father and my mother. That would be beyond grand."

"No, the Sarah and Sam seem to be totally into each other, but whatever they're doing it's married sex, so," Emily smiles. "There's something to eat here, I assume."

We follow Bethany to the kitchen. "Coffee, soda, peanut butter. There's left over paella we ordered at least three or four nights ago. And lots of bread and cheese and egg whites." She is rummaging in the refrigerator, and lining up jars and packages on the counter. "Capers, wasabi mayonnaise, vitamin water, organic ham slices, stone ground mustard, dark chocolate." She waves her arm, "Help yourself. Oh, and cooking sherry and an open bottle of, let's see, Chateauneuf."

She heats up the questionable paella, and we each make little canapé sandwiches with the bread, cheese and ham and sit in wonderfully comfortable chairs at the breakfast table in a sunny alcove off the kitchen. Bethany uses one of the extra chairs as a footrest.

"Okay. Let's get down to the basics. Olivia, you first."

"Daughter of a Korean grocery family in Queens New York. We sell it all, in small packages and jars, the kind of stuff you buy on your way home from work or when the kids text and say you're all out of jelly. Our fame is my mother's fresh salads and the produce we keep outside surrounded by those strips of plastic that are pretend walls. I have a sister who is married, a father who is dead and a mother who is at the cabin right now. She's the real poet, and I am the thief. Oh and I'm in law school, second year, and on spring break."

And then I head in a direction I didn't even know was possible. Maybe because the afternoon sun has warmed my back. Maybe because I'm with two women I barely know. Maybe because my mother is the new mother I never knew existed who writes poetry and fucks men she knows for two days. "I'm an accidental virgin. The boy-man I was going to fuck forgot to bring condoms, and I can't have my life interrupted with a baby so I only blew him. Someone told me she got salmonella that way, which I really don't believe." I take the last bite of my bread and pour some wine.

"I don't think I've ever been a virgin," says Emily. "At least not in spirit. Had my first boy when I was fourteen, and I've never heard that thing about salmonella. My parents are divorced. My father's an asshole but I love him. My mother is probably a bitch but I love her, too. I have a half sister, Lily, who is so sweet you could vomit. I give poems away to people I don't know which I'm hoping will lead to all kinds of fame and my fuck-bucket list includes Olivia here. But not your mother, either of your mothers. Sorry." She picks up my wine glass and takes a swig. "Okay. Bethany, now you."

"Bethany Louise Trout. Junior in college right here in Colorado. I'm what's called an Army brat even though we're Air Force. I grew up in New Jersey, but on base. I know, I know how do we have this kind of money for this kind of house, but let me assure you not everyone in the service is poor. My Dad's grandfather was a liquor wholesaler. My Dad's father was a general in the army. My dad retired as a colonel. My mom's father owned a bunch of local newspapers. So there you are. We masqueraded as average."

She begins putting food back in the refrigerator. "Now about this whole virginity thing. I actually had a friend who went the virgin route with the daddy's-little-girl-party and the pearls, but not my style. I've only had one boyfriend, Brendan, who's still my boyfriend although he's doing his junior year in Belgium. Salmonella? Really?" Bethany looks out the window. "Anything else you girls need before you head back?"

"Could I take a shower?" I ask. I've been thinking about it ever since I walked into the house, imagining the kinds of bathrooms a house like this must have.

"Sure," Bethany doesn't even hesitate. We head upstairs to her bedroom and she points to her bathroom. "Everything you could ever want is there, and feel free to use it all. My only deal is, when this weekend is over, I want to know every little thing that happened."

I hang a towel on the hook and carefully lay my clothes on the vanity counter. I am soaping my hair when the glass door opens and Emily steps into the shower. "Want your back scrubbed?"

Her hands are in my hair massaging the shampoo into my scalp and then we are under the shower together, rinsing my hair and getting her wet.

She hands me the loofah, "Here. Scrub me down a little."

But it is too coarse, and I put it aside, pour some bath gel into my palm and spread it gingerly over her back and down her sides. She turns around and places my hands on her breasts. It is the first time I have ever touched a woman, and I am tentative and careful. Emily is not. She massages my nipples and strokes my belly and my thighs. The water and soap are sluicing between our bodies. I don't know what to do. I do whatever Emily does. At first it seems to hardly matter and then it matters a lot, and we sink down to our knees in the shower so we won't fall.

Suddenly, I am holding onto Emily and laughing and then Emily is laughing so hard she is hiccupping, and we slither over to the faucet and turn off the water. We haul ourselves up and somehow manage to drop the towel onto the shower floor.

We dry off with two clean towels and get dressed. We can see long shadows out the bedroom window. Bethany calls up from downstairs. "Hey you. It's getting late. Better hurry."

We head for the kitchen.

"You missed all the fun," Emily is putting on her boots.

"Oh I know, but it's not my thing. Besides, the shower's not big enough for three." She hands us a flashlight. "*The woods are lovely, dark and deep.*"

"*But I have promises to keep,*" "Emily kisses her on the lips. "Bye sweet Bethany."

I give a little wave, and we are off down the steps, heading back into the shadowy forest.

KEEPING GOOD WATCH

"'*The moon was a ghostly galleon*,'" Sam intoned as he stepped off the porch with the rifle no one, not even Sarah, knew was hidden in the cabin. Unlike the hunting rifle Russell had brought, Sam's was a high-powered military grade weapon. He trudged through the sudden snowfall to check the level in the propane tank. "Oh shit," he tapped at the gauge with his flashlight. "What have these people been doing in there? We're down about three quarters."

A sudden change in air pressure whipped down the valley, and he stepped out into the meadow to look up at the mountain. The sky was a river of stars. A wolf howled. An owl swooped past his head. For just a moment he felt the slightest unevenness in his gait as if the ground had shifted.

Far up the slope he could see two animals lumbering across a ridge. He raised his rifle to site them through the scope. The larger bear trudged steadfast diagonally across the snow face. The smaller one, that must be the cub, followed, but he lost footing and set off a roll of snow that paused at the ridge and then spilled over the edge taking him with it.

Sam saw the larger one look back and then turn around and gallop across the slope. The bear dug into a mound of snow, sniffed and then abandoned it and began on another. "He's over there," Sam whispered and trained his sight on where he thought the missing cub might be, willing the adult to follow. But there was no way to communicate with the bear. She became more frantic as the minutes passed. Sam watched for a half hour as the sky clouded over and snow began to fall.

The bear rushed from mound to mound, finally digging frantically in the place where Sam thought the cub was buried. There the bear stopped. She lay down slowly and stuck a paw deep into the hole. Sam watched her as she swung her arm back and forth, slower and slower. Sam couldn't know whether she had found the cub or was exhausted. Her head drooped and her body went limp.

CABIN LIFE: DAY FOUR

At seven in the morning Sam calculated the amount of snow that had fallen overnight. He could see the porch rails. He could see the outline of the steps. He had been diligent about shoveling every two hours the evening before so the porch itself was clear. Now that the snow had stopped and the air had warmed, he relaxed his vigilance, leaned the shovel against the cabin wall and went inside. He was in charge of breakfast and he chose the classics—scrambled eggs, hash browns and bacon. Edgar was awake and crouched in front of the fireplace arranging the logs for the morning fire.

"One long won't burn; two logs might burn; three logs can burn; four logs will burn," he recited under his breath, and as the fire took hold he turned to Sam. "How's that."

"Looks good to me, but I'm afraid we've gotten ahead of ourselves since we're the only ones awake."

"Not for long." Edgar picked up the fireplace poker and the log tongs and clanged them together five times. "Let's see if that works."

Jacine wandered into the room wearing a long sweater over her pajamas.

"Oh, you slept here," Sam sniggered.

She ignored him and picked a plate off the open shelf. "I will eat before it gets cold."

Edgar clanged the poker and tongs again, but no one else came out of the bedrooms.

"Let's just divvy this up before it's ruined. I'll make more for the others."

They ate on the couch in front of the fire.

Jacine stood. "If nobody minds, I will take the first shower; get the best water."

"Not at all. Go for it. I'm going to wake Sarah."

Edgar was piling the dishes in the sink and mumbling again. He turned to Sam. "Not to disparage your hospitality—yours and Sarah's—but what are we doing here? Aside from drinking and shooting off guns or rather helping people who know nothing about shooting guns have their testosterone moment."

"Don't matter to me," Sam smiled. "I have no skin in this game. This is all Sarah. And her need to justify rebuilding this cabin," he said, breaking off a piece of a stale muffin and waving it around the room before shoving it in his mouth. "We probably should have had more children."

"Or a dog," Edgar suggested.

"You have kids?"

"Two."

Sam nodded. "I'm going to wake Sarah."

"A boy and a girl. And grandkids. Two of those. A girl and a boy. The perfect American formula. You know, like Dick and Jane and all that. In those books in grade school."

Sam nodded again. "So, your wife? Is she home? You could have brought her you know. There doesn't seem to be much poetry going on here. I'm sure she would have felt very comfortable."

"She died. Ruth died four years ago." Edgar wanted to remind him he'd already told the group this but he realized Sam was probably never interested enough to listen in the first place to what he said or what anyone said.

"Oh, I'm sorry," Sam swept some crumbs off the table. "But you're still working right. It keeps you busy, huh? Sure."

Edgar nodded.

"I'm going to wake Sarah."

Sam made breakfast again at nine for Sarah and Olivia and then again at ten-thirty, when Russell drove up.

"So, are we actually going to make some poems today?" Russell had taped his directives onto the log wall once again. "Where's Emily?"

"Still sleeping, I think."

"What we have here is a very questionable commitment to poetry, folks."

"Well, what do you do when your students don't write?"

"I fail them."

Sarah laughed. "I think what you meant to say was you inspire them."

"Have you noticed there are some people who cannot be inspired?"

"I can be inspired," Emily wandered into the room. "But not right now. I have bed hair, and I'm hungry. Did I miss breakfast?"

"Yes," Sam said decisively.

"Okay," she looked up at the ceiling and then positioned herself under one of the beams. "Lunch is just an hour away. I'm going to shower. If that's okay. I mean why wouldn't it be. Okay, I'm going to shower."

"So, are we waiting? Because if we're waiting let's go do something else."

"What else is there?"

"A walk. Bird watching? Fishing? I know we have poles."

"The stream is still frozen."

"No, it's not. I heard it yesterday. It's running, or at least trickling. Although that's not really fishing depth. But we can go look at it in any case," Sarah was pulling on a pair of rubber boots from the row she had organized under the window. 'There should be a pair here for everyone if you're not too particular about size. You don't even have to dress that warm. It's above freezing and it's only going to get warmer."

"There's only one pair even close to our size here, and I think my mother should have them." Olivia stuck out one foot for inspection.

"Oh my god, your feet are the size of my palm." Sarah held her hand up to Olivia's foot. "What size do you wear?"

"Four usually. Sometimes four and a half."

"Where do you get shoes? The children's department."

"Yep. There and some of those high end designers. They make really small sizes." Olivia laced up her sneakers. "These will do. They have really thick soles. And flashing lights."

Boots, coats, sweaters, gloves. They tramped out the door and stood on the porch looking at the snowdrifts.

"How deep is this?"

"Maybe two feet."

"Ugh! Over my knee."

"I'll go first," Edgar offered. "Walk in my footsteps."

They filed across the meadow and up the berm that had been yesterday's rifle target. The snow had some crunch to it and people meandered for fresh patches into which they could sink their boots. Someone called out, "Snow angels!" It was Emily, bounding after them, her unbuttoned coat swinging wildly. She was wearing the only pair of boots left in the cabin, which, somehow, were mismatched in both size and color. She dashed into the open meadow, flung herself on a patch of untrammeled white and sawed her arms above her head.

Sam went next, then Sarah, Olivia and Edgar. They were laughing and coughing as they flapped their arms and legs in the snow. Jacine shuddered and plopped herself down haphazardly, creating such a wide circle of damage it was impossible to discern an angel.

Russell stood at the top of the berm looking back at them. In their overstuffed ski jackets they looked like flailing turtles stranded on their backs. He squatted down on a flat rock and whistled at them as the group evolved into snowball making. Olivia looked up at the whistled command and then turned back to stockpiling snowballs with Sam.

Russell could see he was beaten. He had hoped to get them out in the snow just long enough to feel the full bite of the cold, then shepherd them back inside to do the thing he needed them to do—write poems. Write bad poems he could turn into mediocre ones, write mediocre ones he could turn into good ones, and write good ones he could turn into great ones. That was the goal of *frombadtoverse,* after all. The entire two years of nurturing this group was to get them to a point where he had enough material for his book.

"What a fucking waste of time," was his assessment of the entire retreat. He glared at the poets and casually began to lob chunks of snow at them.

Emily was sitting up and surveying the landscape. She rose to her feet in one graceless move and dropped down next to Russell. "Useless, aren't we."

"More than." Russell nodded. "I should have known this would be a total cluster fuck."

"Oh I don't think we've reached that level. You're the only one who has scored so far. And Jacine I guess."

"What's your preference?"

"I can't decide between Olivia and Edgar."

"Not Sam? Not Sarah?"

"What? The innkeepers?" Emily shrugged. "Too much proprietorship and too much competition between the two of them. It feels like *Master-of-the-House*." And she hummed a few bars off-key.

"Did you think you'd get any writing done when you signed up for this thing?"

"That wasn't the goal. I can post about this when I get back to civilization—or not. Or I can write six poems about it, one for each of you, like *The Canterbury Tales*. Sort of like the opposite of the poetry stand. I'll write poems for people who never asked for them. Besides, what makes you think I haven't been writing?"

"Have you?"

"You'll see."

"Well, send me something."

Russell stood up and whistled again. "One last try."

Edgar hit him with a snowball. Edgar hit every one of them with expertly crafted snowballs using a sidearm throw that walloped knees, thighs and backs with city-street precision and produced the result Russell had been unable to achieve—to get the poets to their feet and moving even if it was solely for inept attempts to fashion their own snowballs.

Russell pulled Emily to her feet. "Let's get ourselves back to the cabin, light a fire and have alcohol at the ready."

"Okay, I'm done," Twenty minutes later Edgar pushed open the cabin door, leaned against the jamb and pulled off his boots. "I hope you two have been doing something productive while we were outside hitting each other in the head with snow. These people have no concept of the art of the snowball. They have no molding techniques and no throwing skills. It's appalling! What are we drinking?"

Jacine staggered in after him, red-faced from the cold, followed by the rest of the poets.

"We've got three bottles of bourbon left, one scotch and four bottles of wine," Russell spread his arm indicating the array on the kitchen table as the others came in. "No mixers though." He stuck his head into the refrigerator. "Oh, I correct myself. We have club soda and cola. And one, two, three, four half bottles of wine. Don't you people know how to consolidate?" He grabbed two open bottles of white and poured one into the other.

"What are you doing?"

"You can't mix like that."

"Oh, I'm sorry. Do you think this wine has any provenance? I bought it at the local mini-mart. I defy you to tell the difference between any of this crap. Let's just say, instead of a half of chardonnay and a half of pinot grigio, we now have a full bottle of a varietal. Besides, it's our last day. This is the time to get truly shitfaced." He poured six glasses of the newly minted wine and handed them around.

"I need to get warm."

"Yeah. Me too."

There was a general crowding around the fireplace and a clear willingness to cross personal space standards as Olivia and Sarah squeezed into one chair and Emily and Russell, in a now welcome pairing, sat nestled into each other on the floor. Edgar added two logs to the fire and sat on the end of the couch, as Jacine, who was lying down lifted her legs and put them down in his lap.

Sam put on an apron, placed a towel butler-style over his forearm and handed around a tray with chunks of cheese, a sleeve of crackers and an open jar of olives in one hand and a full glass of bourbon in the other that was clearly meant for him alone.

"Oh, waiter, I need more wine." That was Sarah. Sam gathered all the bottles and put them on the low table in front of the couch. "Help yourself. I'm going to shower to get warm since you people have eaten all the fire. And anyway, it smells like wet wool in here."

"Okay," Russell pushed himself into a sitting position. "Let's each say something amazing."

"What the fuck does that mean?"

"Don't try to resurrect this meeting or whatever it is so late in the game," Edgar said. He was rubbing Jacine's feet. "In my opinion, it's been a total failure."

"In general or because you didn't get fucked?"

"First of all, how do you know I didn't get fucked?"

"Okay, show of hands. Who fucked Edgar? See, not a single hand."

"That's not accurate. Sam's in the shower."

"Okay, show of hands who did get fucked? Sarah you've got two hands up."

"One for me and one for Sam, although I won't say with whom?"

"Whom." Three people corrected.

"Is there any food in this?"

"What's left in the fridge?"

"I'll look." Sarah pushed herself out of the chair. "Plenty. Potatoes, a half a ham, lots of cheese, carrots, mustard, an amazing amount of raw chicken and some leftover something." She opened the foil and smelled. "Never mind."

"I'll cook," Edgar moved Jacine's feet.

"Me too," that was Emily.

As they got up, everyone else rose and rearranged themselves into new configurations. Olivia sat at Jacine's feet and let her rub her back. Sarah piled plates and utensils on the table and began folding cloth napkins to look like birds.

"So, something amazing, anyone?" Russell ripped the paper poetry inspiration list off the log wall, threw it into the fire and sat down on the ottoman. "No, you pikers? Okay, I'll start. I'm actually part Navajo."

"Why is that amazing? And how does that advance the goal of this group?" That was Olivia.

"Ah, the dormouse has spoken."

"Nothing has happened this entire retreat that has anything to do with poetry, Russell. What amazing thing do you have to say about that? Except of course that my mother got laid. Which I guess is pretty amazing."

"There's still hot water," Sam stopped rubbing his wet hair with a towel. "Oh man, I see I'm waaay behind here. What do I need, more alcohol or is it my turn to confess?"

"Oh, we're not confessing our own little sins, we're calling out other people."

"Anyone call me out yet."

"No, we've only just begun."

Russell combined two bottles of red and passed the mixture around.

"This is such swill," Sam announced.

Emily was holding a pepper grinder. "Dinner is almost ready. And I forgot to ask is anyone allergic to anything?"

"Feathers. All my jackets have to have poly fill. In fact I probably should have made that clear before I came here," Olivia was rubbing her eyes.

"Latex. And I'll say no more." Sam gave a wide-eyed smile.

"I meant food you assholes."

"We know." Three people said.

"What are you cooking?"

"Chicken cacciatore. Lots of it. So eat it all unless you want it for breakfast tomorrow."

Russell had two open bottles of red wine in his hands.

"Oh no you don't. There will be no more mixing. I call the bottle in your right hand."

"I'll take the left. The rest of you suckers can drink the bourbon and the scotch. And drink it all unless you want it for breakfast."

"Okay. I'll say something amazing." Edgar was waving a butcher knife in the air as he passed unwashed plates to Jacine. "I know how to throw knives."

"Everyone knows how to throw knives." Sarah paused dramatically. "Oh, you mean *without* hitting anyone."

With a flick of the wrist Edgar buried the knife in his hand in the wall over the fireplace. "Precisely."

"How do you do that?"

"Two techniques. One by holding the blade and the other by holding the hilt. Want to try?"

Emily put out a hand and Edgar instructed. "I want you to move your whole arm and flick your wrist at the end. Now! Before I give you the knife. In fact, all of you do the same. I'm too drunk to teach you separately."

They practiced diligently.

"What are we aiming at?"

"My best advice would be that wall over the fireplace. You can go one at a time. Stand behind the couch so you've got about seven or eight feet in front of you."

One round and three knives hit the wall. Three failed, with one left standing upright in the couch cushion.

"Okay, let's go again. And Russell and Sarah, don't bring your arm all the way back, just as far as beside your head. Oh my god not all the way back like that!"

"Oh, jeeez. Where's my knife? It fell out of my hand. I really am way too drunk to be doing this. Where is that fucking knife?" Sarah was whining.

Olivia held up her leg and reached for the knife that was imbedded three inches in her foot.

"DON'T TOUCH THE KNIFE!" Edgar and Sam yelled. "DON'T TOUCH THE KNIFE!"

Olivia pulled her hand away and spent a few seconds staring at the knife.

"I'm sorry, I'm sorry. It was my knife. Oh my god I am so sorry!" Sarah cried. She turned to the rest of them. "Help. Anyone. Help?"

Jacine pushed Edgar out of her path. She carefully examined the foot and pointed to the couch. "Someone carry her."

Russell and Sam each cradled Olivia under an arm and a knee and carried her to the couch, settling her in with her foot on the coffee table.

"I need rope or towel or something."

Sam untied the robe he was wearing and handed her the belt. Very gingerly, Jacine wrapped the tie around Olivia's foot twice in front of the knife and then twice behind the knife. She threaded two figure eights around the foot and motioned behind her for another belt. Edgar tore a dishtowel into strips.

"Is that sterile? Do we need alcohol? I am so sorry!" Sarah moaned. "We need a doctor. Don't we need a doctor?"

Russell was putting on his coat. "No, we need a hospital. I'm taking her to the hospital. They'll have to do surgery."

"Surgery? Surgery?" Sarah was shaking her head. "I made such a mess that someone needs surgery."

Sarah had Olivia's sneaker in her hand for the uninjured foot and Jacine unlaced it and put it on.

"We should go to the hospital now."

"I'll pull the truck up to the porch. Get her in on the driver's side so she can slide across and lean against the passenger door. Then she can put her foot in my lap."

"Is that safe?"

"No, actually the safest thing would be if no one had dropped a knife into her foot but here we are."

Jacine had her coat on. "I am coming."

Russell shook his head. "There's no room and you are not sitting in the open truck bed. We are going straight to the hospital. They will remove the knife and stitch her up, and we will be back by morning." He turned to Olivia. "Are you okay?" Olivia nodded. "You see, she can speak for herself."

"Is it okay if your mother stays here?"

"Omah," Olivia spoke to her in both English and Korean. "It's okay. I don't want you sitting in the open truck back. You'll get bounced around too much. I'll be fine. It's really numb right now with all the bandaging you did. See, I'm not even crying."

Russell backed the truck into a snow bank, made a U turn and headed slowly down the road.

The five people left wandered back into the cabin, all energy dissipated. The frenzy of alcohol drained out of them. Jacine, crying quietly, lay down on the couch. Emily crouched on the floor beside her and stroked her arm.

URSA MAJOR

"What a fucking mess," that was Sarah. "And it was my knife. It slipped out of my hand."

"It could have been any of us," Sam soothed. "We should never have been throwing knives." He glared at Edgar.

"You know, "Edgar said thoughtfully. "It wasn't my knife that wound up in her foot. *I* know how to throw knives. It was the rest of you pussies who don't know how to do anything that made this mess." He smiled at them all, raised a wine glass he picked up from the kitchen table and downed it. "What the fuck is in this anyway."

"That's my glass, I think. It's some mixture of scotch and something else."

"You see, that's what we needed—wine charms," Sarah was giggling. "If we each had wine charms we'd know which glass was which and, and…." And she started to howl.

Emily picked up the call, "And, we'd have been much more civilized because we each had our own glass and we would have sipped carefully and never gotten drunk enough to throw knives. And in case you haven't noticed, this knife thing has killed our last night of sharing and creativity. Because we've all written so much poetry. And who the hell are you people anyway? Now that Russell's gone, let's stop pretending."

"Are you serious? Poetry is my life. I live to write. I've been published exactly—*no where*. Come to think of it. So what am I doing here?" Sarah said. "Oh yeah, I live here."

"No you don't," Emily accused. "You live in a much bigger house with five bathrooms just a mile away."

"Two actually, two miles," Sam corrected.

"Oh, I'm sorry, Mr. Innkeeper. What exactly are you doing here? Oh yes, in case we need more toilet paper. Or wine charms! Which, actually, is what your missus thinks is missing from this shindig." She looked at Sarah, "You and my mother have a lot in common."

"Okay. I'll confess," Edgar said. "I caused an accident on the George Washington Bridge that tied up traffic for hours and may have even killed someone. I needed a release from my misery and poetry was it."

"I'm sorry? You caused an accident that may have killed someone?"

"Yeah, I ordered bricks and they weren't tied down on the semi properly. The truck jack-knifed and the bricks went into the river. On the way they took down a green Toyota. Someone had to be in that car even though the divers said the car was locked up tight. The police said it probably broke down and was left, but I know I saw someone!" Edgar banged on the table and picked up another glass. "Now whose is this?" And drank that one, too.

"I'm going to bed. Sam, you coming?"

"It's the shank of the evening. Isn't that what they call it? And what the hell does that mean? There's no going to bed in poetry. We are all going to sit here and confess the unconfessable," Edgar insisted.

Jacine flopped down on the couch. "I sleep with Russell."

"We know. Everyone knows."

"I wanted to sleep with Olivia." Emily shrugged.

"I'm cut to the quick," Edgar touched his heart. "I thought you wanted to sleep with me."

"That too."

"There's still time."

"I can't. You've become an asswipe."

"Only now I've become an asswipe. You mean until now I was someone a lot more fuckable? How can I redeem myself?"

"That ship has sailed."

Edgar waved a glass in the air, "That ship has sailed! Now *there's* a poetry topic. Let's all write a poem about that-ship-has-sailed because that ship sailed for me a long time ago although I don't think I knew it until very recently. Like maybe, oh, two drinks ago. Who said alcohol deadens the senses?"

"I know how to do a few things. Two at least as near as I can remember." Sam asserted.

"What are you talking about?"

"You said we were all a bunch of pussies who didn't know how to do anything."

"That was three conversation ago."

"Yeah but three short conversations ago. It's still in the air, and I know how to do a few things."

"Like? And not job related. Those don't count."

"I speak Arabic. I can ride a unicycle. I can do Irish clog dancing."

"Okay to the last two. Arabic is job related. That's like saying I can lay bricks."

"So, what can you do?"

"I can knit. I can stand on my head. And, of course, I can throw knives."

"Okay my turn," Jacine stood up. "I know how to make *kimchi*—-"

"Job related."

"I know how to make money in stock market."

Sam and Edgar shrugged. "Emily?"

"I can tie a cherry stem with my tongue."

"Now there's a skill," Sam and Edgar said at the same time and made high-five motions. "And a gateway." Sam added.

"And," Emily added. "I know why we are all here."

"Do tell."

"Okay. I will. We are all here because we are misfits. Not that we don't fit in with society. We all have enough social skills to get by." Emily raised her hand and began ticking statements off on her fingers. "We know how to say the right thing and we know how to do the right thing—missing wine charms notwithstanding. We are competent people who have relationships and jobs. We have homes and cars and the right books. We see the right movies; we listen to the right music. We probably recycle and eat organic and give to charity and volunteer to serve thanksgiving meals and all of that stuff."

Emily stopped, picked up a half-full glass, held it to the light and then downed it. "We are misfits because we don't fit into our selves very well. We are like those wooden shape puzzles. We can't find the right place for our shape. Most people probably can't find the right place for their shape but we are misfits because we know it. All of us think we are someone other than who we are."

She looked around the room. Sarah and Sam were standing across from each other at the kitchen table. Jacine was looking over the back of the couch and had started to cry again. Edgar was crouched by the fireplace reaching for another log.

Emily continued, "I bet the one thing we love to hear most is 'I've never met anyone like you.' And I bet the one thing we hate to hear most is 'I've never met anyone like you.' We are thrilled we are different and afraid we are not different enough. So, Edgar. I'm ready to fuck you now."

There was a clunk and a scraping noise on the porch.

"Well. They're back soon." Sam walked over to the window. "Oh shit. It's the bear."

"So what. We're in here. He's out there. It's not like he can unlock the door or anything."

"The 'anything' is he can break a window."

"Why would he do that?"

"Because he can't unlock the door, idiot."

Sam and Edgar looked through two different windows to see the bear pacing back and forth on the porch. "That's not Cubby," Sam advised. "That's the mama."

"What does she want?"

"She's looking for her cub."

Edgar reached over to the doorjamb and caught the rifle by its muzzle. "Did he say it was loaded?"

"Yes." Two people said.

"Should I shoot him?"

"Can you kill him? If you can't kill him, don't shoot him."

"Can *you* kill him?" Edgar offered the rifle to Sam.

"Probably. But I can't shoot him through something. I'm not a sniper. If I shoot through the window, I shatter the glass, and if I shoot through the door it could alter the trajectory. Maybe wait."

"It's a she I told you," Sarah whispered.

"All bears are a 'he' when you have to kill them."

The bear marched to and fro on the porch sniffing into the corners and then sniffing at the door for a few more minutes. She ambled over to the window and stared in as Edgar jumped back. "Give me the rifle."

"Not a chance."

"Well, what are we going to do if she comes through the window? I'm right here. Give me the gun!"

Sam shrugged and handed the rifle to Edgar as the bear turned, paused for a moment and then ambled down the stairs.

"Okay, now's the time."

"The time to do what? Shoot her when she's leaving?"

"For certain. Maybe she's going to get reinforcements!" Edgar joked. "Okay. Stand down everyone."

"Holy shit. 'Stand down?' Go back to what you were doing. Oh yeah. Emily was about to fuck you." Sam turned to Emily, "Or is he on your shit list again."

"I don't know. That rifle adds something."

Edgar raised the rifle and shot the bolt. With no hesitation, Sam grabbed the barrel and jerked the muzzle towards the ceiling. The crack of gunfire was deafening.

"What the fuck? Did you think I was actually going to fire it?"

"There's no thinking. You raise a gun and aim it and there is no thinking!" Sam was screaming. "And you *did* actually fire it."

"Only because you jerked it up. I lost control."

"You could have lost control at any point, whether I jerked it up or not. By doing that, I knew where that shot was going." He looked at Sarah. "And let's not even have one word about the hole in the roof."

They heard shuffling on the porch. "I think the bear is back." Edgar looked out the window. "Oh shit. He's here. Right by the window. What do we do?'

"Now I think we have to kill him."

"Are you crazy? I don't know how to kill a bear."

"I do. I mean I know how to kill," Sam was now holding the high-powered rifle.

"Did you always have that thing?" Edgar accused.

"You bet I did," Sam nodded. "We'll give him five minutes. But the second he makes a move for the window, we have to shoot him."

They watched the bear snuffle at one window, then the other and begin to pace back and forth on the porch.

"I think we should push the couch in front of the door," Sarah whispered.

"I think we should go into the back bedrooms just in case he breaks in."

"Are you nuts. I'm not hiding in a room with a flimsy door while a bear is roaming around the house!" Sarah was waving her arms in the air.

Edgar and Sam looked at each other. "I think we have to kill him."

"Are we that drunk. Or crazy. Or does this make sense?"

Jacine sat up on the couch. "I have seen a bear kill. In Korea we have bears. Yes, we do. Many years ago they come down from mountain in winter. My uncle killed a bear."

"Are we allowed to kill a bear?" Emily was bobbing up and down from foot to foot.

"Wait, let me look at my ethics manual," Sam held out his empty hands and opened them like a book. "It says here we can kill a bear that's threatening us and we can also kill a bear that's been fed by humans. Sarah!" and he turned to her. "What's that you said about the construction guys feeding her?"

"I think you have to do this."

"Can't we wait? Maybe we can frighten her away."

"I don't know. Our friend here just shot a hole in the roof and that didn't frighten her. What do you want to do? Bang some pots together? Maybe you want to wait until she's hurling herself at the door, because she will get in. She may not break the door but she will break the lock!" Sam lowered his voice and looked at Edgar. "Everyone else back away. You too Jacine. This is not time for pussying around on the couch. If you thought the knife was bad, wait till you get mauled by a bear."

"When you're ready, I'll open the door," Edgar offered.

"Let's wait till she's at the other end of the porch and is turning around. Then I can aim for her eye." Sam was resolute.

After Sam positioned himself, Edgar swung the door open with a crash. Perhaps the noise startled her, perhaps the sudden light from the doorway confused her, but Sam was able to take a clear shot and then another. They slammed the door shut. The bear kept moving but then sank to the floor at the other end of the porch.

"Holy shit! Holy mother fucking shit! Is she moving? Did I kill her?"

"I don't know. What do we do?"

"The only thing we can do. Get out there right now while she's down and shoot her in the head!"

Edgar held out his hand. "Give me the gun. You're shaking all over."

Edgar opened the door slowly, slid out, aimed carefully and squeezed off a shot and then another. He stood for several minutes with the rifle raised and then lowered it to his side. He walked slowly back inside and slumped against the closed door. "She's dead. Pour me a drink."

"Drinks all around!"

They passed the half-empty bottles.

"I think I'm shit-faced," Sarah proclaimed.

"I think we're all shit-faced!"

"Ding dong the bear is dead," Emily sang, waving her empty glass. "I want to see the bear! I want to see a dead bear. I've never seen a dead bear!"

They opened the door slowly and tramped onto the porch.

"God. She's so big. What do we now?"

"Are we supposed to bury her?"

"Are you crazy? How do you bury a bear? What did people do in the old days?"

"They skinned them and ate the meat."

"Jesus!"

The five of them circled around the carcass, touching her gingerly at first and then more forcefully. "Let's get her off the porch. I think we can do it. Just grab something, anything and start pulling."

"I'm not doing that. I don't want bear blood on me," Sarah whined.

"Oh, you don't want bear blood on you!" Sam mimicked. "Here," he slid his hands across a puddle of blood and wiped it in Sarah's hair, recoiled for a moment at what he had done and then smacked his hand on top of his own head. "Yummy! Bear blood for all."

Emily dipped two fingers into the puddle and drew them down her cheeks. "WE are the victors! WE have killed a bear!"

"You didn't do anything," Edgar nudged her into the side of the bear and they both slid down together. There was a second of silence and then they started to laugh. "Now this is poetry!" Edgar shouted. "This is pure poetry!"

"A bunch of poets kill a bear!" Sarah shouted.

"Who killed a bear? Who killed a bear? Not a poet! A marksman killed a bear. A sharpshooter killed a bear. A guy who spent twenty years in the Air Force and never killed anything killed a bear. I KILLED A BEAR!" Sam wiped his hands down the front of his shirt. "And I've got the blood to prove it!"

They sat on the steps of the porch and watched Ursa Major rise in the clear night sky.

Eventually, prompted by the cold air on their blood soaked clothes, they rose slowly and went back inside the cabin and stripped down to their underwear, leaving their clothes and boots in a pile by the door. Sarah handed them each a large pot of water in turn and they sluiced the bear blood off their hands and faces into the kitchen sink.

Edgar picked up the rifle and handed it to Sam. He looked at Emily, "So does that offer still stand?"

For answer, Emily downed a half-filled glass of liquid sitting on the ottoman. "Your place or mine."

Edgar took her hand and led her into the bedroom.

Emily pointed to the beds. "Which one's yours?"

"By the window."

She flopped down on the bed and spread her legs, "Have at it."

"Jesus. Didn't your mother teach you anything?"

"Yes. This." Emily sat up. "Wait, you think mothers teach daughters how to fuck?"

"No, I meant about decorum."

'Did your mother teach you? Or your father?" Emily persisted. "In fact, now I want to know it all. What was your first? With who? Whom? How old? Where were you?"

"In my bedroom, fifteen –she was sixteen—with my foster sister I guess you would call her, and my mother caught us—-in the act."

"Were you naked?"

"Of course. She was furious."

"See, my mother would have laughed."

"My mother was screaming and dragging Natalie off the bed. In my mother's eyes, it was her fault because I had never done anything like this before—of course not, I was fifteen. Then Natalie comes to live with us and quick as we can, we are fucking. Even though my mother said she blamed me, I knew she thought it was Natalie's fault because she was older and she was the one my mother didn't raise. I mean I'm certain Natalie was still a virgin."

"So, what happened? Tell me you became lovers and fucked everyday after school."

"Of course not. What universe are you from? My mother sent me upstairs to stay with the neighbors for a whole month, until one of them died and the other had to move in with her daughter." Edgar was pacing from the door to the window. "And when I had to come back home, she sent Natalie away. I mean it wasn't quite like that. It's not as if she put her out on the street. She sent her to boarding school."

"Is that a punishment?"

"No, of course not. She found a girls' school that took her on scholarship, a good school in Virginia with horses and lots of money."

"And you never saw her again."

"This is the crazy thing. My mother bought a second hand car and learned how to drive. We drove down to her school and visited her every month until she graduated and then she went to the Sorbonne in Paris."

Emily gave him a winsome smile. "Wow! You've told me enough stuff for eight poems, better than what most people can say after years of therapy. We shouldn't have started down this path. I'm sorry I was so glib out there. Really, you're the only one in this whole cabin thing that might have a soul. And actually I would have fucked you."

"But not anymore?"

"Oh no, I still will, but now it will have gravitas." And she closed her eyes and danced her head from side to side to a silent rhythm. "And you shot a bear."

"Well, let's not let an awkward beginning ruin it. May I?" Emily nodded and Edgar reached down and tugged carefully at her flimsy underwear as she reached for his T-shirt.

"There are too many hands in this. You stay still..." Edgar admonished.

"But ...."

"And *silent*. I'll manage from here," he said stripping shorts and shirt. He paused and looked at her.

Emily raised a school hand. "Is this the part where you read me my rights and ask permission to do every little thing? Because it's all okay—except for ass fucking. That's never done on a first date."

"I'll keep that in mind. So may I proceed?"

"Fuck away."

There weren't too many hands and Emily said *yes* and put her legs around Edgars hips.

"Oh my god, your cock is so thick."

"Validation at last." Edgar laughed and carefully rolled off, recognizing at that moment the great disparity in their height and weight.

"I should be on top," Emily offered.

"Give me a minute."

RUSSELL

AWAY GAME

"**O**h my god, oh my god. This hurts so bad. It hurts so bad, and it's numb at the same time. How can that be?" The good thing is I didn't moan in pain until I was in the truck and we were driving away from the cabin.

"The actual wound is numb but the surrounding tissue isn't," Russell explained, shifting gears. "Get it together. We have an hour's ride to the hospital. You can't moan the whole way. The time to moan and scream was when it happened."

I took a breath and another. "I couldn't then. It would have upset my mother. And I've disappointed her too much already."

"Oh my god. What sad tale do I have to listen to now?" Russell rolled his eyes with his voice.

"I stole her poems. I took her all the way out here. I managed to get myself stabbed...."

Russell interrupted, "She wrote some stuff you turned into poems. You took her all the way out here and she managed to get herself ... well you know," he grinned. "And someone dropped a knife on your foot."

"I know her. She will be angry. I've never been her favorite anyway. She is prouder of my sister, who is married and has a baby. And is pregnant again. I HAVEN'T EVEN STARTED!" I was banging on the dashboard.

"Is this the time you have chosen to review your past? I'm sorry but a knife in your foot does not qualify as your life flashing before your eyes."

I looked at him carefully. "Who was your mother's favorite?"

"IS. My mother's still alive, thank you. And honestly, I was and still am her favorite. Out of five of us!"

"Well, you are lucky. My mother may never love me the same after this weekend."

We had reached the main road and Russell shifted gears again. We were speeding down the empty highway. "Let me tell you something about mothers. Once they love you, they'll always love you. No matter what. That switch somewhere in their mother-ship heart has been activated, and there's nothing you can do to stop it. And *your* mother loves you."

"And your mother? Were you always her best child?"

"No. In some ways I was her worst child, but that didn't matter."

"Okay. So tell me your worst."

"Well I'll start with the fact that I wouldn't talk until I was almost four. Now, notice I said 'wouldn't' talk, not 'couldn't' talk. I know I must have done it because my younger brother was born. Or maybe it was because everyone else in my house talked so much." He shrugged. "So that's for starters."

"What else?" The pain in my foot was subsiding.

"When I was in fifteen I transferred from the local high school to one in Denver because they needed me on the football team. I was tall, I was a good runner, and I had great reflexes. There was no school bus, and we lived on a ranch so I could get my driver's license when I was fourteen. I had a truck. I had gas money. I had a football schedule that included lots of practices and away games and when there was no away game, I could always say there was."

"So?"

He flashed his high beams and passed a slow car on the right. "I had two friends who also had a lot of freedom. Every two weeks, we would cut school and take a morning plane to Vegas. We'd hang out until the craps table got crowded enough so we could gamble without being carded. Other kids gave us money. We'd bring back their winnings minus a twenty-five percent fee. And they had to chip in for our plane tickets. It was quite a racket."

"Did you get rich?"

"Nah. By the time we factored in the food we ate and maybe a few prostitutes, we barely broke even. But a fifteen year old being able to do that! We were famous in school."

I actually laughed. "I can imagine."

"But that was our undoing. After a while, too many kids knew about us and we were handling too much money. Like maybe a couple of thousand dollars a trip. We couldn't really keep track of it, and we short-changed a kid one day. By a lot, it turns out. He told his parents; they went to our parents. And it was over. I was suspended from school for a week, dropped from the team. For the rest of the term, my mother drove me to school every morning, spent six hours in Denver and drove me home. No truck, no football, no gambling, no girls. It was a dull, dull life."

"But your mother?"

"Oh, at first she was really pissed. But, she had nothing to do in Denver for five hours so she took classes at the community college in accounting. Five years later, she got her degree. She was fifty-one and the oldest person in Colorado to become a CPA. Now it's much more common."

"And so ended your life of crime!"

"Not a chance. I lay low for the rest of high school, but when I went to college I bought and sold term papers. At one point I had a 'library' of over seven thousand papers."

I could see the hospital sign ahead. I was no longer feeling any pain in my foot. "Wasn't it obvious professors were reading stuff they had already graded?"

"I would sell them to other schools. You'd be surprised how easy it is to tweak a paper about, let's say, candy making in *Bleak House* to lace-making in *Return of the Native*."

We were pulling into the emergency room entrance. "So, you were a grifter. A literary grifter, but a grifter nonetheless."

"I actually never gave myself a title, but I like that one. A literary grifter."

"Are you still?" Two attendants were lifting me out of the truck.

"Maybe."

CABIN LIFE: DAY FIVE

"If you wake up now you can take a shower with the last of the hot water," Sam shook Sarah's shoulder gently hoping this would be viewed as a conciliatory gesture after last night's blow out.

"What!" Sarah rolled away from his hand.

"I'll check the propane tank but I think it's almost empty. I don't know how these people did it. Too much guilty cleansing I guess." He sniggered.

"You included?"

"Not me. I still smell like last night's fight, if we're going to go there."

"Oh yes we're going to go there," Sarah exploded. "You and David! I mean what the fuck. Or maybe that's exactly it—what the fuck. How come I don't know this?"

"Ask him. He's your best friend now."

Sarah shoved the quilt off the bed. "It's so cold in here. Is it even light out?"

"I told you, I think the propane's almost gone. And not yet."

Sarah searched the floor with one foot for her slippers and put them on the wrong feet. "Don't even think about showering with me. You can just stink like the rest of them."

She shot across the room, grabbing the one clean towel. In the bathroom she locked the door decisively, got into the shower, still regretting its small size, governed by the aluminum frame needed to hold the waterproof lining. She turned on the faucet, resigned to suffer through lukewarm water at the beginning in order to have hot water at the end. Throughout the whole frenzy the night before she had been unwilling to ask the one petty question that showed up after the initial confession or bragging or whatever it was that had made Sam, a pillar of discretion compared to David's openness, tell her, "David and I fucked."

"Top or bottom?" That's what she wanted to ask. She wasn't sure which answer was the right one for her.

She felt the shower floor shudder and saw three tiles peel away from the wall and then many more as the world tipped over with a roar.

AVALANCHE

It was Edgar who stumbled out of the cabin wearing only the robe he grabbed off the bottom of the bed and fur moccasins he found by the front door. "Fuck Sarah and her rules," he muttered and peed off the side of the porch into the melting snow. He still had not fully surfaced from the alcohol, the drugs, and the high of the bear killing. The smell of sex and sweat was all over him. He scooped handfuls of snow onto his chest and face. The remnants of bear blood ran down his side.

He'd slept in a fitful stupor and woke before daylight. He'd shaken Emily's leg off him and rolled to the edge of the bed. He did not want to wake her. Then he'd have to deal with the morning-after rush of remorse and bad breath or, worse yet, morning sex, which he hated, even in the best of times. This was not one of them.

She was sleeping the sleep of spent passion, her face soft and expressionless, the mantle of bravado and lust stripped away. He saw with despair what a child she was and tried to calculate her age. He knew she was in graduate school and added every gap year he could justify, but still came up short of thirty. Probably younger than his daughter, although why that was his standard he didn't know.

Now that he was outside, it seemed wise to keep going, away from the cabin. Away from Jacine's drunken crying whenever she surfaced from sleep like the dormouse at the tea party. Away from the shouting between Sarah and Sam that had awakened him. Away from Emily and the Edgar he didn't know.

He slogged toward the berm they had used for shooting lessons, sinking up to his knees in the soft snow. He reached a large juniper about a hundred yards uphill, settled himself against its sturdy trunk and waited for the sun, just visible over the top of the mountain, to reach the cabin.

That's where he stayed as the snow pack broke away and hurtled down the mountain gathering more snow and boulders and trees as it came towards him. The roar of the avalanche, the snapping of the tree trunks and the explosion of the cabin were deafening. The snow caught him from the side, rolled him onto his belly and covered him. Breath knocked out of him, he gasped in panic. Time froze. He lay buried in a layer of snow.

Then he was moving, breathing, knocking snow from his back and getting his head into the clear, crisp, silent air. He got to his knees and he could see Russell's truck down below. He was gasping for air and trying to shout at the same time. He knew Russell was yelling at him but nothing made much sense. Then Russell was pulling his arm.

"Where's everyone else?"

Edgar nodded at the hill where the cabin used to be or maybe still was.

Russell was running back down to the truck. Edgar lurched to his feet and followed him.

OLIVIA

AVALANCHE

My head and my foot hurt so much I have trouble focusing but there is some really busy noise outside the truck. We are stopped somewhere on the side of a road with a hill in front of us. I don't think we can go any farther. But I really don't know so I will go back to sleep for a while until my foot stops hurting. I can see when I look down at it that I am not wearing a shoe. There are white bandages all around my foot and then there's a floppy bag of ice that keeps falling off. It's quite a balancing game, holding my foot in exactly the right position, and it takes a lot of concentration. But, I keep getting distracted. Russell is shouting words and numbers into a phone and someone is banging on the window.

It's Edgar. He's opening the truck door and pulling at my arm.

"Avalanche!" he is shouting.

Maybe he wants to get into the truck with me. I try to move over so he can squeeze in but my head hurts too much. Anyway, instead of trying to get into the truck he is pulling at me to get me out. "Leave me alone." I tell him.

He takes three breaths and then says very clearly, "There's been an avalanche. It hit the cabin."

I look but I see nothing, just more snow where there had already been snow. "Where? Where is the cabin?"

"Under. It's under the snow."

"So where is everyone?" It seems to me it's taking a long time for Edgar to tell me this when he was in such a panic minutes ago, but maybe it's the painkillers or the pain itself that's making it hard for me to listen. I don't see anyone else running around and yelling. I squint so I can see Russell through the windshield setting out flares in front of the mound of snow.

"Everyone. Else. Is. In. The. Cabin."

"That's ridiculous. Why would they stay in the cabin? It's under all that snow."

"Because they didn't get out."

"And my mother is in the cabin?" This seems impossible to me. My mother was standing outside the cabin when we drove away. She wanted to come with us but there was no room since I was leaning against the door with my leg propped up on Russell's lap. He was being really careful not to touch the knife as he shifted gears and backed up.

Even in the Emergency Room people were not touching the knife. Someone put a carton over my foot and taped the top closed to make certain no one touched the knife, until, of course, someone touched the knife but by then I was unconscious.

"Your mother is in the cabin," Edgar nods.

Nothing hurts now. Not my foot, not my head. I grab at Edgar. "LET ME OUT."

He can see my foot with the bandages and the ice pack. He stops helping me, and I fall out of the truck into the hardened snow. "OMAH! OMAH! OMAH!"

RESCUE

The helicopters arrive within minutes. First the rescue squad who drop to the ground as the copter hovers a few feet above. The media follow soon after, but do not land. Instead they circle and film, swirling the loose snow around Edgar and Russell and the three rescue experts as they grab shovels and begin to dig. The clanging sounds are obliterated by the Whomp! Whomp! of the blades.

"How much time?" Edgar shouts.

"Thirty minutes tops unless they're in an air pocket."

"Jesus!"

The side wall of the cabin is partially exposed. It is the easiest place to dig, but they have no assurance that anyone is actually buried there. They dig methodically, abandoning one area where the snow is too dense and moving to another place where they can get through faster. When the helicopters circle out, they can hear Olivia calling and screaming, but they can't hear any sound from within the mound surrounding the cabin.

"How many in there?"

"Four." Edgar is the only one who knows for certain.

"Awake? Asleep? Anyone one wearing rescue beepers? And shut that screaming woman up!"

Edgar and Russell shake their heads. Edgar runs to the truck to silence Olivia. In the distance they can hear sirens, but they know it's going to take time before the heavy equipment and the team with the rescue dogs will arrive.

Someone is yelling into a phone. "GET THOSE ASSHOLES OUT OF HERE. How are we supposed to find anyone when we can't hear anyone?"

It takes more minutes of frantic digging before the helicopters recede. Then they hear the faint sound of banging and scraping. One rescuer grabs a megaphone. "WE HEAR YOU. WE HEAR YOU. KEEP BANGING SO WE CAN FIND YOU."

The banging escalates into a frantic rhythm. Three men head to the exposed side where the sound is the clearest. They dig rhythmically until they reach a broken window. One crawls through. "I can stand in here. ARE YOU IN HERE?" He holds his hand up for silence, and they hear a muffled voice. Another rescuer climbs through the window and begins to dig.

"OH MY GOD. WE FOUND, WE FOUND!"

Sarah is laying sideways, with the wall of tile tented over her. Tiny bits of glass sparkle on her skin and in her hair.

"Don't move," someone says quietly. "We'll get you out of here."

But she is already moving. "I'm all right. I'm all right." She looks at her hands inlaid with slivers of tinsel. "I'm cold."

"We'll get a blanket. We'll get everything you need. Don't move. You might be injured."

Sarah laughs, "You can see every part of me. Do I look injured? Here, I'll wiggle my feet. Just pull me out of here and tell Sam to get me some clothes."

"Is Sam here?"

"Of course he is. He's probably in the bedroom. Tell him to get me some clothes." She looks at both of them. "Why are you here?"

"There's been an avalanche."

"Okay," she nods.

"It hit this house."

Sarah looks past them to the snow piled in the bathroom. "Oh my god. Oh my god," she whispers.

Russell and Edgar have given a just-arrived team a description of the cabin layout and some idea of where survivors might be. People are carefully digging out the mounds of snow around both bedrooms when someone on the far side of the mound yells, "We found someone."

A dog has found a piece of clothing visible in a depression in the snow. An arm, a hand, a torso. Hands reach in and drag at Sam's shoulders until they can clear his head and turn him over. His nose and mouth are clogged with ice, as if his own breath has cemented them closed. Someone clears away the ice and begins chest compressions. Someone else clamps an oxygen pump over his nose and mouth and begins rhythmically inflating his chest.

Russell walks Sarah, dressed in a rescuers oversized jacket and pants, to where Sam is lying. They sit in the open bay of the rescue truck. She watches his body jump after they tear open his shirt and apply the defibrillator pads twice and a third time. Then she slides off her seat and carefully picks her way through the snow, Russell holding her arm, and kneels beside Sam. She can hear Olivia return to screaming every so often, but that seems useless. Instead she brushes some snow off Sam's forehead and whispers into his ear, "Sam, come back to me. Come back to me."

She turns to the two men working on him, "He's too cold. Make him warmer. How can he breathe when he's this cold?" The men keep doing chest compressions, but Russell brings blankets from the truck. She looks up at him, "You're not dead, you know, until you're warm and dead."

After another half hour, one of the men takes her hand. "We're going to have to stop soon."

"Just a few more minutes, please. He'll come back. I know he will."

Two hours later the bodies of Jacine and Emily are found.

ALL OTHERS MUST PAY.

Within hours the police and the coroner were at the Big House where everyone had gathered. They interviewed each of the survivors separately about the cabin, the event, everyone's location and the avalanche. There were conflicting recollections but the police were able to piece together a timeline everyone agreed with. There were a few gaps. Sarah did not explain why Sam was out in the snow in only pajama bottoms. And no one knew Emily's last name, her age or her address.

"I don't understand this, Mrs. Trout. You have a guest at your house and you don't know her name. Was she underage? She looks quite young."

Russell took over. "I know her name, Emily Bishop. She was part of our group. I know her well from years of emails. She's a graduate student. She lives in California."

The police found Emily's home address and phone number at the hotel she stayed in the night before the retreat. When they called Gretchen, she ordered, "Do nothing until I get there."

Jacine's friend, Shirley, arrived the next day with Olivia's sister. "Your mother will be buried next to you father in Queens." She made all the arrangements and was very clear on what needed to be done. No embalming. A simple coffin for the flight. The body to be transferred to the funeral home in Queens. "You are not to call her daughters for anything," she told the director. "They are too distraught. This is the second parent they have lost within a year. If you need to communicate, call me directly."

David Front was there the next day, as well, making funeral arrangements for Sam and attempting to manage the media, whose appetite for the story was intense. The avalanche occurred at just the right moment to garner attention. The middle of April was long past time when the general public would expect news of such a disaster. One that destroyed a cabin, killed three people and offered choice live footage of the rescue scene was a prime viewing opportunity. The cameras captured Sarah being led out of the mutilated building, the rescue crew working on Sam's compressed chest and, eventually, the lifeless bodies of Emily and Jacine partially covered by tarps, the edges lifted by the downdraft of the helicopters.

Reporters at the scene attributed Olivia's bandaged foot to a dramatic escape. Sarah's rescue was described as a "miraculous survival against all odds" even though footage clearly showed that side of the cabin still intact. Emily and Jacine were given supporting roles as innocent victims. Samson Trout became the embodiment of his biblical namesake. "The Walls Tumble Around a Modern Day Samson" headlined one local newspaper. David threw it in the trash before Sarah and Bethany could read it.

Every major media outlet in the country and several in Europe were searching for angles and interviews. The easiest to reach were the first responders, the regional and national weather reporters transformed into avalanche experts, and the locals who were divided into two camps. There were those who said an avalanche in that area was inevitable and were certain it had happened before, in, oh, probably the 90's, and those who referred to the mountain as the William's tract and vowed it hadn't had an avalanche in as long as anyone could remember.

"Ah yes," David mumbled, as he and Sarah watched the news coverage on the local station. "Do you even know these people?"

Sarah shook her head. "I don't know anyone except the guys who built this house."

Even so, there were well-meaning people who stopped by respectfully during the day—Sam's military colleagues, vendors and construction workers, the yoga instructor at the gym, a couple of women who had been meaning to invite Sarah to join them for Thursday "tea" but hadn't quite.

In addition, there was an invasion of trespassers who headed right past the house into what was now a well-trodden path to the cabin to take selfies and souvenirs. There were also people who presented themselves as almost victims—the ones who claimed they'd wanted to buy that cabin, or who hiked on the mountain in summer, or had almost been hired to do the construction work and weren't they lucky because if the avalanche had happened two months earlier they would have been there. There was even a woman trading on a flimsy notion she had once taken a poetry class with Russell Cooney and, had she persisted, might have been on the poetry retreat and "there but for the grace of God."

Gretchen Bishop arrived with Robert, Emily's father. They went immediately to the funeral home to see Emily's body and give detailed instructions on how she was to be cared for and transported. "I don't want her left alone for even one minute. There is to be somebody in the room with her at all times until she is put on the plane," she explained.

"We have some Jewish ladies in Colorado Springs who do that for us, but they say prayers for the dead. Is that all right?" The funeral director offered.

Gretchen nodded. "I want to see the cabin," she told Robert.

They went first to the house. Sarah, David and Russell were there as well as Edgar and Shirley.

"Please, explain this to me. Why was she here? Why are you all here?"

Everyone looked at Russell. "We are an on-line poetry group. We all agreed to meet in person. Sarah offered her cabin."

Gretchen was annoyed, "You went to the cabin to do what?"

"To write poems."

"What does that mean? If you're an on-line poetry group, you write poems wherever you are and do what with them? Share them on-line I'm thinking. So why did you all trek out here? Never mind," Gretchen was dismissive.

Russell began, "Sometimes poets need that extra step in moving ahead with their work—"

Robert held up his hand. "We are off topic here. We want to see the cabin. We want copies of the floor plan for the cabin. If any renovations were done we want copies of the building inspector's approvals and the certificate of occupancy. I frankly don't give a rat's ass why you were altogether, although knowing what little I know about literary weekends, I'm assuming there was a lot of alcohol, drugs and sex." He stared at each one of them.

Russell drove Gretchen, Robert and Shirley to the cabin.

"Oh my God." Gretchen whispered. "I don't understand. Part of it is still standing. Where was Emily? Why wasn't she in that part? Who was in there?"

"Sarah was in there," Russell explained. "Emily was in one of the rooms on the other side. And so was Jacine, I imagine. Sam was outside doing something or other. Sarah thinks he was checking the propane tank on the side of the house."

"And where were you?"

"I had taken Olivia to the hospital because she cut her foot very badly."

"Thank God or she would be dead also," Shirley was emphatic. "And that other guy. Where was he?"

"He was outside for some reason. All the way over on that ridge over there."

"I'm going to tell you something," Gretchen spoke very slowly. "If there isn't one in progress right now, before I leave this town, there will be a complete investigation of why this happened. Why, at five-thirty in the morning, three people were not in the cabin and they all survived, why, of the four people in the cabin, only one survived and why that person is the one who was directly in charge of this disaster of a weekend and this cabin." She took out her phone and began talking photos of the entire scene.

"Send me those, please." Shirley asked.

"Take your own photos! "Gretchen snapped.

■　■　■

"Where do you plan to bury Sam?" David was holding Sarah's hand.

"I don't know."

"Okay. So here's what I found. It's almost impossible for him to be buried at the academy but I'm willing to help you try. Or there is a military cemetery on Pike's Peak."

"Pike's Peak," Bethany was emphatic. "He needs to be on a mountain. That's why we're in Colorado. Right?"

Sarah nodded.

"So, I'm sorry there's something else that we have to think about now," David said slowly.

"David, there are many things we have to think about and talk about," Sarah pulled away the hand David had been stroking. "But none of them right now. Right now is for Sam."

The cemetery was military efficiency at its best and within an hour all the arrangements had been made. Sam's brothers and sister were called. It would take two days, but everyone would be there.

Bethany slumped on the couch and was asleep within a few minutes. Sarah motioned David to the kitchen. "Before you talk about whatever you think is so important, I need to know something. Were you and Sam ever lovers?"

"No, of course not." David reached for her hand. "Is *this* what you want to talk about right now?"

Sarah groaned. "It's a stand-in for all the despair I'm going to feel for the rest of my life. Indulge me. What do you mean of course not? He told me. He told me you had fucked."

"Oh shit."

"Yeah, on the last night. We had *some* fight. Not because you fucked, but because no one," and here she looked at him, "NO ONE. Not my husband nor my best friend ever told me."

"It was a long time ago." He was stroking Sarah's palm. "We don't need to talk about this right now. This is a diversion because it is easier than facing Sam's death."

Sarah pulled her hand away. "How long ago? Yesterday long? Six years ago?"

"No, we were still in college," David sighed.

"That is such bullshit. You didn't go to the same schools."

"Okay, maybe right after that. It seemed like a good idea at the time. And it was only once or maybe a few times, and no we weren't drunk! We were sober and depressed or maybe he was depressed. There was a girl there also, but that wasn't working too well. Then it was over and he met you."

"Jesus. Why didn't you tell me?"

"It's not mine to tell. It was up to him, and he didn't think it was important, I guess."

Sarah wandered around the kitchen, opening and shutting cabinets and re-arranging glasses left in the sink, "Oh my god. How did this happen? He wasn't supposed to even be there you know. But he decided I shouldn't be alone in the cabin with a bunch of people I had never met, and look what happened to him. Look. What. Happened. TO. HIM." She picked up each glass and threw it across the room. "TO. HIM. HE NEVER SHOULD HAVE BEEN THERE. It was my stupid, stupid idea!" She opened a cabinet, found four more glasses and threw them as well. She was sobbing.

David clasped her arms and brought her against his chest. He stroked her hair, "Yes, yes, yes. You cry, baby," he soothed. "You cry as much as you need."

After a few minutes, Sarah shook herself loose. "Want some?" she held out two glasses to David. He shook his head.

"I'll throw glasses later," He paused. "I just want us to be prepared for something." He tapped the counter, taking his time. "I am betting you are going to be sued."

"How can I be sued? It's an act of God."

"*Your* cabin."

"Actually, the cabin that was already here. I just embellished it."

"What do you call embellish?"

"Bathroom, kitchen, closets."

"Be more specific."

Sarah laid the construction plans on the kitchen island, and they bent over them to discuss each detail as if Sam's death, the funeral plans, Sam and David's relationship, had all evaporated into the late afternoon air like dust motes.

"Did you change the foundation? The exterior walls?"

"No. Maybe I made the whole thing stronger by adding more interior walls?"

"That could collapse? We need to speak to the contractor. We need to speak to the building inspector."

"There was no inspector. You don't need one for replacement work."

"Oy vey."

"Is this bad?"

David was thoughtful, "It may or may not be. I'm saying you're going to get sued. They may not win, and by 'they' I mean most likely that young girl's parents, but you're going to get sued."

■ ■ ■

The day after Sam's funeral, a sheriff and a park ranger came to the house. The ranger was very apologetic. "Mrs. Trout, we know this is a very sad time for you and your family, but we have an issue that needs resolving."

Sarah nodded and led them into the kitchen.

"Now that we've cleared away enough snow and debris," the ranger stuttered, "Well, let me start over." He handed her a piece of paper. "As you can see, there is a statute in Colorado that makes it a crime to kill a black bear."

Sarah stared at the paper.

"So, I need to ask you if you had an Order of Depredation to do so."

"A what?"

"Did you get permission from the state of Colorado to kill the bear? We know he didn't die in the avalanche. He was shot. Four times."

Sarah turned around and looked out the window so they wouldn't see her tear up. "This bear was there in October when the cabin was being fixed up. The workers were feeding her and her baby—cub, I guess. Then she wasn't there in the winter and I guess that's because she hibernates. Is that true?" She turned to look at them.

The ranger nodded.

"Well, then she showed up again with her cub. And then she came back the night before the avalanche and she was up on the porch and she was marching back and forth."

"Did she maul the door or the windows? Was she aggressive?"

"She wouldn't leave. I don't know much about bears. If they don't leave and they stand up on their legs and their paws are on the window, is that aggressive?" Sarah was crying. "Why is this so important? Three people died. My husband died. Why are we talking about a bear?"

"I'm really sorry about this, but we've already done autopsies on the bodies as you know and the bear is just this loose end. Russell Cooney gave us a detailed description of who everyone was and where they were in the cabin. So the only piece of information missing is the death of the bear."

"Russell told you about the bear?"

"As best he could recall. He did say you were all pretty drunk. Is that accurate?"

Sarah nodded. Russell knew nothing. He hadn't been there. He never saw the bear come back to the cabin. He never saw the gun being passed around. He never heard the shots fired into the roof. He never saw Edgar shoot the bear. He never saw the frenzied aftermath. Was this his crazy way of taking responsibility? Or of aggrandizing himself?

"I don't know. I don't know. But it is true we were all pretty drunk." There was a question on her face. "That's not against the law, is it?"

The sheriff smiled and shrugged. "Listen, how about this? Since this happened just before the avalanche, right? And give or take it's still within the reporting requirements. Why don't you just sign this report, attesting to the bear's aggressive demeanor and your fears for yourself and your guests." He handed her a paper. "And we'll be done."

Sarah read the paper carefully to make sure she wasn't lying about anything before she signed.

As David predicted, a letter of intent to sue was delivered two weeks after the avalanche, and listed fourteen complaints including failure to adequately ensure a safe environment, failure of the siting and location of cabin in relationship to the slope of the mountain; failure to establish ground stability; and multiple failures of construction materials.

In summary, the cabin on [GPS] coordinates, known colloquially as the Trout Cabin and historically as the Williams Tract, failed to meet the basic standards for a dwelling designed to be used as a property appropriate for human habitation. In fact, said property, from the dates of April 15 until its destruction by avalanche on April 19, was used, in a reckless manner, as a "test" dwelling by the owners, the Trout Family Trust, in order to investigate its viability as a rental property. Particularly egregious is the Trust's and Trustees' continued insistence that these individuals were "participants" in a Poetry Retreat. It is an insult to logic and findings to claim these victims and, in the particular, our client,

Emily Minerva Bishop, were in any way consulted in the construction, choice and use of this building. Instead they were advised in a cursory on-line discussion of its existence and its 'charm.'

The letter requested a settlement of fifteen million dollars.

Sarah cringed when she read it, "Is this all possible? Maybe it's all true, and I really am responsible."

David was more sanguine. "We don't have all our the documents yet. Most of this is supposition on their part. I cannot imagine they expect to go to court. I think they are looking for a settlement."

"So what do I do?"

"Bring me everything you've got, including the mortgage documents and any building plans."

Sarah returned from the office with two file folders. "We only have a mortgage on the house. We bought the land outright."

"Do you have a surveyor's map of the property?"

"I guess so. I know the owner had shown Sam the surveyor's stakes and the cabin, and we had an aerial map done using a drone. And we have a land title. Is that what we need?"

"Show it to me," David was leafing through the papers. He studied the surveyor's coordinates carefully and then turned to the drone survey. "I see a listing of a building foundation and lean-to from the surveyor, but I don't see anything inside the coordinates on the drone survey."

She pointed at the map. "Isn't this foundation the cabin?"

"I don't think so. I think that's the lean-to."

Sarah bent over the map and pointed. "Here it is. Here's the cabin. You can see the chimney and the propane tank."

David grabbed the map and took it to the window. "Look at this. Look at it carefully. Here are the survey marks. Here's the cabin outside the survey marks!" His hands were making excited gestures.

"Well, that's got to be wrong. The owner showed Sam the cabin and explained he had been living in it. In fact, the first time I saw it there was still stuff in it—clothing and some food and unwashed plates. I don't think he'd left yet."

"I don't care what he was doing there. I'm telling you, this cabin is not on your property! It's not on your property and it's not your cabin!" David was triumphant. "Let them sue someone else!"

"But I renovated it!"

"Well, more fool you and maybe whoever owns it can sue you for trespassing and misappropriation or whatever the hell he wants. But you are not responsible for the construction of this cabin! Which, it seems to me, is the underlying complaint of this lawsuit. Let's send a surveyor out and get a report as soon as possible."

The report was delivered four days later. It showed clearly the cabin was not included in the one hundred fifty-three acres Sarah and Sam had bought. It was actually on land owned by the state of Colorado. According to the surveyor, the cabin was built sometime in the 1930's as part of the Works Progress Administration and had been used to house itinerant workers.

"Hire a lawyer. Give him all of these documents and let him deal with this lawsuit. Stop worrying about it and start figuring out what you and Bethany are going to do from now on," David counseled.

"Jesus, I spent all that money to renovate a cabin we didn't even own," Sarah was shaking her head. She started to laugh. "I mean Sam was pissed at all the money when he thought it was ours. Can you imagine what he is thinking now?"

"Yeah. He's thinking you just saved millions." David looked up at the ceiling. "Aren't you buddy? And by the way, Mr. Exactitude, didn't you even look at the survey. Oh no, for the first time in your entire life you accepted someone else's analysis, someone else's word on something. Boy, if the Air Force ever finds out, they're going to exhume your body and give you a posthumous dishonorable discharge for failure to measure or something like that."

"What should I do about Emily and Jacine? The ones who died? Aren't I responsible in some way? I feel responsible. Even if it's called an act of God or an act of nature, I volunteered my cabin or what I thought was my cabin. Am I supposed to pay for their funerals or give money to their families?"

"No," David was emphatic. "You're forgetting you are a victim in the same way they are. Do not make yourself responsible. You are no more responsible than this guy Russell who created the poetry group. You should do something neutral and uplifting for them and for Sam. I don't know what that is, but it will come to you."

Sarah looked out the kitchen window. The sun was settling behind the line of trees just beginning to bud. The line of trees where the well had been dug all those months ago when they had argued about whether to trust the dowser. Russell, the dowser and the poet. How ironic she wound up trusting him much more than Sam did.

"Oh God, I wish winter were coming instead of spring. I want to hunker down for a few months. Flowers are so sad."

■ ■ ■

I was ringing up a sale at the cash register in Fine Foods, when Shirley came in. She stood quietly by until the customer left and then beckoned to me. "Olivia, ask Eugene to take over. That's why your parents hired him. I want to talk to you." She marched ahead to the back of the store where Cecelia and I once had our playroom. It had reverted to a storeroom soon after we went to college, but there were remnants of its former life. The storage benches along the sides still had their stenciled cutouts—TOYS, BOOKS, GAMES—and Shirley motioned me over to one of them.

"It's been three months since your mother died. I can understand you took the rest of the semester off from school, but you cannot, CANNOT, spend your life in this grocery store."

"I can't abandon their dream. It would be so disrespectful. So heartless. This was their life. They worked here six days a week," I was crying. "Even when Father died, Omah came right back here after the funeral, the very day."

The purpose of this store," Shirley lectured, "was for your parents to make enough money to give you girls a wonderful life. To send you to college and to law school." She took my hand. "The purpose of the store was not for you to leave law school and become a grocer! They had dreams for you and if you want to honor their work and their sacrifice, you have to live out your destiny."

"I don't know what my destiny is."

"Well, for now, it's to go back to school."

"It's not in my heart anymore."

Shirley shook her head. I felt compelled to emphasize my reluctance. "Maybe I only went there to please them."

"No, I will not listen to such childishness. Please don't tell me, who has known you since you were born, that you worked hard in college with the goal of becoming a lawyer, and now there is no Omah to please, you are done with it." She wagged a finger, "Life is not like that. Not the life you were trained to lead. Your parents raised you to have goals. To honor them, you must go back to law school and graduate. You must become a lawyer. After that, you can do as you please. You can write poetry all day if you want, but you will be a lawyer writing poetry, not a grocer writing poetry!"

"Do you think that makes a difference?" I challenged.

"Of course it makes a difference. In one case, you're a person of standing who has proven your ability to meet a challenge but chosen instead to pursue art. In the other case, you're a *schlep*—you know what that is don't you?—who fights for a seat on the subway so you can write poems in a little notebook you take out of your ugly shoulder bag," Shirley was emphatic.

I understood exactly what she was saying because I could hear in her words the way I was raised. There was no faltering. There was no stepping off the path that was chosen for you, or, in my lucky case, the path I had chosen for myself. Sacrifices had been made for me to have the life I had. The standing of an immigrant parent was in jeopardy if a child did not honor that sacrifice. The whole purpose of emigrating was to give children a better life, a life that would not be circumscribed by the status of their parents.

In Korea, my mother had been beyond fortunate to rise from a menial laborer who tied bags around pears to preserve their beauty, to a shopkeeper! But, in her mind and in Shirley's, it was only in America her daughters could raise themselves to be professionals.

"How will this work?" I asked. "Who will be in charge of the shop?"

"Ah," Shirley was triumphant. "This is how it will work. Eugene will be in charge of the store on a daily basis. He has worked here for seven years now. He is capable. He is honest. He knows the suppliers, the delivery dates, and the quantity of items. He knows your parents' traditional ways of doing business, and he also knows how business is done now," she paused and smiled.

"Every Friday, Maxwell Mister Lee and I will come to the store and check on the books and the bookkeeping. Maxwell Mister Lee may be my chief complaint in this world, but I will give him credit to say he knows how to run a business. We will check on the books, we will see what is on order for the following week, and we will pay the bills and salaries."

Although, since my mother was killed, Shirley had been everything my mother never thought she was—helpful, kind, and almost loving—I could see now the officiousness my mother had always balked against.

"Once a month and only once a month, you will come down from school and we will have a business meeting with you and Cecelia. We will show you everything and discuss with you both any problems that have come up and any changes that need to be made. That is what will happen until you graduate. Then we will figure out what will come next." She stood up. "In the meantime, when your studies allow, you can write all the poems you wish."

It was not important to tell her I had not written a poem since the avalanche, and I probably never would again. My mother, even with her ungainly language and her half expressed thoughts, was my muse. Her emails came from pure artlessness. Her memories were deep and unprocessed, as if she had never said or thought them before. They were the opposite of the overwrought stuff I made of them. Rereading them, I am ashamed at how I turned them into what other people would think was more acceptable and more poetic. One day, I hope to be able to mine that purity from my own life, but not now.

■　■　■

Russell was in Marissa's office with the newspapers spread out in front of them. He had given an interview to a national publication, and they stared at the headshot lifted off his book jacket cover. There was also a photo of him in front of the cabin, and one of the cabin before its destruction that the reporter had found in the city archives. He had wanted photos of the group on the retreat, but Russell claimed there were none. He knew Emily had been taking photos but he was not going to let Gretchen know they existed just in case they proved damaging. The article was a mash-up of the avalanche and a review of the book, rushed into publication, in the aftermath of the disaster.

Russell titled the book, *Before I Sleep*. It featured Emily Minerva Bishop's last poem, "Miles to Go," as well as poems from all of the members of *frombadtoverse* in their original versions, as submitted in the years and months before the disaster. Woven around the poems was the story of the poetry retreat and the avalanche. The final chapter contained the US Geological Survey report on the cause of the avalanche and Russell's eulogy poem.

"There's another book offer in the works but I'm not sure I'm going to be the first one they approach. I think they'll go for Sarah since it's her cabin."

"Oh, I don't think so. How are they going to get an interesting angle and dig up real dirt? Certainly not from the person who is possibly responsible for the disaster?" Marisa paused. "They're going to go for you or that other guy. Or the mother of that girl. I've seen photos of Emily. Very appealing. Was she that beautiful?"

"Yes. She was quite stunning when you really looked at her."

"Did you?"

"Damn, Marissa, she was way too young, even for me. Although, the other guy, Edgar, did, I think. And he's probably as old." He smiled. "Anyway, as soon as I got the publishing offer—multiples actually—I sent a letter to each of them, or their survivors, with a check for ten thousand dollars to close out their participation in the book."

"Jesus! Are you that devious?"

"Not at all. I explained everything. How I'd gotten offers but no dollar amounts, how I was technically an employee of the university. How, in fact, the university might be the owner of all the poems and the website, and thus entitled to all the money...."

"That is beyond bullshit," Marisa leaned over her desk.

"Maybe yes, maybe no. I don't know that for sure. It was supposition on my part, which I shared with them. If it turns out I'm wrong, what did I know? I'm not a lawyer," Russell shrugged.

"Oh, damn Russell. So what happened?"

"Sarah sent the check back to me with 'VOID' written on it. Edgar cashed his maybe a week later."

"And the others?"

"Emily's mother is not going to take any money from any-one to absolve us of guilt, even if she can never establish whose fault it was. Olivia was going to take the money, or at least that's what she told me. She actually was very apologetic. She said this woman Shirley told her to leave her options open, and she felt a duty to listen since she was her mother's best friend."

"So, what's going to happen?"

"What's going to happen is I'm going to make a lot of money. A lot of money! So much I won't actually need the chairmanship, but I'm going to take it anyway. And then I'll have to give some of the money away, most likely to Olivia.

She'll actually read the book. Emily's mother will never read the book. She will have her lawyer read the book, and he will advise her to go after me for money, but she won't."

■ ■ ■

It was three in the morning. Gretchen lay in bed. The mound of covers kept her from moving. During the past month, she had ordered rolling shutters installed over her bedroom windows so she could sleep in total darkness in the middle of the day, if she needed to. Sometimes she went to bed at sunset. Sometimes she didn't sleep all night and sometimes she would call Robert, Emily's father, at three in the morning. He always answered on the first ring as if he, too, was awake.

"I'm thinking about Emily."

"I know. Me too."

"Do you think about her alive or dead?"

"Both."

"Tonight, I'm thinking about her dead. I lie like her on my back. We made a mistake and I don't know what to do," Gretchen was crying. "Do you know how hard it is to sleep on your back?"

"I know. I can't either."

"Neither can she. We should have had them lay her on her side. Why didn't we think of that? Why didn't we do that?"

"Nobody is buried on their side, "Robert reasoned.

"But we could have told them to do that," Gretchen sobbed. "You can't imagine how hard it is to sleep on you back. I've been trying for hours."

"She'll be all right. She's very resourceful."

"Are you sure?"

"I'm certain. And I can prove it," he was triumphant. "Remember when she broke her ankle when she was five? She had to sleep on her back for weeks and she did it. She figured it out!"

"So she'll be okay?"

"I promise. She'll be okay. She is okay."

"Thank you."

"Good night, Gretchen."

"Good night. Go to sleep. You have work tomorrow."

■　■　■

For a long while, Gretchen would come home every night after work, pull into the garage and get a millisecond of joy before she knew Emily wasn't there and would never be there again even though her little blue hatchback was patiently waiting for her. It was the sweet pain of biting on a loose tooth to see if it could be dislodged before it had to be pulled. But eventually Gretchen knew there was no other way.

A year after Emily's death, she put the house on the market and packed up the things she wanted, including the half-finished quilt they had never managed to stitch. She took Emily's notebooks and the box with every card and drawing and note Emily had ever given her. She saved two of her baby dresses and her favorite doll.

Emily's laptop had already been sent to the attorneys handling the lawsuit. They logged the emails concerning *frombadtoverse,* including several addressed directly to Russell Cooney and four from Sarah on arrival plans, dress advice and logistics of cabin living. A specialist in forensic photo analysis was hired to create a timeline and retrieve hundreds of deleted photos including the ones from Emily's phone where it was found intact in the cabin destruction. Small things sometimes survive.

"Donate the rest or leave it for the new owners," Gretchen told the colleague who was handling the sale. Two months later, Gretchen received the accounting from the realtor, including receipts for the donated furniture. By then she had moved down to the Palisades and bought a one-bedroom house overlooking the Pacific Ocean.

The new owners of Gretchen's house fenced in the pool and took out part of the grass to plant a vegetable garden. Their two sturdy boys made short work of the sandbox and the swing on the side yard. In the rainy winter, that year, the father needed the extra space in the garage for his kayak so the boys were given ten dollars each to empty it out. They piled the detritus on the curb and threw the poetry stand on top.

The pelting rain raised the grain of the wood. The red letters disintegrated. The paint was defused into rivulets running down the street, washing away "**All Others Must Pay.**"

■　■　■

Edgar looked carefully at the return address on the envelope. It was from N. Fouchette, postmarked Strasbourg, France. He was certain it was from his Natalie. He opened the flap carefully.

> *It took me a couple of months to track you down, as you can see. The newspaper articles said you were from New York, and showed a photo of you in front of your apartment building. If you take a photo of a building and use the right app you can find the address! So here I am and there you are. There is too much to write in a letter. We*

are too old to tell our entire life stories in fifty words or less but here is a start. I found my mother. Once I moved to France it was easy. She was still in Fez, but using her grandmother's maiden name.

I must see you. I will come to New York in September. We have a lot to discuss. Please answer me. Below are my email and my phone number."

Edgar didn't answer right away. His intention was not to answer at all, but then there was a night in July when the air-conditioning wasn't working. He wandered down to the river, north of the bridge and watched the lights of the cars flicker in and out as they passed the struts. It had rained recently, which didn't lower the temperature by much, but the river smelled clean and fresh.

There had been many years when he didn't think about Natalie at all. In fact, when he was in college and he and his roommates would number the girls they had sex with, Edgar usually forgot to count her. But, now he thought about Emily and Natalie a lot. He didn't blame himself for sleeping with a woman so much younger. Emily brought back Natalie for him and the wonderful thrill of those scary days in his bedroom before his mother found out. He remembered the shame when they were discovered but also the power of doing something to shock her. The freedom of not being the obedient only child doomed to be known forever as someone who was "good to his mother."

He hadn't been so good to his mother after all, causing her all kinds of upset and turning her into someone who lied to her friends to protect both her reputation and him. But it was his actions that forced her to buy a car and learn how to drive.

To go all the way to Virginia and stay overnight in a motel in order to visit this adopted daughter forced on her by ridiculous circumstances. She no longer looked at him as her reliable Edgar who was always helpful and obedient. He no longer looked at himself as the *schmucky* little kid who was forever carrying other people's groceries or going off on an adventure to the library. The library for God's sake!!

He wrote back to Natalie. Two months later, he was standing on the upper level of Grand Central Station watching the rivers of people crossing below him. He noticed people didn't wander aimlessly. They entered the station at one end and made their way with purpose, heading for the tracks or the ticket booths or out the other side, using the station as a short cut.

There were a few people milling about under the clock, which was a romantic idea left over from the sixties about where to meet a long lost love. That's where he told Natalie to go. And there she was. Wearing a tri-color scarf. He watched her walk up to the clock and stand with purpose looking right and left. Then he watched her move to the other side and look left and right. Then back to where he could see her clearly.

She was fifteen minutes early, so he felt no need to meet her yet. She would wait the fifteen minutes and then she would wait an hour more at least. It had been a long journey for her. He was certain she wouldn't give up just because he was late. And, after all, he wasn't really late. He was there already, just not visible to her. He would stay just a few more minutes and then walk down. He thought about the value of finding a vantage point. How wanting to get home saved him from the brick disaster.

He had, after all, flown down to Tennessee with the idea of riding in the truck back to New York. But at the last minute he decided to fly home instead. There was something about the oppressive heat and the case of beer stored behind the driver's seat that had made the decision easy.

A vantage point had saved his life at the cabin. Truly he had tried to wake Emily, but she was both drunk and stoned, so tired she was sleeping on her back with her knees up and snoring loudly enough that he couldn't—*could not*—he emphasized, sleep. What was there to do but leave the sweaty bed and the dank after-smell of sex and go outside?

Who exactly was he? The boy who had gotten Natalie banished. The man who ignored signals of impending disaster, the guy who started a knife throwing contest, shot a bear who was probably already dead, watched an avalanche from a quarter of a mile away and agreed to newspaper interviews that brought a woman back to a country she had been only too eager to leave years ago.

As he watched Natalie, he knew there was a life waiting for him. Not that it was certain. After all, they hadn't seen each other in forty years, but why had she come all this way? Certainly not out of curiosity. She had a purpose, and it was him.

He watched her pace in front of the clock. It was time. He walked slowly to the staircase. When he turned right, Natalie would be in his arms in a moment. When he turned left, he would be enveloped in the waning light of the September evening.

ACKNOWLEDGEMENTS

First, I want to thank you, my reader, for making the commitment to read this novel. Hopefully it kept you interested, excited, captivated or enthralled until the very end. If you read it for a book club I am delighted someone chose this book for discussion. If you read it on a long plane flight, I hope it either made the time go by painlessly, or helped lull you into much needed sleep. If you read it and recommended it to someone else, I am forever grateful.

This novel comes from four places—deep seated curiosity about things I have never experienced, like avalanches; other people's experiences so compelling I needed to fictionalize them; the need to write something meaningful that expands my understanding of life and the human spirit; and the constant search for excuses to eat chocolate and drink wine while I mull over a page or a chapter.

I began *All Others Must Pay.* in a National Novel Writing Month (NaNoWriMo) frenzy in November of 2016. Thank you to Chris Baty and the incredible writers who started NaNoWriMo in 1999. Once I started and wrote the first 20,000 words or so, a universe of fellow writers kept me going. I could not have completed this novel without the amazing insights and editing skills of my classmates in the OLLI writing program at UNLV . We were guided by Richard Stephen Kram, who is also a member of a quartet of writers—Amber Meyer, Sharlene

Lim Perry, Richard and I—who meet month after month, year after year to read, question, critique and edit each other's work.

I am grateful to others for stories that helped me illuminate the histories of my characters. Thank you Sharon Gainsburg for a story about a Philadelphia grocery store. Thank you, also, to Dennis DuRoff for a great story about underage gambling in Las Vegas. My grandmother Clara told me many stories about how she transitioned from being an immigrant from Bucharest to becoming part of the fabric of New York City life. Those stories helped me embellish the lives of Jacine and Olivia Park. Thank you to the Uber driver who, on a trip to Reagan Airport, told me about the Jewish mystics in Morocco. That story was the impetus for Edgar and Estelle's adventure, later embellished by my friend Noreen Lane's memories of the mystic in her family.

Thank you to friends in Seoul, Korea who took me into their lives and showed me their neighborhoods, their houses, their stories and how to make *kimchi*. The poet Douglas Goetsch, wote an article in *The American Scholar* magazine about creating a poetry stand in Princeton, New Jersey for a group of high school students that inspired the character of Emily Bishop. Quilting expert Eileen Sherman gave me insights into quilt making and enabled me to make my own poetry quilt.

My intrepid traveling companions Marsha Seiden and Stephen Seiden, as well as Myra Cohen, all exhibited enviable patience while I explored Colorado cabins, California cabins, New Mexico cabins and on and on in order to understand the nature of one of the silent main characters in the novel—the Trout Cabin. I have never been lucky enough to live in a cabin, but I have been lucky enough to own several houses, each of which I renovated in some way. All those decisions, triumphs and regrets are featured here.

I want to apologize to the fictional bears (Mamo and Cubby) that were killed in this novel by inept, drunk poets looking for excitement. And I want to apologize to these very inept poets for killing off three of them.

The poems in this novel were all written by me over the course of decades and have now been attributed to my characters. "The Door in the Wall" originally appeared in *Bone Needles, The Selected Poetry of Jan Ashman, Thomas J. Fitzpatrick, Gary Ashman, Ken Wanamaker, Mike Talbert, Sheila Paris Klein.* Zeitgeist Press, 2005. Gary, Jan, Tom, Mike, Ken and I spent many years reading, analyzing, critiquing and even "killing" poems in order to garner the best work from each of us. Thank you also to our editor and publisher Bruce Isaacson. The poem "Going to the Dogs" was awarded first prize in The Sin City Poetry Contest of 2007. "What Dreams May Come" was published in my chapbook, *The Lost Language of Dust*. And in the spirit of true confession, "Loose Men and Tight Women" was rejected by the "Metropolitan Diary" section of *The New York Times*.

I have dedicated this novel to my wonderful family for encouraging me, questioning me, urging me on and actually giving me new places to write when I visited or we vacationed together. A special thank you to Noam Paris for the cover design concept and to Marsha Seiden for the photo of me on the book jacket.

Thank you to my *ad hoc* group of fellow artists and writers over the years. So often a class, a chance meeting, a get-together at a gallery or an art fair, or a group challenge to meet a deadline has led to great creative work from all of us.

Great discussions about books illuminate what makes a compelling story and interesting characters. Thanks to the "Bookies"—Judith August, Joanne Gilbert, Robin Gordon,

Barbara Goldman, Joan Kline, Carole Pockey, Lynn Rosenberg, Marsha Seiden, Charlene Sher, Louise Unell, Susan Lowe Shlisky, and Ardis Weible—for twelve years of book club discussions and, once again, lots of wine and chocolate.

BOOK CLUB DISCUSSION QUESTIONS

1. The theme of this novel is perspective—how people see and experience life through different vantage points—whether physical, psychological or emotional. Discuss how Edgar, Natalie and Sarah each use and misuse perspective.

2. What actions and decisions by the characters are caused specifically because they are all in an isolated mountain cabin?

3. Who is your favorite character and why?

4. Who is the character you like the least and why?

5. Which character had the most self-awareness? Which the least?

6. The Trout Cabin serves the role of isolating the characters from any outside intervention so they can exhibit their best and worst traits. It is a very common theme in literature and movies. What other novels and plays/movies have done the same with their locations?

7. In this novel, which characters actually "pay" something and what do they pay?

8. If you were in this novel which character would you be?